Something Like Love

SOMETHING LIKE LOVE

TRACY BROEMMER

Something Like Love
by
Tracy Broemmer
Women's Fiction with Romantic Elements

Published by Tracy Broemmer
Edited by Lexie Broemmer
Cover by Vanilla Lily Designs
Formatted by Vanilla Lily Designs

One

"C'MON, KID. C'MON." KARRIE MALLORY WRAPPED her fingers around a skeletal wrist, but she kept her eyes trained on the monitor near the head of the stretcher. Sweat glistened on Dominic Wolfe's arms, the taut muscles quivering with exertion. Karrie's heart hammered out of control as Dom hung his head, tucked his chin to his chest, and Lane Roberts, another ER nurse, moved to start rescue breathing again.

"Breathe. Dammit, Jacinda, you gotta breathe." Her whispered words were lost in the bustle around her. She didn't notice the steady beep of cardiac monitors up and down the open ER area. Somewhere nearby a woman was sobbing, but it felt distant, removed from Karrie's world.

A knife of emotion in her own throat, she dragged her eyes from the flat line on the screen and forced herself to look at Dominic Wolfe. Behind the mask, his face looked shadowed and haggard, and his eyes were red as if someone had thrown a handful of sand at him. He caught her gaze. The tiny shake of his head was almost unnoticeable, but everyone around the stretcher had seen it. He glanced at the clock on the wall.

"Time of death, 2:18."

Karrie felt the adrenaline gush from her, as if he had pulled the plug on a drain. Shoulders slumped, she hung her head for a moment to catch her breath. Her fingers still rested on the girl's thin, cold arm. The room emptied; Karrie didn't notice Dom leave. Finally, she stepped away from the stretcher, the toe of her right black and pink Nike stepping on the discarded wrapper of a hypodermic needle. She peeled off first the right and then left latex glove she had yanked on just 157 minutes ago when the girl had been wheeled in by the EMTs. Tossed them in the trashcan in the corner of the room and slipped out.

She used to cry when patients died. When she had first started the ER thing. She should have known watching emergencies that didn't have good endings would bother her. After all, she had hated being in a pediatrician's office, because she hated giving shots to little kids. What the hell had made her think she could deal with possible sudden death on a nightly basis?

She had learned, though. Maybe she wouldn't go so far as to say she had grown immune to it, but she had learned to file it away and go on. Four years in the field had been long enough for her to grow a thicker skin. So what if she had picked up some bad habits through those four years to get her through the long hours when she walked out of the hospital and headed home, and the ghosts of those dead people followed her? Maybe she drank a little too much at times, but she had never allowed it to become a problem. She didn't sleep much, but then that had predated the ER job. And maybe her choice in partners guaranteed she would never find true love, but for a while Karrie had been okay with that, too.

Apparently, she had come full circle, though. The ghosts of those dead people combined with her personal demons were proving to be too much.

She told herself she was done as she hurried to the locker room to shower and head home. She hated the end of a shift on a good night; nights like this were torture. She wasn't going to make it worse for herself by looking for him. Nope. Been there, done that. Drank to it. Put it to rest.

Still, her heart slid a bit in her chest when she saw him. Back pressed to the wall, knee bent, and foot resting on the wall, too, he blinked as she walked by. He had pulled the mask down to hang around his neck. The years had carved lines in his forehead and his jowls, and they were both sexy and shocking. It struck her now, too, that there was more gray in his thick black hair tonight than there had been just a week ago.

"Karrie."

She shook her head, because she didn't have the energy to talk about it. Much less do it. The last time they talked, which had been the night before, Dom had hinted that there was something he wanted to discuss with her. Rather than listen, Karrie had thrown a temper tantrum and told him to get out. Maybe he had been about to tell her that his divorce was final and suggest they get a place together. More than likely, he had been about to beg off their standing Wednesday night fuck because he had forgotten he had to take Marlie to a Daddy Daughter dance or Amy wanted to have a family dinner. At one time, he had promised her that he and Amy were separated and that he didn't see reconciliation as a possibility. She had been thrilled at the thought, and she had waited patiently to claim Dominic Wolfe as hers, to go public with their relationship.

Now, she didn't know what she wanted, but this eighteen-month affair had started feeling cheap and pointless a while ago. Even before her sister had called her.

She slowed her step when she passed him, but when Dom stood up straight and pushed off the wall, Karrie took a step backwards. She watched as he folded his arms over his chest and looked at her with that smug, know-it-all tilt of his chin. She used to think it was sexy. Now it irritated the hell out of her. Suddenly overcome with the urge to smack the arrogance off his face, she smoothed her hands over her hips. Her scrubs were sweaty and gross after that last fight in exam room four, and her neck and her shoulders were stiff and tight.

"Can we go somewhere?" His low voice, gruff now with exhaustion, used to light her up. Now it was like an ice pick stabbing the center of her neck, making the ache almost unbearable. She blinked at him and wondered if he thought she was stupid. That was kind of the worst of it. Not that she had let him use her for sex for the past year and a half. That was bad enough, but then again, he *had* delivered some mind-blowing orgasms in the beginning, so maybe she had used him, too. But if he thought he still had her fooled, that she still believed he had any intention of leaving Amy, that was unforgiveable.

"Dom." She blew out a long sigh and propped her hands on her hips. "I'm taking a few days off." True enough. She hadn't told him, but her boss had approved a vacation. "I'm gonna go home." She spoke softly, but not because she was sad about leaving him. Because *this part*—the idea of going *home*—was new to her, and she was surprised to realize as she said it that she needed to make the trip. She *wanted* to go home and regroup.

Even if it meant facing Leigh, risking her sister figuring out all the secrets best left in the dark.

"Okay." He nodded quickly, as if granting her a night off. Karrie bristled and stepped back again when he reached to touch her arm. "Go home. I'll try to call you tomorrow."

She arched an eyebrow. He would *try* to call her tomorrow? So he was going to head home now. Had he intended to blow her off anyway, or was he just doing so now to save face?

"No. I'm going *home*." She shook her head. "Back to Illinois."

Two

HIGHWAY DRIVING HAD NEVER BEEN HER THING. LONG, cross-country car rides weren't high on her list of thrills. Hundreds of miles of tumbling weeds and sand broken up by mountains and then hundreds of miles of plains and farms didn't turn her on. And stopping at gas stations built side by side with gaudy pink buildings with overhangs and signs with silhouettes of naked girls and the words *XXX/Nude Girls/Adult Superstore* wasn't an item she had ever wanted to check off her bucket list.

But Karrie was surprised to find she didn't mind the drive. She didn't use the travel hours as time to catch up on phone calls. She had already called Leigh last night to let her know she was coming. She would call her mom once she got where she was going. She had told her roommate, Sheena, yesterday over coffee and multigrain toast that she was taking a road trip, and she refused to discuss it with Dom. She didn't even use the highway time as soul-searching time. Not really, anyway. If her mind tended down one of those detours, she threw up a mental roadblock. Turned up the radio and listened to hard rock loud enough to blow her speakers out.

Past New Mexico, somewhere in Kansas, she looked around and decided she liked the desert better than farms. Maybe she would feel differently if she had decided to come home back in May, when the plains were green, and crops were growing. As it was, the late summer temperatures had long since baked the farmland, and all that was left was the stubble of the corn and bean crops along the highway. Maybe she would feel differently, too, on the drive *back* to Phoenix, or maybe she would enjoy the trip home so much she would hate to leave, hate to go back to her real life.

Maybe it had nothing to do with scenery and everything to do with being a responsible adult. Maybe she needed the break more than she had realized.

She stopped halfway through the drive. Mostly, she would have been okay to shoot straight through. But Leigh had made her promise she wouldn't do it. Too risky. Karrie trusted herself; she was an ER nurse in a big city hospital. She had gone well over twenty-four hours without sleep many times. But Leigh had quickly gone from deadbeat exhaustion to amped and frazzled at the thought of Karrie not resting on the drive, and so rather than argue, rather than add to her sister's stress, Karrie had made a reservation for a room just over the Oklahoma border in Kansas.

Even then, she didn't let herself relax. Well, she grabbed a slice of pizza at a convenience store and crashed on the hotel bed to watch *Top Gun* for the seventh or eighth time. But she didn't give herself permission to think. Could be that was the main purpose of this get away, but she had to tiptoe up to that possibility and feel it out. For now, she was happy with the lie she had told Sheena and, even, Leigh.

She *hadn't* told Dom, and maybe he was too thickheaded to consider that she left to take time away from him. From the tragic atmosphere on the job. She couldn't breathe right now, and Leigh's sudden circumstances had been the perfect excuse to take off. Not that Leigh's circumstances were all that different from Karrie's daily grind right now. Still. Something about going home to visit, to offer Leigh and the kids some help, just for a couple of weeks, made her feel good.

Mind-numbing boredom kicked in on day two of the drive. Only so many dried out cornfields she could look at before her brain insisted on thinking. Thinking about Dom, mostly, and if there was one thing she absolutely didn't want to think about, it was Dom. Instead, she forced herself to go the other way. Memory lane. She hadn't ended it with Dom, though she was going to, late-night missing him aside. But he was currently still her present, so Karrie forced herself down memory lane as her little SUV ate up the miles of gray ribbon in front of her.

Leigh had gone to college at home. Karrie always assumed she had stayed close to home because of Brad. Not that her education was subpar; Karrie had always thought Leigh was brilliant, and Karrie was practical enough to know that fancy universities with fancy tuitions didn't necessarily mean fancy educations. Still, Leigh had stayed close to home and dated her high school boyfriend all through college, and then she had graduated, taken a job at People's First Bank, and married Brad.

Karrie studied at a small university a couple hours away. She had dated through high school, but there hadn't been anyone special. She attended school on scholarship, part academic and part athletic. Even though she was close to her family—including both parents and now her stepparents, too—Karrie had thrived away from home. Even after blowing her knee out on the basketball court and hauling her ass around on crutches before and after surgery.

She had gone to Arizona with her college suitemates their sophomore year. The trip had been an adventure that had included pool time with the girls, drinks out with some guys Jeannie knew, a hot three-day hookup with a gym rat she wouldn't give the time of day now, and miles and miles of that dry Arizona heat. Turned on by the freedom, the possibility, and the thought of mild winters, she had gone straight back to the southwest after graduation, and she had been living there since.

No regrets.

Well. Regrets, because everyone regretted something, probably. To some degree. But Karrie's regrets had more to do with the rut she had settled into, not her original decision to move away. She kept in touch with her parents. She visited her mom and stepdad when she came home to visit Leigh. And she tried to get to Texas at least once a year to visit with her dad and his new wife.

Still, she couldn't deny that she was looking forward to this spur of the moment visit. Her trips were usually in the summer, which was kind of dumb now that she thought about it. Why leave the oven for a pot of boiling water? Why not go home when it was a bit cooler and the leaves were beginning to turn? She missed the display of autumn her hometown offered, and it made her sad now to think that even though this trip was later in the year, she was still going to miss the prettiest part of the season when the leaves changed and started to fall.

Her phone chimed with a message. There was a time when she would have checked the text, just peeked at it to see who it was from. But when she left the hotel this morning intent on finding coffee—thankfully she had found a coffee shop that served at least the Midwest's most mediocre cup—she had forgotten to take her cell from her purse. If nothing else, her years as an ER nurse had taught her never to dig around in a purse for a phone that she shouldn't be looking at anyway while driving. Karrie had seen some fatalities and some injuries possibly worse than fatalities due to texting and driving accidents.

Drunk driving. Distracted driving. Reckless driving.

Drug overdoses. Domestic violence. Bar fights. Gunshot wounds. Stabbings. Rape victims.

Overwhelmed by the stream of memories from the ER, memories she would rather not take home with her, she gave herself a mental shake. Odds were the text message was from Leigh. Entirely possible her sister was even testing her to see if she answered while she was driving.

But maybe it was Dom.

The thought niggled at her. She tried to think about old things. High school. Hanging with Leigh and the other girls on the team. The parties she and her friends snuck into that her parents always seemed to find out about anyway. The time she drank too many wine coolers and got sick in Leigh's bedroom. Thankfully, Leigh had shoved her toward the metal Chicago Bulls can in the corner of her room and saved the pink carpet.

Pink carpet. Karrie shivered now in disgust. Not at the memory of vomiting those disgusting wine coolers into the trashcan, but at the memory of Leigh's room all done in that gross cotton candy pink. What the hell had she been thinking? Cotton candy pink carpet and bedspread. Shams. And posters of Michael Jordan and the Chicago Bulls tacked up all over her walls.

Karrie laughed softly. Maybe it was a wonder Brad married Leigh. She had been a girly, pink-loving, uptight, and hard-ass Chicago Bulls fan.

What if it was Dom texting her? Asking if she had left to go home yet? Suggesting dinner somewhere? Okay, most of the time when Dom suggested dinner, he meant sex. But they *used to* do other things together. Things had gone south, and now that Karrie was looking, it seemed like they were near the equator and close to burning up and not in a sexy, fun way, but in a five-alarm destructive sort of way. But he had kind of loved her once, right? They had had something real.

She wondered how badly Brad was hurt. Leigh hadn't been great about keeping in touch with the updates. The phone calls were vague. In fact, the only reason Karrie knew anything more than that Brad had been in an accident was that her mom had let things slip. Not the whole story, because Karrie was pretty sure there was a lot more to the story than Brad had wrecked a bike on Kramer Highway and sustained serious injuries. But Leigh's account had been along the lines of *Brad was in an accident.*

The bike thing intrigued Karrie. She couldn't imagine her sweet, quiet brother-in-law on a bike of any sort, unless it was a Huffy or a dirt bike, and she knew no one rode a bicycle on Kramer Highway.

Her cell chimed again. Karrie gripped the steering wheel tighter and reminded herself of the last kid brought in by bus after a texting and driving accident. The car had been wrapped around a stoplight. The kid had severe brain trauma, and as far as Karrie knew, he was still in a rehab facility.

"You can wait," she told herself. If it was Leigh, she would be seeing her before the night was over.

And if it was Dom, maybe her absence would do his heart some good.

Well, probably it would do his dick some good, although Karrie wasn't altogether sure that he wouldn't go find someone else to satisfy his needs.

But maybe the trip, the absence, might do *her* heart and head some good.

Three

Leigh's house always looked the same to Karrie: cozy and inviting. No matter the time of year, Leigh always had some seasonal decoration on the little front porch or around the light post in the yard. Brad was particular about the yard, though Karrie knew that Leigh was outside helping him cut grass and trim weeds and bushes more often than not.

Today, though, none of that seemed to be the case. Karrie hunched over the steering wheel in the driveway and tilted her head to get a better look at her sister's house. The gutters were full—leaves and maybe helicopters—and the downspout at the corner was missing altogether. The yard itself needed to be mowed, and though it was September, there was nothing fall or Johnny Appleseed—yes, Leigh was *that bad* with decorations that she sometimes put up apple cutouts in her windows—or Halloween about the house.

Surprise mingled with wariness as she finally reached to tug the key from the ignition. Maybe it was a good thing she had come home for a visit. Looked like maybe Leigh might need more help than she had let on. Karrie sighed and reached for her purse. She clipped one handle but just missed the other one. Frustrated, she fell back against the seat and watched her belongings spill out of her purse to the floor on the passenger side. Her phone. Chewing gum she forgot she had. A tampon. Lipstick. Two ink pens. Interesting. Half of that stuff she wouldn't be able to find if she spent ten minutes digging around in her purse.

With another deep breath—after all, wasn't going to do anyone any good if she hustled around out here and knocked on Leigh's door in a huff for no reason other than dumping her purse—Karrie pushed herself up in her seat and then leaned over to pick up her things. She scooped the tampon and pens up and tossed them back into her purse. The lipstick had, of course, rolled all the way to the passenger door. Karrie gritted her teeth and pushed off her door with her toe to give herself a little umph.

"Ouch! Dammit!" She fell forward as the door opened away from her foot. With a quick glance over her shoulder, she saw her sister and her nephew where her door should have been.

"I think your butt's gotten bigger," Leigh announced. Karrie dragged her eyes away from Leigh's, checked out her own butt in the bright red athletic shorts, and then flicked her eyes to her nephew's. Too young to be embarrassed by his aunt's ass sticking in the air, Gino simply offered her his signature crooked grin.

"Dude!" Karrie twisted around to sit upright, bumped her head on the rearview mirror, and dropped the lipstick. She glanced back as it rolled back to the passenger door. It figured it had to be one of her more expensive tubes. She rolled her eyes. She had to remember to walk around and grab it from that side of the SUV; otherwise, she would forget it was there and end up losing it.

"Aunt Karrie, I—"

"You lost a tooth, man!" She scooched over the seat. Leigh dropped her hands on Gino's shoulders and pulled him back a step as Karrie jumped out of the SUV. "Where'd that tooth go?"

Already a bit long and lanky at five, Gino giggled as Karrie hunched over to give him a hug. She closed her eyes and reveled in the feel of a pair of skinny five-year-old boy arms wrapped tightly around her waist. She never forgot how much she missed the feeling, but she never quite remembered how good it felt to hug her nephew and niece, either.

"The tooth fairy took it, Aunt Karrie." His uncharacteristically deep voice brought a low rumble of laughter from deep in her belly. She ruffled his hair and leaned over to kiss the top of his head.

"Yeah? What did she leave for you?"

"Five bucks."

"Five? Five bucks?" Karrie lifted her chin to look at Leigh. "Five bucks? Seriously?"

Leigh grinned and shrugged as she stepped forward. "That's the going rate, Aunt Karrie," she said as she threw her arms around Karrie and pulled her close. "Mom gives 'em twenties." She said it low enough that Gino didn't hear her, but Karrie drew back to look at her with a frown.

"You're skinnier," she said, because of course their mother gave Gino and Hazel twenties if they lost teeth at her house.

"Am not," Leigh argued, "and your butt really doesn't look that big."

Karrie mouthed the word *wow* and shook her head. "Thanks, I think." She glanced down at Gino again and smoothed his straight brown hair down over his forehead. He needed a cut. She had grown used to the shaggy hair. Even not getting to see him as often as she liked, Leigh had always been great about sending photos of both kids. Gino's shaggy hair was cute, but today it was too shaggy. Sliding quickly from the style—if kindergartners were into style—to unkempt.

"Where's Hazel?" Karrie looked around, but her niece wasn't waiting in the wings to welcome her home. Leigh's flinch was hardly noticeable; there and gone so quickly, Karrie thought she might have imagined it. But when Leigh bit her lower lip and slowly dragged her teeth over it, Karrie decided the flinch was real.

"She's um…" Leigh cleared her throat and shrugged. Karrie studied her sister curiously as she looked down at her son and then lifted her chin to look at Karrie again. "In her room."

"Can I go play?" Gino tugged at Leigh's hand.

"Not gonna help Aunt Karrie with her bags?"

Karrie snorted softly.

"Oh, I see." She nodded. "You're working me for tip money. You wanna take my bags in for me, so I tip you. Savin' up to buy something? Gonna put my tips with your five bucks from the tooth fairy?"

Gino scrunched an eye up and looked at her like she was crazy.

"Whatcha gonna buy? New car? Maybe a Corvette?"

"What's a Corvette?" he asked with a frown.

Karrie groaned. She cupped Gino's face in her hands and leaned over to kiss the tip of his nose.

"Dude. You need to come and live with me in Arizona," she told him. "I can show you all sorts of cool things."

"Can Mommy come?"

Karrie chuckled and looked up at Leigh, but she was struck with dread when she saw the pained look on her sister's face.

"Of course she can come." Karrie turned her attention back to Gino. "Wanna carry my purse inside for me?"

"Will I get tipped for that?"

Karrie laughed as she turned away from him and reached back into the vehicle for her purse. This time, she was careful to grab both straps. Gino took it with a grin and scurried in between Brad's Ford truck and Leigh's minivan in the garage to the house.

"So—"

"How many bags did you bring?" Leigh interrupted her.

"Why? I'm not tipping you."

"I'll grab one." Leigh ignored the joke and stepped around Karrie to get to the back of the SUV. "I hope you don't mind. I put you in that little basement bedroom—"

Karrie watched as her sister busied herself at the back end of the SUV. She reached to open it and ducked inside to start pulling Karrie's bags out. The basement bedroom kind of sucked as far as spare room choices went. It was small and a basement room, so no windows, and also, it always felt a bit damp. Even with a dehumidifier running.

Leigh and Brad had lucked out with the house when they bought it. A master suite and three additional bedrooms and another full bath, all upstairs. New carpet, new roof. The asking price had been lowered to make it just at the high end of affordable for them, and they had debated for a day before their real estate agent goosed them to force a decision. The four bedrooms worked great: the master suite for Leigh and Brad, a decent-sized room for each kid (though Hazel's was a smidge bigger and rightly so, since she was the oldest), and a spare room. For when they had an overnight guest. Which was always Karrie.

Leigh stepped back and stood up straight as she lowered Karrie's black suitcase to the driveway. She shot Karrie a look as if to ask her what she was doing, and Karrie—still wondering why she had been stuck in the basement—reached out to swing the driver's door closed.

"Is that okay?" Leigh asked as she joined her at the back of the vehicle. Karrie watched her chew on her lip again. Noticed two small grooves between Leigh's eyebrows. She couldn't swear to it, but she didn't think they had been there on her last trip home. Which hadn't been *that* long ago.

"Sure." Karrie nodded. Had to be a reason she'd been shoved away to the basement. Maybe they were redecorating. Or maybe they had turned that spare room upstairs into a man cave for baseball watching or a sewing room for Leigh. Except Leigh wasn't any more familiar with the business end of a needle than Karrie was.

The grooves disappeared, but Leigh still worried her lip with her teeth. Karrie opened her mouth to say something, though she had no idea what. No idea what was going on in Leigh's life, and she was a bit apprehensive now about what she would find inside the house. She wanted to offer Leigh comfort, but she sensed now wasn't the time for it.

"How did you get away from your guy?" Leigh asked, and Karrie's heart surged with a flash of hurt and panic so strong, she winced and looked away. "Karrie?"

When Leigh gouged her elbow into her side, Karrie turned to her.

"You okay?"

"Yeah, why?" She shrugged and looked down to realize she had pressed her hand to her chest.

Leigh arched her eyebrows in question.

"I had convenience store pizza last night for supper and today for lunch," she mumbled. "And I think I need an antacid now."

"You keep eating like that and your butt is gonna get bigger."

"Stop worrying about my butt," Karrie said with a soft laugh. "I'm here to take care of yours."

Four

THE SUN STILL LIT THE BACKYARD AND WOULD FOR A while to come, but in the house, Karrie could only see where it tried to peek around the edges of the closed vertical blinds on the sliding glass doors. The four-top table where Leigh's family gathered for meals was covered with scattered newspapers and what Karrie guessed was mail. She wondered if she had interrupted Leigh in the process of reading it as some envelopes were opened and piled with letters and some were still sealed and stacked.

September weather was fickle in the Midwest, but Karrie thought it was gorgeous standing out in the driveway with Leigh and Gino a moment ago. The temperature had reached the mid 80s earlier, according to her weather app, but just a moment ago, a lazy breeze had stirred only pleasantly warm air and the leaves still in the trees. By contrast, the house felt ridiculously hot and reminded Karrie of sitting on her own little cement patch of patio in Phoenix.

The other thing she noticed immediately was the lack of sound. Not like things were muted, like a TV with Gino's cartoons or music Leigh might have been listening to when she realized Karrie was in the driveway. The house was silent, and the stillness was tight and uncomfortable. Karrie watched Leigh step past her and head to the basement stairs to put her bag away.

With a glance toward the family room, Karrie took a reluctant step and finally, she inched her way down the stairs, wondering if she should have started this visit with her mom before coming to see Leigh. It was obvious something was wrong and just as obvious that Leigh didn't want to talk about it.

She pulled her second suitcase behind her over the shag carpet—another thing to love about the basement—to the bedroom doorway. Looked around as she moseyed. The other end of the basement was the toy room, though Karrie doubted Hazel appreciated calling it that. In the yellow glow from the light in the stairwell and now the lamp in the bedroom, she decided nothing had changed. Leigh had told her several times since she and Brad bought the house that she wanted to redecorate the basement, but they had agreed it could wait while they dealt with other expenses. Like Hazel's orthodontist bills.

"Leigh." Karrie situated her bag in the corner of the room and turned to watch her sister fuss over the other one as if she were parking a car in a tight space rather than pushing a suitcase on rollers to the corner of a tiny bedroom.

"Hmm?" Leigh eyed the bag and then leaned over to set it on its side.

"What's going on?"

"I was just going to order pizza for dinner tonight, but if you had pizza last night and again today, we could do something different. I could run and pick up some subs—"

"Gas station pizza hardly qualifies as pizza." Karrie waved Leigh's concern away. "What's the—"

"I thought you were going to take better care of yourself."

Karrie opened her mouth to argue, but when Leigh stood and turned to face her, she simply closed her mouth. She had promised Leigh the last time she was home that she would start eating better and get more sleep, although there really wasn't much she could do about that, was there?

"I am." The words came out more like a question than a promise, and Leigh cocked her head and gave her a pointed stare. "I am. Most of the time. It's hard to eat salads on the road."

When Karrie didn't back down, Leigh hunched her shoulders and drew her arms up to hug herself.

"I'm sorry," she said quietly. "I just….there's so much, Karrie. I don't wanna have to worry about you, too."

"So much?" Karrie whispered. "What's going on? What haven't you told me?"

Leigh stood in the middle of the room, arms crossed over her chest and her hands wrapped around her upper arms as if she was cold. She licked her lips, hesitated as if she might say something, and then shook her head.

"I need to get upstairs—"

"Why's Hazel in her room?" Karrie tried again. "Is she in trouble?"

"What?" Leigh yelped, clearly surprised by the suggestion. Karrie knew better; Hazel and Gino were good kids. Leigh rarely raised her voice to either one of them. She couldn't imagine what Hazel would have to do to get banished to her room.

Then again, she wouldn't have imagined that her niece would blow off her homecoming tonight, either. Unless Hazel was suddenly at the age when all adults, including aunts, were just not cool enough to be around.

She didn't want to admit to Leigh that she was a little bit hurt that Hazel hadn't come outside to greet her or come looking for her yet.

"Let's go upstairs." Leigh dropped her hands to her sides. She walked out of the room before Karrie could say another word.

"Well." Karrie sighed and took a quick look around. The basement room afforded her more privacy, but she didn't need it here. Not to mention, the room upstairs had a lock on the door, so she could have privacy if she wanted it. At least the upstairs room had windows. This one was dark and gloomy, and the bright glow from the lamp only seemed to make that worse.

She gave a dramatic shrug of her shoulders and finally followed Leigh. With a flip of the switch, the room went dark. Karrie trailed her fingers over the banister as she went back upstairs. The higher she climbed, the more her heart sank. She had dragged her feet a bit when Leigh first called about the accident. Trusted that if it were bad, Leigh would tell her so. But once she made up her mind to come home, she looked forward to it. She had wanted to see Leigh and Brad, to help her sister out for a few days. And she had hoped she would find some time to find herself, figure out what she wanted from life, from Dom, while she was here.

The anticipation she had felt on the last few hours of her drive had turned into a restless dread. Leigh didn't want to open up to her, Hazel hadn't even greeted her yet, and she was stuck in the basement bedroom. While she wouldn't deal with any work stress on this trip home, now she wasn't sure her vacation was going to be a good thing.

She found Leigh in the kitchen. The overhead light was on, which made the room a bit more bearable. But it wasn't enough. The blinds on the door should be drawn, and Karrie wished even the door itself was open.

"Where did Gino go?" she asked when she noticed her purse on the table. Had it been there a minute ago when they walked through the first time? Possibly. She had been a little more disturbed by the state of the kitchen than curious about where Gino had run off to with her stuff. She reached for it now, and even though her stomach felt a little sick at what she was doing, thinking, she stuck her hand in to fish for her phone.

"He's in his room."

Karrie froze, her body bent over the table and her hand in her purse. She looked at Leigh with only her eyes. What the heck was a five-year-old boy doing in his room on a perfect fall day? Why wasn't he out in the backyard digging in the dirt or climbing on the jungle gym?

"Leigh—"

"So. Are you hungry?" Leigh cleared her throat. She leaned on the counter for a half second, and then before Karrie could answer her, she turned and opened a cabinet. Karrie watched silently as she rummaged through boxes of macaroni and cheese and spaghetti and Hamburger Helper meals. While Leigh wasn't looking, she took a quick peek around the kitchen. The bowl Leigh usually kept filled with fresh fruit was not on the table nor on the counter. There was no banana tree by the refrigerator.

Her fingers closed around the phone in her purse, and she moved slowly to stand straight again. Looked back at the cabinet Leigh was still digging in, though she didn't appear to be doing much besides shoving things around and making a mess. Karrie saw a package of chocolate chip cookies, a box of graham crackers, and a bag of chocolate candy on the second shelf.

"Want me to go grab—"

"No." Karrie's voice was firm, and she felt like it echoed in the kitchen. But it still took Leigh a moment to turn and look at her.

"Okay." Leigh shrugged. She took a deep breath and then ducked her head and rubbed the bridge of her nose. "I can throw some—"

"Leigh, no." Karrie sighed, disgusted with herself for not being clear. "I'm not hungry right now. I'm fine."

Leigh stood with her chin still tucked into her chest. When she nodded and turned her face away, Karrie realized she was crying. She fought the urge to go to her and put her arms around her. In the past, Leigh might cry, and Karrie would give her a hug, and they would talk and all would be right—enough—in the world. But something told Karrie that times were different now. Something had changed. Karrie didn't know what exactly was going on; but something had changed, and Leigh wasn't ready to share it with her.

Nursing her own hurt feelings—double whammy now after Hazel had blown her off and now realizing that her sister was kind of doing the same—Karrie set her phone on the table. Part of her wanted to look and see if Dom had called or texted. But she was a little bit glad to have a reason not to look. If he had called, he could wait a little longer for her response. If he hadn't, she wasn't sure she wanted to know yet.

"Are *you* hungry?" she asked as she opened the blinds. She squinted as she worked the lock on the door. Shot a quick glance back at Leigh to find her leaning on the counter again. She was back to working her lip with her teeth, but she wasn't crying.

"No."

She spoke so quietly, Karrie barely heard her. Door unlocked, she slid it back and drew in a deep breath of fresh air. Still with her back to Leigh, she listened to the traffic on the road out back, relieved to be back in the land of the living. How could Leigh stand being cooped up in the house like this? How long had it been since she had the door open? Windows open?

"What about the kids? Is it time for them to eat?"

When Leigh didn't answer, Karrie turned to look at her. She hadn't moved, but when she felt Karrie watching her, she took a deep breath to puff her cheeks up and then let it out slowly.

"Yeah."

"Okay." Karrie nodded. "Both of them still like mac and cheese?"

"Of course."

If Leigh wouldn't let Karrie listen, she would do something else to help. Starting with fixing boxed mac and cheese for her niece and nephew. She wasn't a foodie, but she could boil water and macaroni like a boss. When Leigh didn't move and Karrie needed access to the cabinet right behind her, she simply took her sister's hands and led her away from the counter. Leigh sat at the table and watched her.

"Tell me about Brad." Karrie took a pot from the cabinet and filled it with water. She glanced at Leigh as she put it on the stove and turned the burner on. "What kind of injuries do you consider serious?"

Five

SHE FIXED THE MAC AND CHEESE FOR HAZEL AND Gino, and when Leigh ate just a little bit, Karrie breathed a small sigh of relief. Her sister avoided her eyes all through the two-minute conversation about Brad's accident, because turned out, there was a hell of a lot more to the story than some injuries sustained in an accident. Their mom's version had been a bit more accurate, though she had also been stingy with details. Leigh avoided Karrie's eyes through dinner, too, probably because she knew Karrie was pissed for being left out of the loop. She was an ER nurse, for Pete's sake, and she had had no idea how badly her brother-in-law had been hurt.

She should have been home a hell of a lot sooner. She *would* have come home immediately if she had had any idea he was critical. As it was, she had hem-hawed around long enough that her sister could have lost her husband, and Karrie had assumed he was in a cast and missing a few weeks of work.

Furious with Leigh and their parents, too, though Leigh insisted their dad didn't know how bad it was, Karrie practically threw the dishes in the dishwasher and then she went downstairs to unpack and change clothes. Anger and grief and helplessness made a volatile mix on her already messed up stomach. And

Karrie suspected they hadn't even broached the deepest part of the story; she suspected there was more to it. But when Hazel had finally shown her sweet little face—slack jawed and sad rather than sweet tonight—Leigh had become tightlipped, and she had refused to discuss it again when Karrie asked after dinner.

Dom hadn't called. The only message on her cell was from her roommate. And that call wasn't good news. Karrie listened to Sheena's message twice, certain she heard her wrong. Nope. Sheena had a visitor today—Karrie didn't know who it was, and it didn't matter—and the visitor's dog had peed in Karrie's bedroom. Sheena wasn't a slob, but Karrie was curious why her bedroom door had been open in the first place. She wasn't sure she trusted her to clean the carpet to her satisfaction. Nothing like the prospect of going back to the smell of dog urine in her bedroom.

When she went back upstairs, Leigh caught her before she could step outside. Karrie noticed the way Leigh's eyes darted suspiciously around the neighborhood and then to the sky—already heavy with darkness. Karrie tamped down her irritation when Leigh suggested maybe she should wait until tomorrow to run, as if she were only planning to run for exercise and not to exorcise the ghosts she dragged home with her. And all the new bad feelings she hadn't seen coming, because she had never thought to watch for threats from her family.

Her thoughts turned to Hazel as she took off at a jog. Thirteen was a tough age for anyone, definitely tough for a girl, and that much harder for a girl whose normal family life had taken such a hit. Karrie had swallowed the hurt from earlier when Hazel latched on to her in the kitchen and hugged her so tightly, she couldn't breathe. She had wanted to comfort her niece, the same as she wanted to comfort Leigh. But all of them were skittish with their new normal, and Karrie was afraid to overwhelm them, so she simply held on right back and dropped a kiss on Hazel's cheek before the girl ducked away and zoomed back into her bedroom.

She and Leigh were close when they were younger. Four years apart in age, they had gone through the ornery stage when Leigh was in junior high and decided it might be more fun to be mean to Karrie instead of nice. The rough patch hadn't lasted long, though, and they confided in each other as they got older.

Except, did they? Really? Okay, maybe Leigh called to tell her when she was pregnant the third time and wasn't sure she wanted another baby. She had sworn Karrie to secrecy, as if Karrie would hang up the phone and text Brad or announce Leigh's ambivalence toward a third child on social media. And maybe Leigh had called to cry to her when she lost that baby and swore on a stack of bibles—figuratively, because who had a stack of bibles in their house—that the miscarriage was her fault because she hadn't really wanted to do the diaper and bottle thing again when Gino was three.

But did Karrie confide in Leigh? Well. Sure. Sometimes. She couldn't exactly call and disclose all the gory details of a bloody scene in the emergency room. That would violate HIPAA laws, and Leigh wouldn't expect that any more than Karrie would do it. But there were nights when Karrie called her after losing a kid or a mom or a grandpa in the ER. There were nights when she would call her big sister, and in a whisper that sounded like wind over gravel, she would ask Leigh to talk to her. Tell her a story. Leigh knew what those calls were about without a single detail, and Karrie could picture her sister sliding from her side of the bed and tiptoeing out of the room she shared with Brad. Curling up on the sofa or even going out to the deck to talk Karrie through her waking nightmares.

But Karrie *didn't* talk to Leigh about her personal life. She had mentioned Dom in passing, but never more than his name. That they had gone for dinner. Or taken a walk in the moonlight. Leigh didn't know Dom was the attending physician in the ER. Or that he was married. And had children.

And Leigh *hadn't* asked Karrie to come home. When Brad had been rushed to the ER in the back of an ambulance, Leigh had shouldered all of it without once telling Karrie how dire the situation was.

She moved quickly from a jog to a run, and when she realized how close she was to her old high school, she finished in a sprint. Collapsed gracefully to sit on the sidewalk outside the gymnasium. Ducked her head and sucked in oxygen while concentrating on sweating out the pain. Because damned if she was going to cry. There was a lot more going on than Leigh had admitted to, and Karrie sure as hell wasn't going to waste the tears or the energy yet.

When full dark descended and the lights came on in the gym, she realized someone was inside. Curious, and if she were honest, lonely for the past, for a time when she and Leigh were close or maybe more to the point, when she *believed* she and Leigh were close, when things were so ridiculously simple, she climbed to her feet and yanked the big glass door open to go inside.

She heard male voices, but she didn't see anyone in the gym. Probably coaches or a coach and the athletic director talking in the A.D.'s office or maybe in the long corridor between the gym and the office. Whatever. Karrie had no idea who any of the current coaches were, didn't particularly care.

The familiar smell of the floor wax hung in the air, and she wandered the length of the gym with her fingers fluttering lightly over the railing around the upper level. Though no one was around, she heard the squeak of shoes in the stop and start, tearing up the floor on a breakaway and the sound of a layup and a basketball banking off the backboard and dropping through the net. The roar of the crowd and the pep band's version of the school fight song.

She and Leigh had lived on this court. They had lived and died. Sunk three-pointers and free throws and missed layups and fouled out here on this court, in this gym. Karrie walked the length of the gym twice, fingers on the metal pipe railing, eyes on the floor—waxed to a shine, though even from where she paced a whole cheering section away, she could see the scuff marks and gouges years of athletes had put there—and then when she was still alone and her head was still pounding with all the things she wanted to leave behind, she ducked and climbed under the railing and down the bleachers to the floor.

From the new vantage point, she could hear two different conversations going on. She glanced up and saw two older gentlemen on the upper level she had just left, although they were closer to the doors that led through to the heart of the school than the main door she had come in. Obviously, they hadn't seen her. Rather than ask permission, she simply trained her eyes to the painted lines on the floor and walked them with the same finesse as a tightrope walker.

Dom and the teen girl they had lost just the other night had no place here. Eyes on the toes of her Nike shoes, she could almost pretend they were the old white Nike court shoes that the team had worn when she went to school here. Her brain played out scenes from the hundreds of games she played back in the day. The shot she had thrown up at the buzzer at the end of her freshman year that banked off the backboard and bounced into the bleachers. The sound of the buzzer and the heartache that had dragged her to her knees. Her heart ached with the memory of letting her team down.

She made it halfway around the court when she happened to lift her head a fraction of an inch. A round orange ball half hidden under the end of the bottom bleacher caught her eye. Because the basketball was out of season, she stopped and looked around the gym. Fall in the Midwest, at least in the area where she had grown up and gone to school, was volleyball season. Just to be sure she wasn't going crazy, Karrie threw a quick glance over her shoulder. Sure enough, the net was stretched across the court. She had played, and she had a decent bump, but her true love was the backboard and the net and the orange ball.

Figuring whoever was here would escort her out when they needed to lock up the gym, she stepped off the black court line and crossed the small area over to the home team's bench.

Karrie dribbled the ball twice and put it up with finesse. The ball swished through the net and bounced back at her. Before taking another shot, she huffed out another breath and lifted the hem of her t-shirt to wipe the sweat from her forehead and then dab around her eyes. Hurt like hell to get sweat there, and it made it hard to see sometimes.

Brad had been a football player, which had been convenient for Leigh. She had been able to go to most of his games, and when his season was over, he'd been able to watch Leigh play. Brad was steady like a brick wall, just enough sway to stay standing. Karrie knew for a fact he had been a big support to Leigh when their parents divorced, and their dad moved away. Leigh and Dad had always been close, and his move had been hard on her.

Karrie thought about that now as she dribbled the ball low and tight to the floor. Picked it up and put it up in a smooth jump shot. Her parents had divorced when she had gone to college. She wondered from time to time how long they had been unhappy. If they'd stuck through years of a bad marriage together for herself and Leigh. Hard to say. They seemed friendly enough now, and since Karrie had been gone, the divorce hadn't been as hard for her as it had for Leigh. In fact, she wasn't sure she had even told Dom about it. They talked some about their families, but they had never had that relationship where they dug deep for purchase and held on for life.

That strong and steady Brad Avery was now laid up in a rehabilitation hospital blew her mind. She had envisioned a broken leg, maybe a cast from hip to toe decorated with Gino's artwork. Maybe raccoon eyes and stitches over his forehead that would leave him with a scar that would turn his clean-cut good looks into rakish and sexy. Possible brain trauma had never crossed her mind. Probably because Leigh had failed to mention it. *Possible brain trauma.* That's exactly how Leigh had said it earlier, too. The conversation which had wrapped up in two minutes or less had been ridiculously cool and heavy on medical jargon.

Karrie snagged a rebound and put the ball back up, welcoming the pull in her muscles. She hadn't worked out in ages. And she hadn't done this kind of thing—a thing that involved a basketball and a court—since she left college. The adrenaline and the sweat and the sound of the ball pounding the court were like a much-needed fix.

Had Leigh spoon-fed her those words because they were Karrie's language? Had she said *hematoma* and *swelling on the brain* because they would appeal to Karrie? Because she needed Karrie to answer in the same language? Because she wanted Karrie to assure her everything would be okay?

She couldn't. Surely, Leigh understood that Karrie couldn't just blindly reassure her that Brad would make a complete recovery. Even after seeing him and talking to his doctors, assuming Leigh wanted her to, she wouldn't assure Leigh anything. It sounded like Brad's condition had been touch and go since the emergency responders had found him, and part of Karrie resented Leigh for wanting such a promise. She had come home to help, and she would do *anything* for her sister. Anything but give her and her kids false hope.

Part of her—and that was another thing, so many parts of her right now, she felt like she had splintered into millions of pieces and as if she wouldn't find herself until she was whole again and she wasn't entirely sure that was *possible*—still wanted to know what the hell Brad Avery was doing on a crotch rocket. Karrie hated the damned things. Had since she lost a friend in high school. Semi versus crotch rocket. The venue had been the main street in town, and every damned living person in town had come out to watch the medics try to peel Clark up from the street. Karrie had been there; Leigh's fingers threaded so tightly through hers, she thought her hand would break. What the hell had Brad been thinking? What if Leigh had watched his rescue? She hadn't—she told Karrie that—but still. She probably thought of Clark and the blood and his body parts strewn over Maine Street and wondered what the scene of Brad's accident looked like every damned time she closed her eyes at night.

Karrie huffed out another breath and considered quitting for the night. Trouble with that was, she wasn't sure she would have an opportunity to come back to the gym. And now that she had put up some shots, she most definitely wanted to come back. She would gladly pay her last dollar to rent an hour here every night just for some alone time. The ball, the board, and her hand. The old memories soothing away the new stuff. The adult stuff.

Ball on her hip, arm curved over it to hold it there, Karrie leaned forward a bit and sucked in a deep, cleansing breath. She almost laughed when she saw that she had pressed her left hand down over the edge of her shorts and pulled them tight. Same thing they'd all done when they were lined up at the lane for foul shots.

She missed her friends, too. Her friends. Leigh's friends. All the same.

Aw, hell, Karrie. You're alone now. Admit it.

So alone, she actually missed Dom. And Dominic Wolfe had stopped being a comfort, safety, to her a long time ago.

She missed Leigh. She hadn't come home expecting her sister to gush at her feet with gratitude. But she hadn't expected a clipped recitation of Brad's injuries delivered so matter of fact, either. She'd come home to *help*, and she wanted Leigh to lean.

"Look at that gorgeous ass."

The quiet words carried all the way to the gymnasium floor. Karrie stood up, flipped her blond ponytail over her shoulder, and turned around.

"Who the hell is that, and where the hell has she been all my life?"

Six

Daxton Law forgot how voices carried in this gymnasium when it was empty. He had been listening to Jed Isles talk for the better part of an hour, but it wasn't like he could stop his boss from rambling, was it? His eyes were nearly crossed in his head. They were walking toward the gym; more to the point, Jed was heading toward the exit and escape was in sight. And then Jed, who was the athletic director at Holy Trinity High School, had started talking about the upcoming Bump and Spike girls' volleyball tournament, and Daxton had worked his ass off to keep a lid on the yawn. He honestly didn't care much about girls' sports, and there was a six-pack of longnecks in his fridge calling his name.

And then he saw her. Well, to be exact, he had seen that fine round ass sticking up in the air. The athletic shorts stretched just so over what appeared from up here to be perfectly taut muscle. Isles was talking about their starting seniors and the total number of kills they had together, and Dax's dick was checking out that ass. Ready to roll, for damned sure. Luckily, he was wearing loose-fitting athletic shorts himself, or his boss might have noticed the party in his pants. Which would be a problem since they were discussing high school students.

However, he had forgotten that maybe commenting on a fine ass in front of his boss wasn't exactly a good idea. The same way he forgot how voices carried in here. And now, the body that connected to the fine ass straightened up and turned slowly to look at him. What looked like miles of platinum blond hair were pulled into submission in a ponytail, though a few pieces had revolted and now curled around a model's face. High cheekbones and a strong chin and blue eyes that flashed with annoyance. If voices carried, so did the drop-dead waves emanating from the hot little number down on the court.

"Now you've done it."

Dax broke the eye contact with the woman on the court long enough to glance at his boss. He was surprised to see the smirk on Jed's face. Reminded himself that even though he was his boss, he was a guy and not an *old* guy who might be stuffy and stodgy about respecting women but one who would notice a damned fine ass when he saw one.

"Good luck, Law." Isles' mouth didn't even move when he spoke. Daxton watched him walk away and then looked back down at the court. She was gone. Heart in his throat and his dick in serious protest—he had hoped to at least get an up-close look at her to see if she was as gorgeous as she appeared to be—he aimed a frantic look around the upper level of the gym. Nowhere in sight.

The door at the opposite end of the gym swung closed, but Dax could see Jed outside through the small glass square, not the girl. He stepped closer to the rail, wrapped his fingers around it, and leaned in to listen. Nothing at first, and then he heard her footsteps on the stairs. He turned that way, to his right, as she appeared. She had pulled the elastic out of her hair, and he was right; the long, blond waves tumbled over her shoulders and framed her face.

Her cheeks were spotted with cherry red dimes. Since she wore a look of disdain, he assumed the red spots on her cheeks were from anger rather than physical exertion.

"Hey." He wriggled his eyebrows at her, but nothing in her glacial expression melted. "I've never seen you around here before. I'm Daxton Law."

She arched her eyebrows up, as if in disbelief, but she simply stared at him.

"I'm the boys' basketball coach," he told her. The cool blue eyes disappeared for a moment when she blinked, and then they were back again. Steady and intense. Dax had no idea how long she had been in the gym, and though she had been holding a basketball when he noticed her on the court, he didn't know if she had been dribbling or shooting or just holding the ball. He dragged his eyes down over her body, careful not to linger at her breasts, though he sure as hell wanted to. Her skin was dewy, rather than sweaty, but damned if she didn't smell good.

Something rich and heavy that kind of wrapped around his brain and paralyzed him.

On the way back up her body—her legs were just about as delicious as her ass—he realized she hadn't reacted. She still hadn't said a word. In fact, it was suddenly a bit chilly in the gym. Pretty sure that had everything to do with the blonde standing in front of him and nothing to do with the a/c in the building, Dax raised his eyes to hers and swallowed hard.

"Um." He shrugged and grinned sheepishly. "About what I said…"

Finally! She tilted her head and narrowed her eyes at him.

"Takin' it back now, Dax Law?"

Her voice was thick and smoky and brought to mind lazy afternoon sex. Because she was naked in his head, his eyes took another ride south and this time stopped at her breasts. The top of a black sports bra peeked out over the top of her black tank top, her girls wedged tightly together creating some spectacular cleavage.

"Oh, hell no," he mumbled. "No takin' anything back."

Her skin—the skin on her arms and legs, as well as her neck and that impressive cleavage—was sun-kissed. Daxton took a moment to imagine his lips grazing over the same spots the sun touched, but when she cleared her throat, he jumped and lifted his guilty face to meet her eyes.

She studied his face for a moment. Nodded to herself and then turned to walk away. She muttered something; Dax wasn't sure, but it sounded like she called him a dick.

"Wait!" he called as he hurried after her. She didn't slow down. Didn't turn around. Just walked—no, marched might be more accurate—head high, chin in the air toward the exit. "What's…you didn't tell me your name."

He was right behind her when she hit the release bar on the door with the palms of her hands. No rings. Clean, short fingernails. Slender but toned forearms. She didn't look back at him as he stepped outside behind her. He couldn't leave yet. Since Isles had already taken off, Dax had to turn the lights off and lock up the gym.

A quick glance at the parking lot tanked his last hope. No car. No license plate to get so he could at least find out who the hell she was.

"What's your name?" he called out as she got further down the sidewalk.

She turned—a perfect pivot that made him wonder how she handled a basketball—and leveled him with a cool stare.

"Puddin' and tame," she said sweetly. Sarcasm thick like syrup dripped from her words.

"I'm serious. Did you walk here? Who are you?"

She smiled, but it was a little bit cold and vicious.

"I don't think names matter to guys like you, Daxton Law."

Something in the way she said his name gave him a chill. Not in a sexy way, but more like nails on a chalkboard. Unpleasant, to say the least. He ignored the dread that curled around his shoulders like a sneaky, up-to-no-good cat.

"What does that mean?"

Damn. He hated the way his voice curled up at the end. Like he was desperate. Sure, he was intrigued as hell by her, and yes, he was still caught up in the thought of a lazy afternoon in bed with her. But he wasn't desperate. He had any number of women he could call to get rid of the wood this woman apparently didn't want.

"Will I see you again?"

Her unladylike snort hit him like a freight train. But even that wasn't enough to cool him off.

"Not if I can help it."

She winked.

Son-of-a-bitch. She swung that hammer down on his coffin and winked while she nailed him. He watched, mouth still hanging open, as she gathered her hair and pulled it back again and then turned and took off at a light jog. Her ass didn't wiggle so much as glide, but Daxton found himself watching all of her—not just the luscious curve at her hips—as she got further and further down the sidewalk.

When she was out of sight, he finally turned to go back inside and lock up. His dick was still hard and thick as he made his way back around the pit and down the hall to the athletic offices. Isles had flipped his light off and locked his door, but Dax had planned to sit down for a while and go over an article or two on a new defensive play he was interested in. Mind on offense now, particularly on ball handling skills and pretty, ringless hands, he turned the light off in his office and pulled the door closed.

She had called him a dick.

He puffed up his cheeks as he slid the lock into the doorknob. She was right. He was a dick. No apologies. His philosophy on women had always been something like do 'em and dump 'em. No woman he ever dated or slept with had inspired in him anything other than sexual arousal. Not even his ex-wife.

"Yeah, she'd agree with you, blondie," he mumbled. He rattled the door. Satisfied that it was locked, he stuck his hands in his pockets and stared at the blue glow through the window on the door.

Dammit. He had left his laptop powered on. On his desk. With a sigh of frustration—damned if that little blond number hadn't gotten under his skin—he unlocked the door again and stepped inside.

Yep. He was a dick. If that chick was a school mom—no fucking way that hot body had a kid in high school—or a school sister or anything related to this school, he had no business sniffing around her. Didn't matter how curvy her ass was; she was off-limits.

Tell that to his dick.

He powered the laptop down and then picked it up.

Still hard like a steel rod, he carried the laptop across his office.

Still.

Still. She had said he was a *still* a dick.

Which meant, she had thought that about him sometime in the past.

Which meant…she knew who he was.

Seven

KARRIE TOSSED AND TURNED FOR WHAT FELT LIKE days, but she eventually slept. Not well, but she slept. There were some dreams, but at least these featured cornfields and basketball courts and not flatlines and severed arteries spraying the ER. She woke with a start and groped for her phone. Hand falling to the bed and fingers curling around the edge of the mattress, she pushed herself up and climbed from the bed in one fluid motion.

Where the hell was her nightstand? Her clock? Phone? She blinked and made her way to the end of the bed where she stubbed her toe on the heavy wooden post.

"Ouch." She bit her lip and hobbled around the bed. She remembered then. She was home. She was at Leigh's house, sleeping in the frigging basement because Leigh was in the process of setting up the spare room upstairs with a hospital bed. For Brad.

"Shit." She attempted to perch on the edge of the bed, as she would at home, but this bed had the ornate posts and footboard, and she ended up sitting awkwardly on the footboard. With a sigh, she crossed her right foot over her left knee and rubbed her toe.

Brad. She should visit Brad today. It made her feel guilty that the thought of seeing her brother-in-law laid up in a rehab facility made her sick with dread.

"You have to do it," she whispered to herself. "Grow up."

Still, thinking about the smell of the hospital, the smell of blood and sweat and alcohol, made her want to vomit. She was on a mini vacation. Throwing this in her face wasn't fair.

"Fair?" she mumbled. "Jesus, Karrie, really?"

She shivered, though it wasn't exactly cold in the basement. But the shorts and t-shirt she slept in were damp—probably sweat, although she thought it felt a bit humid down here, so maybe her bedclothes and pajamas were wet because of the humidity. She lifted her head, hand still wrapped around her throbbing toe and looked around the dark room. She could just barely make out the dark shadow of the dresser across the room where she left her phone last night so she could plug it in. No clock. No windows. No idea what time it was.

Her phone buzzed, and she wondered now if that's what woke her up. She stood and inched her away across the dark room, hands outstretched. She wasn't afraid of the dark, but she would rather not sacrifice another toe to blindness. Her fingers found the dresser, so she tapped her way over the top of it until she found her phone.

7:47.

And a text from Dom. Her voicemail icon was lit up with a little red flag, too. Karrie pushed the home button and then the text icon. Dom's message was at the top of the screen.

Called to hear your voice. I miss you.

Interesting. She considered listening to her voicemail. Because if she were being honest, she *kind of* missed him, too, and she loved his voice. Finger hovering over the icon, she lifted her head when she heard thundering footsteps overhead, followed by a peal of laughter and then a sharp, angry wail.

She wanted coffee. And daylight. God, the darkness down here was unforgiving. Phone in hand, though Dom's message momentarily forgotten, she shuffled her way across the room to the door. She almost went straight upstairs, but she decided it might be wise to use the bathroom down here and stay out of Hazel and Gino's way.

The bright yellow light in the bathroom was torture, and Karrie feared she might be blind when she left the room. Business taken care of, she studied her face in the mirror over the sink as she washed her hands.

Daxton Law.

She watched her lips curve up with amusement. He had grown up to be an even better-looking man than he was a teenager. Still a dick, though. The fact that he had commented on her ass and then not recognized her when he looked her in the eye spoke volumes.

Sure, she looked different. They all looked different, because they had grown up. But if he had ever really looked at her when they were younger, he would have at least thought she looked familiar. Instead, then as now, guys like Dax were too busy eyeing girls' boobs and asses, and apparently, still had the social IQs of dicks.

She blinked her bloodshot eyes and leaned closer to the mirror to study the skin around her mouth. No lines. God, no. She hadn't even hit thirty yet. She didn't need any lines around her mouth or her eyes. Before she got carried away with her self-examination, she remembered that Dom had called her because he missed her, and she remembered, too, that she wanted coffee.

Her sister was yelling upstairs when she opened the bathroom door. Karrie flipped the light off and then stood, blinking, into the inky black family room. She was going to have to find some sort of nightlight or risk more personal injury. She had no idea how long she would be here; Leigh had been so stingy with details, well, with everything last night, Karrie didn't know if she was even wanted. Much too early to make plans beyond the next day or two.

But this basement thing sucked, no doubt about it. She picked her way through the room again and finally reached the dimly lit rectangle where the stairway was. At the bottom, she looked up into the lighted kitchen and drew in a big, deep breath.

"Mo-om!" Gino's yell stabbed her head just behind her eyes. At least she smelled coffee. Maybe she could get a cup and step outside. Sit on the deck for a few minutes. Listen to Dom's message. She wouldn't call him back. That was a promise. But wouldn't hurt to listen to someone miss her for a second, would it?

"Mom, Gino hid my social studies notes!"

"Gino Andrew—"

"Hazel hit me!"

Karrie looked around the kitchen as her foot hit the top step. Neutral zone for the moment. Two backpacks on the kitchen table. Both unzipped, a mess of papers falling out of one of them. Karrie assumed it was Gino's.

She tiptoed around the table, eyes on the prize. A full pot of coffee, the machine still burping and hissing as if it had only just finished the magic.

"Both of you, get your bags and let's go—"

"But Mom—"

"I've had it. Let's go."

Karrie took a dainty porcelain mug from the hook under the cabinet. She set it down and then splashed the liquid gold over the pale pink rose pattern.

Wondered for the hundredth or maybe thousandth time what had possessed Leigh to register for this ugly tableware. The cups were tiny, and they felt fragile. Then again, in all the years Leigh and Brad had been married, only one of the hideous cups had broken.

"Can I go to open gym tonight?"

"No."

"But Mom."

Karrie turned and rested her back on the counter. She lifted the cup—reminded her of a little tea set she and Leigh had when they were little girls—to her mouth and sipped. She swallowed the coffee and breathed appreciatively. Her eyes fluttered closed. At least her sister knew how to make good, strong coffee.

"Hazel, I said no. There's no point now, is there?"

"My friends are going…" Hazel's words faded away, and suddenly, Leigh appeared in the kitchen.

"Sorry to wake you." Her tone was borderline cool, and then Hazel was there behind her. Her pale cheeks were ruddy and red in spots; it was obvious she had been crying.

"You didn't," Karrie assured Leigh, although she wasn't sure Leigh heard her.

"Bus is down the street!" Gino bellowed as he flew into the kitchen. Karrie watched, half-entertained and half-horrified, as he snagged his backpack from the table and ran for the back door. Hazel ducked her head so her limp brown hair swung forward to hide her eyes. She picked up the backpack Karrie had assumed belonged to Gino and made her way to the door without another look at Leigh.

Gino already gone, the screen door banged as Hazel disappeared right behind him. Outside, the bus lumbered to a stop in front of the house. Karrie propped her right foot on her left shin and stared at Leigh silently. Without a word, Leigh ducked out the back door, presumably to make sure the hellions got on the bus.

Left alone in the house, stunned by what she had just witnessed, Karrie stared at her phone and considered calling her mom. Maybe she had some idea who the hell these people were who were living in Leigh's house and where Leigh and her family had gone. Deciding she wasn't ready to talk to her mother at this hour, because talking to her mother would surely involve personal questions she didn't want to answer, she pushed off the counter and moved to the sliding glass door. As she had last night, she opened the blinds first and then the door. A cool gray day greeted her.

Rain would be good, she thought as she stepped outside. But even this beat that dry, unrelenting heat in Phoenix. She took another drink and rolled her eyes at her cup. Another swallow, and she would need a refill already. The wooden deck was rough under her feet. She eyed the swing warily.

The cushioned pillows on it were faded to a worn out blue and orange. A spider had spun a complicated web around one end. Thankfully, the spider appeared to be long gone, but the idea of getting hung up in the silken web made Karrie shiver.

Passing on the swing, she made her way across the deck to the only lounge chair there. The frame was still shiny metal—Karrie thought this might be the chair Brad and the kids had given to Leigh for Mother's Day last May—but there was already a stain in the navy-blue fabric high on the back of it. She settled into the chair, the sounds of laughter and childish voices in the air. She assumed the voices belonged to the kids getting on the bus, and she wondered if Leigh had come back inside yet.

She didn't love Dom. Not anymore. He had promised so much in the beginning, and then given too little, and now each time he said the things she had once yearned to hear, she heard the emptiness in his tone rather than the words he didn't mean. But not loving him and not needing him were two different things at the moment.

Part of her wanted to pack up and head right back to him. At least their go-nowhere relationship was familiar, and therefore, easy. Well, easier than this, maybe.

Just as she tapped the voicemail icon and lifted her phone to her ear, the door behind her slid open.

"Karrie." Dom's voice in her ear was sexy and warm. But Leigh stood over her now, so she tapped end and lowered the phone to her lap. Rather than sit, Leigh leaned on the rail and avoided Karrie's eyes.

"You shouldn't have come."

The whisper was louder than Gino's shrieking just moments ago. Eyes on her sister, Karrie rolled her lips inward and nodded slowly. Leigh glanced at her, but she wouldn't hold eye contact.

Karrie tried to breathe around the knife in her throat.

"And why's that?" Her voice was tight and small, and the tears she refused to cry last night threatened now. When Leigh didn't answer her, she dabbed at her eyes and searched her mind, her heart, for something to say. Coming up empty, she laid her head on the chair and closed her eyes. "I saw Daxton Law last night."

"Lucky you," Leigh mumbled.

"Anybody else still around?" She blinked her eyes open to look at Leigh.

"I don't know, Karrie. Haven't had a lot of time lately to worry about it."

Chagrined, Karrie raised her eyebrows and looked away. She nodded. Felt that ache in her throat again as Leigh moved back toward the house.

"Leigh."

"What?"

"Why did you tell Hazel she can't go to open gym?"

"Because I have to work. And I can't just leave to pick her up. I need her here to watch Gino—"

All of that might be true, but there was more to it, and Karrie knew it. She shook her head as she twisted around on the chair and climbed to her feet.

"But none of that's new. And you said there was no point anymore."

Leigh blinked at her.

"Why? Why would you say that? To Hazel?"

Arms crossed defensively over her chest, Leigh looked at Karrie with glassy eyes and shrugged.

"Some of the girls go there to play. Practice."

"Basketball?" Karrie tilted her head. She felt a little prick of adrenaline pulse through her at the thought. The memory of the ball in her hand last night.

"Any sport," Leigh said simply. Karrie nodded. Maybe it was just a safe way for kids to kill some time in the afternoon after school. And maybe some of them did actually use that time to practice their sports. Her niece wanted to go there to practice basketball. Hazel wasn't a natural athlete, but the girl worked her butt off trying to learn the sport and improve her skills. Because she wanted to be like her mom.

"So, why would you say that to her? That there was no point?"

"Well, when their coach is laid up in a rehab center hooked up to life support, kinda puts a damper on the whole season, doesn't it?"

Eight

THE BELL JANGLED OVER KARRIE'S HEAD AS SHE stepped inside the café. She glanced up at it—how could the wait staff here stand the noise? She would take a hammer to it before her first day working here was over—and then swept her gaze around the well-lit, yet homey interior. Jada's House, like so many of the fun places here, had not existed when Karrie still lived at home. Therefore, she was always tickled to go to the trendy places her mom chose when she was home for a visit.

She found her mom holding court at a table for two on the east wall. Thankfully, the ladies she currently entertained were gathered around her, rather than seated at their table. Karrie had run into that issue more than once. Her mom was an exercise instructor at a local gym. Mid-fifties, the woman was a petite little bombshell that all the men still ogled and all the women still wanted to be.

Add to that the fact that she was nice, that she was happy and always had a smile to give, and there was always a flock of people around her. Karrie often spent the first five or ten minutes of their lunch dates or coffee outings standing just outside the circle, somewhat proud of her mom and somewhat annoyed to have to take a number just to see her.

"Karrie!" Tawny Koenig's face lit up when she saw her daughter just inside the door. Tawny, ash blond hair cut in the ever-popular stack, scooted her chair back as if to stand. The women surrounding her turned as one and fussed at Karrie much the same way her mom just did as she made her way across the café.

"Hey." Karrie offered them all a tight-lipped smile. She was glad her mom had friends, but it made her uncomfortable to be treated as something special simply because she was Tawny Koenig's daughter. "How are you?"

"When did you get in?" her mom asked as she stood to hug her.

"Last night."

"Why didn't you call?"

"Ugh. Just." She shook her head and licked her lips self-consciously. The women watched her with bated breath, as if she might impart words of wisdom for them to live by. Tawny patted her hand as they eased away from each other. Karrie set her purse on the table and sat as her mom said her goodbyes and shooed her friends, fans—who knew?—away. "I was tired. I had hoped Leigh and I could talk."

"And how did that go?" Tawny asked quietly, but Karrie could tell from the sharp arch in her brow that her mother already knew the answer to her question.

"It went so well that I went for a run. And ended up shooting baskets at school."

The smile that flashed over her mom's face was so bright, Karrie almost reached to dig her sunglasses out of her purse. Instead, she fidgeted with her table service, only to meet her mom's eyes and drop her hands to her lap.

"Do you get to do that often?"

"What? Get blown off by my big sister?" Karrie tried and failed to tamp down the sarcasm. "No. I don't, actually. And it sucks."

The waitress, apparently another fan or friend of her mom's, approached with two menus printed on pastel green cardstock. Karrie perused the menu while her mom and the woman spoke for a moment. She always got the Cobb salad and a cup of tomato soup when she was here, even if it was ninety-five degrees outside. Today, though, she decided it was time to mix it up. After all, she had taken a vacation—a real vacation, which was unheard of—and she intended to tell Dom when she got back that they were through.

Time to step out of the box and live a little, Karrie Mallory.

She felt her mom's eyes on her as she studied the menu. Apparently, it was go time, and she wasn't sure what she wanted. Well, she did know what she wanted. And that was a change. No more letting things slide. No more reacting to life as it roared past. Karrie was ready to live.

"I'll have the Fuji apple salad," she announced. She laughed softly when her mom's mouth went slack with surprise. "And what's the soup of the day?"

"It's—"

"No." Karrie shook her head as she handed her menu over to the waitress. "Never mind. I'll take a cup of whatever it is. And tea, please."

Her mom eyed her curiously as the waitress walked away. She must have decided to ignore the elephant at the table with them.

"Play ball," she said as if their conversation hadn't been interrupted, first by Karrie's own sarcasm and then by the appearance of the waitress. "Do you get to play much in Phoenix?"

Karrie picked up her water glass and sipped from it.

Too tired and maybe too worried—definitely too confused—to keep up the sarcasm and the hard feelings over Leigh's attitude, she shook her head.

"No. I haven't done that in ages."

"I miss those days." Her mom's voice was soft and wistful, and the memories, her old life, old family, tugged at Karrie's heart.

"Me, too." She cleared her throat. "I saw Jed Isles there last night. With Dax Law. What was he doing there?" Jed had been the boys' basketball coach when Karrie was in school.

"Jed's the A.D. His daughter just got married."

"Isn't she, like, ten?"

Karrie ignored the little knife twist in her heart. Maybe it seemed unfair that girls so much younger than her were getting married, but it wasn't. Karrie had made her choice. She had focused on her education and then her career. But the no regrets thing stopped there. Because she had also walked into her relationship with Dom Wolfe with her eyes wide-open. Married man with children at home. And she'd been naïve enough to believe their relationship was different. When Dom told her in the beginning that he and his wife were separated and that he intended to file for divorce, she had signed on the dotted line. She would have bought ocean-front property from him there in Arizona, too, if he had suggested it.

Now she knew better.

"Did you talk to Daxton?"

The question pulled her away from stewing over Dom, anyway. She snorted and cleared her throat. Shook her head.

"Um. Not really."

"You didn't?!" Her mom's sincere surprise baffled her.

"No?" Karrie shrugged. "Mom, he was older than me—"

"Well, he still is, hon, but you could talk to the man."

"The man," Karrie started, "made a comment about my ass and then continued to dig a hole and bury himself."

Her mom only laughed.

"He's not so bad."

"If you say so." Karrie shook her head. She wondered why her mom was defending him. Dax had hung out with Leigh and Brad when they were younger, and Karrie remembered him being cute and rebellious. Maybe he had pictured himself as the new James Dean, but Karrie had hung out with his younger brother, and though she never missed a chance to look at Dax when she could, she hadn't been convinced he was all that tough.

"His brother's a police officer now. Somewhere in Missouri."

"I think I would rather coach basketball," Karrie mumbled. "Speaking of which. Mom. What is going on with Leigh? What—why did Brad—I don't get it."

She leaned halfway over the table, anxiously awaiting whatever her mom might say, ready to latch on to whatever explanation she offered. When her mom only stared back at her, Karrie slumped back in her seat and sighed.

"I don't know, Karrie. Leigh's not talking. She's not accepting help from any of us."

"That makes no sense."

Her mom shrugged helplessly. She looked up when their waitress returned with their drinks. Karrie took that moment to study her mom, relieved to see that she looked good. Healthy and happy. The same as always. Unlike her sister.

"She used to be so on top of everything. Ya know?" Karrie cocked her head. "Like, she had schedules for everything. Every activity was on the daily schedule. She probably had times penciled in for sneezing and laughing. I'm not kidding—"

"I know that." Her mom's nod was slow and precise.

"And now, she's like…I don't even know. I don't recognize her. The house? Have you been over there lately? I don't think she's had it open in weeks. The drapes and blinds were all closed. The air was on, but the thermostat's on seventy-eight. There's…and the kids. She was grouchy with the kids, and they were demons this morning—"

"She's had quite a shock, Karrie," her mom reminded her. "What's happened to Leigh is *your* day-to-day normal. But this is her family. This is her husband. The father—"

"I know that." Karrie took a deep breath. "I know that."

It irritated her that her mom assumed working in an ER setting could make her cold and heartless enough that she wouldn't feel for her own sister during a time like this. But because she wasn't the issue here, nor did she want to be, she swallowed down the irritation and reminded herself she was worried about Leigh.

"I guess it's not even any of that." She spoke quietly, exhausted already, and she had only just come home. "I don't understand why she doesn't want me here."

"Of course, she does—"

Karrie shook her head. "This morning, she looked me in the eye." Okay, not exactly, but still. "And said I shouldn't have come."

Karrie's throat tightened on the last word, but she got it out. Eyes burning with tears, she stared at her mom and waited for her to make it better. For her to explain why her sister would say such a thing. Why Leigh was referring to Brad's condition in clinical terms.

When her mom swallowed hard and averted her eyes, Karrie's heart slid south in her chest.

"Mom?"

"I don't know, Karrie," she whispered. "She's pushed me away, too. She doesn't want me at the house."

"Do you see the kids?"

"Yes. I pick them up from school sometimes. And they come over. But she doesn't want anyone around the house."

Karrie sighed. She dabbed at her eyes and then tucked a strand of hair behind her ear.

"I was hoping she would confide in you."

Karrie raised her eyebrows. "Doesn't seem likely."

"Keep trying."

"I will."

Their lunches were delivered during that lull in conversation. Karrie wasn't sure she could eat after her mom couldn't reassure her everything would be okay. But, the soup of the day, which appeared to be cheesy asparagus, promised to be warm and comforting, so she spooned a bite and then moaned appreciatively.

"So." Her mom kept her eyes trained on her fork as she stabbed at her salad. "What's going on with you and your boyfriend?"

Karrie nearly choked on the soup. She blinked at her mom and wondered what Dr. Dominic Wolfe would think of being referred to as her boyfriend. Sophisticated, made of money, and sexy besides, she doubted he would appreciate it.

"We're not seeing each other anymore."

She was surprised at how good it felt to say it out loud. She just prayed she would have the guts to say it to his face, to tell him they were through, when she went back to Phoenix.

Nine

Dax pulled the key from the ignition and eyed a group of kids as they walked in front of his truck. He glanced at his phone as he climbed down from the cab and swung the door closed. It wasn't quite three-thirty, so he was right on time to meet Matt Ware, who coached the junior high-aged Warrior Basketball travel team. The high school team was well-known for its winning record; Dax had been at the helm for three years, and for two years before that, he had been an assistant coach. One thing he had admired about his predecessor was the way he kept his finger on the pulse of all the younger club teams and evaluated the boys individually. The high school team had almost been hand-picked through the years. No wonder they carried the winning record as long as they had.

Besides coaching the varsity basketball team, Dax was also the IT guru at the high school. As much as he liked technology, there wasn't a whole lot of excitement in keeping the school's IT department going. The beginning of the school year was always busy, and getting new parents set up to use the online grade reporting system tended to take up a lot of time. And of course, now and then a student or two decided to use their iPads to cheat on exams or send inappropriate messages to other students. But Dax much preferred the afterschool part of his job to the regular office hours.

The day was cool and gray, but he had rolled his sleeves up early on. Now, as he walked up the sidewalk toward the squat, red-bricked building, he tucked his hands in the pockets of his trousers. He had spent some time last night working out the specifics of a new defense, but mostly, he had wasted the rest of his night trying to figure out who the blonde with the nice ass was. He had finally decided she looked a little familiar, but he never had come up with a name.

And then he wondered if he just told himself she looked familiar because she seemed to know who he was.

More to the point, though, would he ever see her again? Colson wasn't a big town by any stretch of the imagination. Honestly, Dax liked that. Just right for a guy like him. He had enough room here to stretch out and soak up the fun, the good vibes, but the pace of life here was more enjoyable. Chicago had been a bit too frantic for him. As had Keely, his ex-wife. Colson wasn't slow or backbeat, though, which most of the time was a good thing. He wouldn't be able to stay in a town that was still and dry like a ghost town or just a small town like in the movies.

But a small town like in the movies might assure him that someone would know who the girl was. If he lived in Shepley, a town of nine hundred about twenty-seven miles north of Colson, he could slip into the coffee shop and mention the blonde—he would have to leave out the part about her great ass, because saying stuff like that in public in a small town would be frowned upon—and someone would either know her or at the very least, do a few minutes of sleuthing and then provide him with a name.

The hallways of St. Anne's were only dotted with kids or small groups of kids at this time of day. Dax high-fived a few of the guys as he headed past the principal's office toward the gym. Matt Ware didn't have an office here, but Dax knew he would find him in the gym. The Warriors travel club didn't belong to any particular elementary school. It was a community team that drew from all the area elementary schools. But Matt Ware spent most of his time at St. Anne's. Dax supposed it was most convenient for him since his kids attended school here.

Ware sat on the bleachers, a clipboard on his knee and a pen in hand. Dax moseyed through the gym toward him, but he kept his eyes on the boys under the far basket. They were running a passing drill. Dax was pleased to see some crisp chest passes.

He ducked when he heard a squeal and turned in time to see two giggling girls hurrying toward him. They chased a runaway volleyball. Dax didn't get volleyball. Sure, he knew the rules, but he didn't get how it was fun. Still, he did like the kids, and the girls always wanted to flirt with him. He would never flirt back, but he did talk to them and every word out of his mouth seemed to make them swoon.

Too bad adult women didn't seem to feel that way about him. Like the blonde at the gym last night.

Dax reached back and palmed the ball. He grinned as the girls neared him and tossed the ball to the one in front.

"Hey, Molly."

"Hi, Mr. Law." The girl was breathless, though he doubted it was from running across the court after the ball. She turned away quickly, but not before he saw the furious blush flood her cheeks. Dax chuckled, stuck his hands back in his pockets, and continued across the gym. Now he watched a group of four girls under a side basket on the far end of the gym. Two of them didn't look bad. The other two were painful to watch.

"Is this St. Anne's or the Colson free zoo?" he asked as he stopped at the bleachers in front of Matt Ware.

Matt, eyes on the clipboard, grinned and shook his head.

"Actually, it's getting to be a little bit like daycare."

Dax pursed his lips as he swept his gaze over the gym. There were at least thirty kids here.

"That's the idea, though. Right?" He looked back at Matt. The school had opened the gym for more than one reason. Sure, it was a great opportunity for kids to come in and be active and practice a sport. It was also a good option for parents who worked and couldn't find or couldn't afford after-school daycare.

Matt whooshed out a resigned sigh as he set the clipboard and pen aside.

"Yeah. It is." He nodded. "I guess I shouldn't complain."

Dax knew Matt spent a lot of time here in a volunteer capacity. He also knew there was a school employee here somewhere who supervised the gym activity.

"You know of any new kids here?" Dax hoped he sounded casual. He had no desire to share the story about how he had dined on his foot last night. He just hoped Isles didn't feel the need to share the story.

Matt crossed his arms over his chest and pressed his lips together. "Yeah," he finally answered, but he drew the word out to be a good five syllables at least. "New family started here in August. They have twins in first grade."

"Yeah?" Dax tried to picture the woman in his head. He supposed it was possible she had first grade twins.

"Mm-hmm. They moved here from Michigan, I think."

Dax wondered how to ask what the mom looked like without giving himself away.

"Two boys. Curly red hair like Little Orphan Annie. Dad's bald as the day's long, but their mama's got a whole lot of red hair. Smart little guys, too. They're gonna get pretty familiar with the principal's office before this year's over, I would guess."

Dax grinned. Question answered. He was disappointed but relieved, too. He needed the blonde from last night to be single. Completely unattached. Looking for some fun, no strings attached, if he could choose.

He stepped to his right and put his hand out to stop yet another runaway ball, this one his favorite kind. He dribbled the orange Wilson basketball and offered Hazel Avery a small smile when she jogged hesitantly toward him. Now there was a kid he felt sorry for. And there was a kid who most certainly didn't belong on a basketball court.

He sent her an easy bounce pass and flinched when she muffed the catch. Felt a flash of guilt when she winced and waved her hand. He had jammed her finger, even though he was careful with the pass. Cheeks bright red, she scrambled after the ball and turned her back to him.

"How's Brad Avery doing?" Dax asked Matt as he watched Hazel trot awkwardly back to the group of girls under the side basket. "Anything new?"

"Not that I know of." Matt shook his head.

Dax hung his head and blew out a sigh. He wasn't sure which was worse. Imagining Brad laid up in the hospital indefinitely with possible brain damage or imagining his wife and kids at home trying to make sense of how their family had been blown apart so suddenly.

Ten

KARRIE IGNORED HER PHONE AS GINO WOBBLED ON his bike to the end of the driveway. He did okay until he remembered that his dad wasn't behind him, holding the back of the seat. Then the fear got him, and the bike wobbled uncontrollably. Karrie had caught him three of the four times he had gone down. She had to hand it to him, though. He climbed back on the damned thing after scraping his knees up. Hadn't cried, and that kind of broke Karrie's heart more than crocodile tears would have. He had simply studied the scratches on his knees, dabbed at the blood that had risen to the surface of the broken skin, and then rubbed his hands together and climbed back on the bike.

Maybe they were all like that. Maybe they were all okay, until they remembered Brad wasn't behind them, watching over them. Leigh had moments this afternoon when she seemed normal. She still hadn't said much to Karrie regarding the accident itself or the circus act Karrie had witnessed that morning. But she asked about her lunch with their mom. And she had caught Karrie up on some of the gossip around town, even though earlier today Karrie's comment about Dax Law and her question about other people they went to school with had been met with disdain.

"Where's Hazel?" Karrie asked as Gino made his way past her again, studiously eyeing the pavement in front of him.

"In 'er room," he answered without so much as a glance.

"Why? It's so nice out here." She stretched now, arms above her head, and looked around. The basketball goal post was still at the side of the drive. The net was gone, but the rim and backboard were still attached. "You guys should appreciate this weather. Phoenix is still hotter than—"

Gino blinked at her as he hit the brakes. Karrie smashed her lips together as she jumped forward to catch him. He didn't fall, though. He simply put his foot down on the drive and held the handlebars firmly, as if he had been riding forever instead of just a few months. Karrie wouldn't ask, but she assumed Leigh hadn't been outside with him much since the accident.

"She's always in 'er room," Gino mumbled.

"Will she come out? If I ask her to?"

Gino shrugged. He stepped off the bike, dragging and banging his right leg over the bar. Karrie flinched as she watched him scoot and hop backwards and took a deep breath when he appeared to be steady on his feet again.

"I dunno." He put the kickstand down and walked toward the garage.

"What're—? Gino, what're you doing?" She followed him and watched with a frown as he dug through an old refrigerator box that had apparently been designated as his toy box.

"Collecting ants." The tone of his voice suggested she was ridiculous for not knowing what he was going to do next. She watched him pull a bucket and a magnifying glass from the box.

"Collecting—? You're collecting ants? In a sand bucket?"

Gino shot her a look over his shoulder as he crossed the drive and then lowered himself to kneel at the edge of the concrete. Karrie sighed. She was all about helping him ride his bike or tossing a ball—any kind of ball—or even a frisbee, but she had never thought of herself as an ant collector. Or any sort of bug collector. She wasn't totally on board with *becoming* a bug collector, either.

"Where's your basketball?"

"It's flat," Gino answered without looking at her. She started to groan out loud, but when he did look at her as if he was going to comment, she flashed him a big smile. "Hazel's is in the garage."

"Hazel's? Bike?"

Okay, she could work with that. She wanted to spend time with Gino or Hazel or both of them, actually. But more than that, at the moment, she needed to move. Dom had called her twice today. The first time she had just been leaving lunch with her mom, and with her mom's nosy questions about him still ringing in her ears and her irrational anger with his unwillingness to give more than he had ever promised her, she had no desire to talk to him. The second time was about three minutes ago.

She missed him. Well, she missed the physical contact. Couldn't really claim she missed being with someone who cared about her, because no matter what the hell was going on with Leigh, she knew her sister cared. As did her mother. But she missed the status quo, and therefore, talking to Dom right now would not be a good idea. She might cave. She might say things she had no business saying. Again. Telling Dom she loved him the first time had been reckless. The third and fourth and seventeenth and hundredth had just been flat out stupid.

"Her ball." Gino sounded put out when he answered her.

"Hazel's ball." Karrie nodded. She grinned when Gino's answer and her question finally clicked. "Oh. Good."

She waited, thinking he would put the ant collecting on hold for a moment so he could get Hazel's ball for her. When seconds passed and Gino didn't so much as glance at her, she sighed and moseyed into the garage.

"How's school?" she called over her shoulder as she ducked her head into a cabinet that looked promising. No dice. She had assumed she would find Hazel's basketball, at the very least, some of the kids' toys. The cabinet apparently belonged to her brother-in-law. She straightened and turned to look at Gino. Head low over the bucket—was he looking for ants in the garage?—he had no intention of answering her. "Gino."

"Yes?" he asked with a sigh. She waited until he looked at her before she spoke again. His wide-eyed stare was filled more with boredom than innocence.

"How's school going?"

"Fine."

"Fine?"

He nodded. Continued to stare at her, though he didn't seem inclined to say more.

"Mm-kay." She nodded and smiled. Gino, one knee resting on the cement floor and one knee bent and tucked under his chin, dropped his gaze back to the bucket and dismissed her. Karrie propped her hands on her hips and looked around the garage. What had happened to her nephew? To all of them? She felt like she had slipped into an alternate reality; the people in this house looked like her family, but they were all like pen and ink outlines of the people she loved.

With a sigh, Karrie glanced at Leigh's minivan. When she noticed a small dent in the front quarter panel, she moved to touch it, as if she could read the story of her sister's life in the imperfect metal. She looked over her shoulder, but Gino was still busy with the ant collecting. Although Karrie didn't think he had any ants, which only made her feel worse. She had gone from favorite aunt status to backseat to a bucket and a magnifying glass in the space of a few minutes.

After a half-hearted search of the garage, she found Hazel's basketball. Sadly, it had only enough air in it to bounce just below her knees when she dribbled it. She tossed it back into the corner where she found it, dusted her hands off, and headed to the back door.

"Gino. I'm gonna go find Hazel."

"'kay." He nodded, eyes still on the bucket. She stood for a moment, wondering if he ever moved from that spot when he hunted ants. With a shrug that was wasted on Gino, she pulled the door open and stepped into the kitchen. She drew up short when she found Leigh on her knees in front of the refrigerator.

"What's…what're—what're you doing, Leigh?"

"Scrubbing the fridge out." Leigh spoke as if it should be obvious to Karrie what she was doing. Karrie wasn't crazy about the task, but she did it on a sort-of regular basis, and she never had to be on her knees to scrub anything. Had someone spilled something? Maybe Gino spilled his apple juice? That would be sticky and could possibly call for some elbow grease.

"Where's Hazel?"

"In 'er room." Head in the fridge now, Leigh's voice sounded flat and muffled. Karrie blinked at Leigh's response. Since when did Leigh let her kids just waste their days away? No, she hadn't ever been the mom to make them sign up for tons of activities; they always just wanted to be on the go, whether it was for art classes or piano lessons or ball practice. And when they weren't on the go for organized activities, the kids were always outside doing something that kept them active.

Karrie slipped around the kitchen table and out of the room. She heard music coming from Hazel's room and cringed. Some kind of pop boy band. She listened to the same kind of stuff when she was Hazel's age, but her tastes in music and pretty much everything else had changed. For the better, she decided when she stood in front of her niece's closed door. She knocked softly and then a bit harder. When she thought she heard Hazel answer, she twisted the doorknob and opened the door slowly. Her heart sort of splintered, poked her lung or something, because when she saw her usually bubbly niece flopped out on her bed staring at the ceiling, it hurt to breathe.

"Hey." She inched her way into Hazel's room, completely aware that this might be a mix of things.

The bad mojo in the overly pink bedroom might be a combination of the horrid decorating—looked like Pepto Bismol, and while the stuff had worked for stomach aches when she was a kid, it was the grossest pink she had ever seen and that was saying a lot, considering how ugly Leigh's childhood room had been—the usual funk and angst of being a tween girl, and the deal with her dad. Karrie had suggested to Leigh that they go and visit Brad when her sister had come home from work. Leigh had simply said no.

Hazel rolled her head on her pillow to look at her. No tears. No frowns. Her face was so smooth and blank, it could have been a mask.

"How was school?" Karrie asked as she approached her bed.

"Fine." Hazel shrugged. Karrie bent her knee and lowered it to the bed to perch there. She dropped her hand on Hazel's thigh and noted how skinny the girl was.

"Wanna go shoot some baskets with me?"

"No."

"How come?"

Another shrug.

"You went to the gym after school, didn't you?" Karrie cocked her head as Hazel met her eyes. She nodded. Karrie wondered how that had happened since Leigh had told her no this morning, but she wasn't going to ask Hazel. "Worn out from shooting there, huh?"

"Nope."

Karrie waited for Hazel to say more, but she was quiet. Karrie took a long, deep breath. She swept her gaze around the room. Decided if she lived in town, she would offer to help Hazel redecorate.

"Got a lot of homework?" Karrie tried again.

"Nuh-uh."

"Wanna go for a walk?"

"No. I'm tired."

Karrie rolled her lips inward to hold in the questions, the worries. The longer she was here, and God help her, it had only been a day, the more concerned she was. But the questions and the concern were better directed at Leigh.

"Mm-kay." She nodded. "I'm gonna…" She wasn't sure what she was going to say or do. She rolled her head on her neck and looked back at Hazel. Her heart dropped a bit in her chest when Hazel turned over to lie with her back to her. "Go for a run."

"'kay."

Karrie slipped out of Hazel's room, grateful to leave the boy band behind, but her heart was heavy to leave Hazel alone. She moved quickly through the kitchen, ignored Leigh, and banged out the back door. Gino was gone, so she moved to the back door of the garage and peeked out to find him. Satisfied that he was safe when she saw him by the fence in the backyard, she walked out the front of the garage and took off at a jog.

She didn't stop to consider where she was going or think about seeing anyone in particular until she had run two blocks, the sound of her feet slapping the pavement soothing her. She had turned in the direction of her old school, and suddenly the thought of banging a ball around a backboard for a while was more appealing than anything else on the agenda.

She laughed at that.

There was nothing on her agenda. Because her sister wouldn't even come clean and tell her what the hell was going on, let alone loosen the reigns and let her help.

She wasn't necessarily running toward Dax Law. Yep, the guy was smoking hot, and that smile last night had made her tingle in parts she didn't care to think about. She wouldn't mind looking at him again, as long as he kept his mouth closed and didn't make another rude comment about her ass.

Nope. She wasn't running toward Dax Law. She was still running away. She had just added to the list of people she was running from.

Eleven

Dax had heard and ignored the dribbling of a ball earlier. He was a basketball coach, after all, and the pounding of the ball on the court had become background noise a long time ago. He stopped typing now and stared at his computer screen. He was in the middle of an email to the varsity coach of a team in the quad cities, trying to finalize a schedule change for a game later this season.

Later this *basketball* season. Which started in November. As far as he knew, it was still only September. Fingers still hovering over his keyboard, Dax moved his gaze to the small calendar on the corner of his desk. Yep. September all month long, a good ten days left. Definitely not basketball season.

Volleyball. The girls had practiced earlier this afternoon, right after school. For the boys, it was football and soccer season. Therefore, no one should be dribbling or banging shots off the backboard. Not that the boards rattled, but again, Dax was a basketball guy. He recognized the sounds when he heard them.

Maybe…

Slowly, almost as if he were in a trance, he dropped his hands to the arms of his chair and rolled it back away from the desk. He stood and moved around the corner of the desk and out to the door. Yep. Still heard the dribbling.

Maybe it was the mystery shooter from the other night. Maybe if he didn't do something stupid, like comment on her ass, she would talk to him. His whole body hummed to life when he saw her down on the court. Her platinum blond hair was pulled back in a messy ponytail, but the messy was cute, as much of a turn on as her ass had been the other night when she was leaning over at the foul line, her tight little butt sticking up in the air.

Dax slipped his hands in his pockets. Rather than stand up here and watch her and risk missing an opportunity to talk to her, he moved swiftly down the steps to the gym floor. She was at the far end of the court, and Dax watched through the volleyball net as she launched a three pointer. The board didn't rattle, because the ball swished through the net without touching it. Impressed, he arched his eyebrows and watched as she moved to rebound her own shot and power it up again from under the basket.

She looked familiar. Curious now, besides interested, Dax moseyed across the floor and wondered what she would do when she saw him. Technically, he supposed she was trespassing. But he didn't see the harm in it. They didn't have open gym time scheduled, but on the other hand, there weren't any hard, fast rules against someone shooting baskets when the gym was open. However, if she were a stranger who happened in to do some shooting, the administration would probably frown on it.

But Dax was pretty sure she wasn't a stranger.

She banked a shot in, reacted in time when her rebound went wild, and snagged it with her fingertips. Dax watched her pull it in for a tight dribble and then work the ball smoothly between her legs. No stranger to basketball, that was for damned sure.

This time when she spun to shoot, she noticed him. Rather than put the ball up again, she pivoted on her toes and held the ball against her hip, arm draped over it. He noticed—all in a split second—that she was breathing heavy, her cheeks were flushed with an energetic pink, and her fingers were bare. Oh. And that her eyes were narrowed at him, eyebrows ready to slide into a frown.

"You're back."

Okay, as small talk or flirting went, that sucked. But maybe it beat starting out with a comment about her ass. Quite possibly she had taken that as an insult. Or maybe she was touchy about sexual comments and harassment. A lot of women were sensitive about comments or whistles now, though Dax hadn't meant any disrespect. Just hard not to say something when he saw something he liked.

She licked her lips and huffed out another long, deep breath as he stopped to stand just a few feet from her.

Despite the beads of sweat on her forehead, she smelled fresh and sweet, like oranges. Dax wanted to move closer just to breathe her in, but he reminded himself that would be a bad move.

"Kicking me out?" she asked quietly.

"No." He shrugged.

"Come down to take me on?"

One blond eyebrow slanted upward while the other lowered. Interesting. A bit of a challenge, maybe. An invitation and a warning issued all at the same time.

"Best of ten free throws?" he suggested.

"Well, sure, but I was thinking a little one-on-one."

Dax's mouth went dry. Glad for the loose-fitting sports shorts he wore, he looked away. Dragged his eyes up the wall to the old scoreboard and forced himself to think about molecules. And gray matter. And parrots. Anything except a little one-on-one with this piece of work standing in front of him.

"You think you can handle me?"

He looked back at her when he thought it was safe. Found out he was wrong when she arched both brows and walloped him right in the pride with a look that said *are you kidding?* and a little snort that escaped her very pink, very wet lips. Paralyzed, Dax watched the tip of her tongue dart out to stroke over her lips again.

He wondered what she would taste like. If he licked her lips right now, would he taste oranges? Or was that something in her shampoo or lotion?

"Law?"

He snapped out of his thoughts, again grateful for the loose fit of his shorts, and stepped back from her. She watched him, though, eyes reading his mind if the look on her face was any indication.

"Do you know me?"

The words came out small, and he hated that. That and the way she grinned, as if she was amused.

"Do you?" He propped his hands on his hips.

Rather than answer him, the girl looked over her shoulder at the basket. Dax took the opportunity to let his eyes roam down over her shoulders and her breasts. Saw the moment she went from relaxed to ready as she cupped her palm around the basketball, still pressed to her side.

"Are you in?" She looked back at him.

"Sure." He tossed his hands up to indicate he was ready. He could play for a while. The only thing he had left to do here was finish the email he started earlier, and that involved clicking send. Then again, maybe he should read it over and make sure he hadn't typed something about the blonde who had just challenged him to a game of one-on-one. She had gotten under his skin after seeing her just one time.

Totally possible he could have typed some thoughts into that email. Totally not a good thing if he had. He would definitely read it again before sending, and he decided he would go easy on her now, so she would come back again. "Gotta take it back. Half court?"

She shrugged and pushed the ball at him.

"Just don't get hung up in the volleyball net."

"You play?"

She shrugged and turned her nose up just the slightest bit. "High school. Not enough cardio for me."

"What's your name?" he asked her. He took the ball from her as they moved back toward the volleyball net. "Your ball first."

She snorted softly and raised her eyebrows at him.

"Why's that? Because I'm a girl?"

He shrugged, but before he could respond, she cocked her head at him and continued, "You blew it yesterday, Dax Law. With the comment about my ass. You can't give me a line about ladies first and call it even."

"For the record," he pushed the ball at her again, "I was talking to Jed. Not you. And I whispered—"

"You didn't, really, though," she argued.

"Not to mention that I was *admiring* your ass. I didn't mean to insult you."

She moved around him and put the ball against her hip again.

"You can't just walk around commenting like that on women's bodies."

"We've been doing it since the beginning of time, Blondie."

"Blondie?"

"You won't tell me your name, I'll call you Blondie." Dax settled into a defensive position. "And also? Women check out men's bodies just the same damned way men look at women."

"Possibly," she agreed. "However, women know how to whisper. And—"

Dax opened his mouth to argue, to defend himself. Voices carried in this damned gym. Not his fault. But she shook her head and plunged into her second point, effectively cutting him off.

"You don't *know* if *I* would make that comment about *your* ass."

"I bet you get compliments all the time."

"Are you kidding me?" She cocked her head and stared at him with angry eyes. "Compliments?"

Dax raised his eyebrows and nodded.

"A compliment would be telling me I look nice today.

Or commenting on my jump shot. Not *look at that ass*. Or *look at that babe*. Or *check out that rack*."

Dax stood up straight and threw his hands up in defense.

"I did not say a word about your rack." Naturally, his eyes dropped to said part of her body as his mouth formed the word.

Blondie shrugged and offered him a closed-mouth smile.

"Okay." He nodded and stepped closer to her. "So you're telling me that when a guy finds a woman attractive or sexy, she would rather he say she's got a nice jump shot than to say that she has a damned fine ass or that he loves her curves or that her lips look like they would taste like sin?"

Blondie's eyebrows jumped in disbelief. Her mouth dropped open around the shape of the word *wow*.

"Are you married?" she asked with a quiet laugh. "You're not married. Are you?"

"Why?" He would like to think she was asking because she was interested, but the smirk on her face told him otherwise. She was laughing at him. Again.

"Because those lines are bad."

"Who says they're lines?"

She giggled. "You used to be cool." She shook her head. "What happened to you?"

"What?"

"You had game in high school." She shrugged almost apologetically, but she was still laughing.

"Wait." He reached toward her to hold her up, to keep the game from going anywhere. His fingertips stroked her wrist, and Dax felt the zing of electricity shoot up his arm. Apparently, she didn't feel it, because she put the ball down in a tight dribble, moved around him, and laid it up for two points. Dax watched her move, his eyes drawn to her legs and her ass again. She had a pretty shot, but the best part about it was her sweet firm ass in the blue athletic shorts.

"You need to work on your defense a little bit, too." She cleared her throat as she rebounded her own shot and slung the ball at him in a crisp, underhanded pass. Brain still in a fog from the zap of awareness at the skin-on-skin contact, he caught the pass easily and copied her move from earlier. Rested the ball against his hip and draped his arm over it to hold it in place.

"Doesn't count."

"Excuse me?"

"Doesn't count."

"What do you mean it doesn't count? I just scored two points."

"I said wait."

"You're kidding, right?" She grinned, eyebrows jumping again in disbelief. "Really? Are you gonna call time or tell me you aren't ready every time I score?"

"Oh, I'm gonna be damned good and ready the next time you score." Gaze locked with hers, he nodded. He had to give her credit. She didn't blush, but her eyes went wide with surprise, maybe. Or if he was fooling himself, he might say interest.

Hands on her hips, she settled into a defensive crouch and shot him a feisty grin.

"Well, at least you're acknowledging that I am going to score again."

Dax felt a flicker of recognition as he put the ball down in a dribble. Eyes still on her, he had a flash of a younger, skinnier version of the same girl. Same position on the court. Playing her heart out, running her ass off, though admittedly, he hadn't done much looking at her ass back in the day.

He moved slightly, faked right, and then dribbled behind his back to go left. She moved with him, hand out not quite skimming his stomach. She shuffled easily, keeping the toe of one foot aligned with the heel of the other, sliding with him as he worked his way closer to the basket.

When he pulled up for a jump shot to the left of the lane, he assumed she would back away and let him take the shot. He should have known better. Blondie went up with him, hand up to block the shot. She wasn't tall enough, and he got the shot off, absorbing her body against his as she crashed against him.

"That's a foul," he told her, though he didn't mind. The feel of her breasts against his chest as she slid down his front made him consider challenging her to a game of football, so they could have more contact.

"Pansy," she mumbled as she turned to the basket. She thrust her hips back to box him out, but his shot swished through the net for two, and Dax's eyes were on her ass again, so close to his body he had to step backwards to give them both a bit of space.

It hit him suddenly. He knew exactly who she was, and he wasn't sure what he thought about that flash of heat he felt just a moment ago when she had pressed up against him.

Twelve

WHEN NEITHER OF THEM MOVED TO PICK UP DAX'S rebound, the ball bounced toward the bleacher section under the basket. Karrie moved to chase it down, but she stopped short when she heard him.

"What?" She shrugged. "What's wrong?"

"You're Leigh Avery's little sister." His voice was a little soft, which made him sound a little starstruck, and that made Karrie snort again. "Karrie, right?"

Dax Law had graduated with Leigh's class. Karrie had always thought he was cute, changed her mind when he was a senior and decided he was hot, and knew from the word go he would never give her a second glance. Leigh had always been the knockout back in their school days. Pretty blue eyes and honey blond hair. Karrie had been stick thin, all bony angles, and a tomboy down to her toes.

Dax hadn't been around a lot when she was younger, but he was in Leigh's bigger circle of friends, so Karrie had seen him now and then at their house or at football games. He was always the guy to pull her ponytail and tease her about her freckles and any boy in a two-mile vicinity.

He was also Adam Law's brother. And Adam Law had run around with Jake Spencer. Karrie and Jake had gotten biblically acquainted when she was seventeen and then tried to bend themselves to fit into a relationship that neither of them wanted. When it had proved too awkward, they had agreed to just be friends. Karrie hadn't talked to Adam Law or Jake Spencer since the summer after she graduated from school.

She hadn't been referred to as Leigh Avery's—or Leigh Mallory's—little sister since that summer, either. Irritated now to be molded back into that old role, she chafed at his words and then shook her head and turned to go after the ball. It had rolled to a stop at the bleachers, and Karrie leaned over to get it, knowing Dax was looking at her ass again. It was stupid to let it bother her now, just because he finally figured out who she was. Especially since it had been just a little bit fun and flirty before.

"Karrie?" He arched his eyebrows in question when she dribbled back toward him. She met his eyes and nodded curtly as she passed him to take the ball back near half court. "You played volleyball."

"Never said I didn't," she answered. "But I liked basketball better."

"Did you play in college?"

"Basketball? Yep." She nodded. "Played until I blew my knee out."

He cringed. His gaze lit her up as he dragged it down over her shoulders and her hips and stopped at her legs.

"ACL?"

"Yep."

"What do you do now? Are you visiting? You don't live here, do you? I would have heard that. If you had moved back."

"Why would you have heard that?" she asked with a frown. Maybe she had been a big deal back in the day, but the same sort of big deal all the other student athletes had been. Nothing noteworthy in her adult life.

"Well." He shrugged. "Leigh."

She rolled her lips inward and took a moment to let her sister's name fall away before she spoke. When she was a kid, she had been crazy about Leigh, and she had always been thrilled to be recognized as Leigh Mallory's sister. But things had changed. She was an adult now. An independent woman who had been living out from under her sister's shadow for several years. She didn't fit back inside that same shadow quite the same anymore.

And the fact that Leigh had been less than forthcoming about Brad's accident and that Leigh had been closemouthed and less than welcoming when

Karrie had come home to help rubbed her the wrong way.

"Do you see a lot of Leigh? Now?"

She hated to ask. For a number of reasons, Karrie hated to ask Daxton Law if he saw a lot of her sister. For one thing, it made her sound desperate. A little bit out of the loop. And another, she didn't want to owe this guy a damned thing. He was a high school heartthrob, sure, but Karrie also thought he was cocky and arrogant, and at the moment, she wasn't sure he had changed much since what he probably considered the glory days.

He shifted his weight on his feet and then inched forward. Ready to defend. As if he thought this game was going to continue now. As if she gave a damn about beating him after being reminded that her sister's life was a mess, and her hands were tied to do a damned thing about it.

"Mmm."

If she hadn't been watching, she would have missed the slight shrug of his shoulder.

"Not really. Nobody really sees Leigh these days."

Their eyes met. Karrie was surprised to see a hint of compassion in the deep, rich brown. She was also unsatisfied with his answer, both because she knew Leigh wasn't getting out and that bothered her, and because Dax had given her the impression he and

Leigh were still friends and saying that no one saw her these days wasn't really an answer to her question.

"You know. With Brad…"

Karrie nodded. She cleared her throat. Dax and Brad had been friends. She considered asking him about her brother-in-law, but again, she held back because she didn't want to admit to how little she knew about what was going on.

"So." He sort of nodded at the ball in her hands. She had all but forgotten she was holding it. "Are you just back to visit her?"

"Yeah." She licked her lips and looked around the gym. She wondered what time it was. Seemed like she had been here a while. Maybe she should get home and see if Leigh needed her to do anything. Or maybe see if there was anything she could do for Hazel or Gino. "I'm gonna…" She frowned and gave herself a mental shake. "I should go."

"Why?" He waggled his eyebrows at her. It was suggestive and sort of cute and sort of funny, but the reminder of Leigh and that situation had drained her. "Seems suspicious that you have to leave as soon as I tie the game."

She offered him a tired smile and stepped toward him. Dax only stared at her when she offered the ball to him.

"You're not off the hook," he argued.

"Maybe I'm taking it easy on you," she suggested. "I have the feeling getting beat by a girl would really be a blow to your ego."

"My ego?" he repeated. "What about my ego? And who says you can beat me?"

"I can." She grinned at the look of horror on his face. "Trust me. And if I remember correctly, the collective male ego here back in the day was awfully fragile."

"Collective—what? What're you talking about? You can't just leave."

When Dax wouldn't take the ball from her, Karrie lowered it to the floor. She looked at him again as she turned to leave.

"I need to go check on Leigh."

She wanted to call the words back as soon as they were out of her mouth. Leigh had made it clear that whatever was going on in her house was none of Karrie's business. Surely, if it wasn't Karrie's business, it wasn't Daxton Law's business.

"Will I see you again?"

The question stopped her cold. She looked at him over her shoulder and arched an eyebrow at him. This wasn't a date. This was an *oh, hey, you're shooting baskets, can I play, too,* thing. Not at all a situation where the guy asked the girl if he would or could see her again.

"Wasn't a date, Law," she finally announced.

"Tie game," he reminded her. "Bragging rights at stake."

She turned to him but started walking backwards toward the stairs out of the gym.

"Let's just pretend I won," she answered.

"I would much rather play it out."

"Goodnight, Law." She gave him her back again. Felt his eyes on her as she walked away.

"Goodnight, Blondie."

She wouldn't have liked the nickname, but she decided as she jogged up the steps that it was a hell of a lot better than being *Leigh Avery's little sister*. Too bad he figured it out. Well, no, wasn't so much that he realized who she was. Too bad that he had referred to her as Leigh's little sister. The whole world had come crashing back in on her and all the good her run and her time on the court had done her were long gone as she left the school.

Knowing Leigh wasn't going to automatically change speeds when she got back home, that she wasn't going to gush with gratitude for Karrie being there, she walked through the parking lot. What was the hurry? None of them wanted her around. She considered going to see her mom, but she wasn't much in the mood for that, either.

That left Dom. There was a time when just hearing his voice would make her feel better. Now the sound of his voice only reminded her things were never going to change, and she had done it to herself. Still. Dom's voice right now beat her own voice bouncing around in her head, worrying about her sister and her husband.

She walked out of Leigh's house earlier without her phone. It had been incredibly freeing, and she felt lighter on the jog to the school. Now, though, she wished she had it. Not because she was worried Leigh or the kids would see anything on it that she would rather keep to herself. It was password protected, and she couldn't imagine any of the three of them pulling a random code from their heads to figure it out. Not to mention that she doubted any of them would be interested enough to notice it on the counter in the kitchen, let alone pick it up.

No, she wished she had it because she would call Dom. She had no idea where he would be now, and odds were, she would only get his voicemail. But at least she could hear his voice and quiet her own.

Thirteen

It was full dark when she headed up Leigh's driveway toward the house. Karrie wasn't naïve, nor was she stupid. She was always aware of her surroundings, but she felt completely at ease being out alone after dark back here at home. Not that bad things didn't or couldn't happen in smaller towns. But living in the Phoenix area for the past several years had changed her frame of reference. As frustrated as she was with her sister and the kids, she was happy with the quiet here, with the slower pace.

The living room was dark behind the sheers, except for the flicker of the TV. Karrie wondered what Leigh was watching. Something she always watched, or had she picked up a TV habit just to get through the nights without Brad around? The overhead garage door was open, but Leigh hadn't turned on lights for her. Karrie trailed her fingertips over Leigh's van, slowed to stroke her hand over that dent in the quarter panel, and wondered again why Brad was riding a motorcycle when he had the accident. If there would have even been an accident if he had been in his truck.

Okay, that was pointless. There was absolutely no way to know the answer to that question. However, there was a reason for Brad being on the bike. She could figure that out. She could hammer at Leigh until she broke down and told her what was going on.

The only light in the kitchen was the small nightlight under the microwave. Karrie stepped inside, reached blindly for the button on the garage wall to close the overhead door, and then cautiously pushed the back door closed. The TV was turned so low, she couldn't make out any noise. The smell of garlic hung in the air. She glanced around the room, but there were no dishes or pans to be seen.

Her phone was right where she left it. She picked it up and glanced at it. The thought of heading down to the basement bedroom didn't appeal to her, so she crossed the kitchen silently and slid the screen door back.

"Wow. Finally decided to come home, huh?"

Startled, Karrie nearly dropped her phone as she stepped out onto the deck. Catching it and trapping it against her stomach, she looked around without an answer. Leigh sat in the lounge chair Karrie had claimed the night before. Karrie glanced back at the house and wondered who was up. It was just after nine, which wasn't really that late for Hazel. But it seemed odd that Leigh would sit out here and let Hazel sit in the dark by herself with the TV down so low she couldn't possibly hear it.

Unless Leigh didn't realize the TV was on.

"Who's watching TV?"

Karrie's voice was thick with an unnamed emotion she wasn't familiar with. Kind of felt like dread. Nerves. Anxiety. Since when did she feel anxious about talking to her sister?

"No one." Leigh looked at her for a moment and then looked away.

Karrie considered Leigh's answer and nodded slowly. She looked at her phone, still pressed against her stomach. So much for sitting out here for a few minutes before lugging her ass down the steps to the dungeon.

"I turned it on, because Hazel likes it."

Karrie stared at Leigh, waited for her to elaborate. When she didn't, she moved to stand at the railing of the deck, the same as Leigh had last night.

"What is it?"

"What?" Leigh looked at her as if she was a stranger and she had just appeared out of nowhere. "Oh. Um. Not a particular show. It's just…" Leigh huffed out a tired sigh. "The TV lights. She has her door open. The lights…" Leigh's words trailed off. Karrie watched her shrug and then shake her head.

So the TV lights gave Hazel some comfort. And rather than crawl into bed with her daughter and put her arms around her and hold her, Leigh was content to let the flickering lights of an abandoned TV do the job for her.

"'kay." She nodded. It wasn't okay, but it was so far from something her sister would have done six months ago, just *three* months ago, that Karrie didn't even know what to say. "I'm gonna—"

"He texted."

"What?" Karrie felt a surge of excitement, electricity roll through her. If Brad had texted, maybe he wasn't as badly injured as Leigh had led her to believe. Right?

"Your boyfriend." Leigh nodded at Karrie's phone. "Dom? Is that his name?"

"You read my texts?" Karrie asked quietly. Again, she wasn't particularly worried about it, because the odds of Dom mentioning his wife in a text or email or call —or ever—were very low. But she still felt violated.

"Your phone buzzed while the kids were cleaning up after dinner. Hazel picked it up."

Karrie raised her eyebrows.

"Okay." She took a deep breath and considered her phone again. She wanted to ask what they had for dinner and not just because she was hungry. She wanted to know what Leigh had fed her kids. "I'm gonna—"

"What's he look like?"

"What?"

"Humor me. What's Dom look like?"

It crossed her mind that she could tell Leigh to go to hell. Something was going on in this house, and Leigh seemed determined to keep it from Karrie. Even after she had driven here to help. Why should she confide in her? Even if it was something as simple as what Dom looked like.

"Um." She looked around and then leaned on the rail. "He's—"

"Sit down."

"What?"

"Sit down. You look like you're ready to run out of here again."

Karrie sighed. Leigh watched her, her gaze heavy and uncomfortable, as she heaved herself onto the swing, careful to dodge the spider web spun around the end by the house. She stretched and sighed again. Decided the pillows on the swing might be faded, but they were comfortable, and the night air was pleasant on her bare skin.

"Where did you go?"

"What?" Stretched out on the swing, Karrie closed her eyes.

"When you left earlier. Where did you go?"

"Just went for a run."

"You were gone for a couple of hours."

"Surprised you noticed."

When Leigh didn't respond, Karrie opened her eyes. From the swing, she couldn't see Leigh well. Just her profile. She watched her silently, wondered why she had decided to freeze her out about whatever was going on.

"Are you hungry?"

"I'm fine," she lied.

"We had spaghetti," Leigh continued. "I made a plate for you."

That quickly, the kernel of hurt inside her melted away.

"Thank you," she said quietly.

"So?"

"Hmm?" Karrie lowered her right leg to the deck and nudged her toe on the wood. She closed her eyes as the swing started to sway.

"What's he look like?"

"Oh." She pressed her lips together and conjured Dom in her mind. "He's…got…really…handsome?" She laughed softly. "Hands. Slender fingers. Elegant. He has elegant hands."

"God, Karrie." Leigh laughed softly.

"What?" Karrie propped herself up on her elbows to stare at Leigh. "He does."

"I didn't ask what you like about him—"

Karrie rolled her eyes. "He's a doctor. And I spend a lot of time looking at his hands."

"Hmm." Leigh pursed her lips. "So you work with him?"

"I do."

"Okay. So he has elegant hands. How about his face?"

"Little bit angular," Karrie said quietly. She dropped back to lie on the swing. Considered Dom's face. The fact that he had aged since they had been together. His face was more angular now, leaner than it had been a few years ago. His eyes were often tired, if not haunted, and gray now mixed with the black in his thick hair. Didn't matter. He was a beautiful man, and even though she didn't love him anymore—didn't want to think about him anymore—she might always feel a little something for him.

"So, you're seeing a guy with elegant hands and an angular face."

Karrie flicked her lips up in a lazy smile. "He's got dark hair. Thick. Longish. Because he doesn't take the time to get it cut." She loved it when it was long enough to brush his collar and always felt a little bereft each time Amy flexed the wifely muscles, and Dom came to her with a new, neat trim. "He has dark eyes. Thick lashes. Thick eyebrows. He's not a big guy, but he's wiry. Tough."

"Do you live together?"

"No."

"You don't?"

Karrie propped herself on her elbows again to look at her sister. The suspicious look on her face made Karrie chuckle.

"I know you tell Mom you aren't living together—"

"We're not living together, Leigh," Karrie said quietly. "We aren't home that much anyway. No time."

"So you get a lot of—what? Locker room quickies?"

Sadly, Leigh wasn't that far off the mark. Maybe not locker room, but she and Dom had long since moved beyond lying together in bed for hours on end—in their free time—and rarely had an hour together these days. An hour left little room for making love and talking over their days. No more cooking together. They had never done a lot of public dating, but there had been weekends when Dom had all but moved in.

"Something like that."

"Don't you want more?"

Karrie's laugh was a little rough around the edges. She dropped back to lie flat on the swing and took a deep breath. She hoped Leigh couldn't see her, couldn't read her mind. Hell yes, she wanted more. But she had finally grown up enough to see that she wasn't going to get it. She would never get what she wanted with Dominic Wolfe, because he was never going to leave his wife.

"Yeah." She smacked her lips together. "Yeah, I do."

"But what?" Leigh pushed. "He doesn't?"

"No, he doesn't." Karrie hated lying. She desperately wanted to tell someone that she had made the most basic mistake a single woman could make. That she had gotten tangled up with a married man. Allowed herself to believe the standard line, that he was planning to leave his wife. She hadn't just believed it. She'd swallowed the whole big, damned lie, and then, she had gone and fallen in love with him.

And now she was falling out of love with him. Hurt like hell, and what was worse was doing it alone. She had never confided to her friends that she was in love with Dom; she never confided to her sister or her mom that she was involved with a married man. So what if she was crawling away from her past, from the only man she had loved? Alone? She deserved it. Anytime she decided to feel sorry for herself, she thought about Amy, Dom's wife. How must she feel?

Because Karrie knew she wasn't the first younger woman to fall for Dom. And when they were done—well, when Dom got the message that she had moved on—she would be easily replaced.

"He asked you to call him."

"What?"

Leigh cleared her throat.

"Hazel said his text was him asking you to call him."

The urge to hear his voice was gone now. Her phone was on her belly, her hand pressed over the top of it. She mumbled okay, but she had no intention of calling him. Not now. In fact, she should delete his number from her phone. Couldn't delete it from her memory, though.

Leigh made a noise that was half sob and half laugh. Karrie lifted her arms over her head and blinked at the night sky above her. She saw three stars. Wondered if there was rain in the forecast. If it rained tomorrow, she wouldn't run outside. She wouldn't see Dax.

"I thought—"

Dax? Where the hell had that thought come from? Who cared if she ever saw Dax Law again?

"What?"

Aware that Leigh had said something, and she missed it, Karrie closed her eyes. Dax had told her he commented on her ass because he liked it. *Jerk.* Who walked around saying stuff like that to women? Then again, she had to admit he was right. If he had said something to her about her shoes or her hair, she would have felt old and frumpy. She would have felt like he was complimenting her mother. Maybe it was sexist as hell, but it was a bit of a thrill to know a guy like Dax Law liked her ass and had given her a once over tonight on the court.

Was that the same as a stranger whistling at her on the street? She had flipped more than one guy the bird for less. It felt different, though. Maybe because she knew Dax. Maybe he was an ass, but he was a familiar ass. Besides, he had a point, too. Women checked men out, too, all day long. Hard to get a feel for what his ass looked like in the loose-fitting athletic shorts, but she sure as heck approved of the tight pull of his t-shirts over his broad shoulders.

"I keep expecting you to call and tell me you and Dom ran away to get married."

Karrie snorted. "Nope."

"Or for you to come home engaged."

"Not happening, Leigh."

"Because you don't want it to?"

"Well, no, not now." Still lying on the swing, Karrie shrugged. Once upon a time, she thought Dom and Amy would divorce, and that she and Dom would set up house. Maybe she had never planned a wedding, but she had hoped for that very thing. "I don't wanna marry someone who doesn't love me."

"He doesn't love you?" Leigh's voice was sharp.

"No." Karrie sighed. He had never loved her *enough*, and as far as she was concerned, that was the same as never loving her. She had wasted enough time being loved second best. Time to move on.

"I miss Brad," Leigh whispered.

Karrie winced. She swallowed down a knot of loneliness for Dom and guilt for thinking of herself when her brother-in-law was fighting for his life.

"I wanna see him, Leigh. Let me go with you to visit him."

The night was quiet. Karrie heard Leigh moving around. Heard her clear her throat, and she assumed she was trying to control her emotions. When minutes had passed and Leigh hadn't answered her, Karrie turned to her right. Leigh glanced at her as she swung her legs over the side of the lounge chair and stood up. Karrie waited for her to say something, but her sister only crossed the deck and slipped inside.

Fourteen

"KARRIE."

"What?" Karrie snapped. "Hand me that bottle, will you?"

Karrie groped behind her for the bottle of window cleaner as her mom handed it to her.

"What are you doing?"

"Do you know how to get the drapes down in the living room?" She sprayed the cleaner on the sliding door and started swiping at it with the paper towel in her hand.

"What?"

"The drapes," Karrie said as she turned to look at her mom.

"Sweetheart, what are you doing?"

"Washing Leigh's windows." Karrie looked from her mom to the bucket of soapy water at her feet. Seemed pretty obvious to her what she was doing.

"But *why* are you washing Leigh's windows?"

Karrie blinked at her mom—sporty and stylish today in simple jeans and a gray Calvin Klein sweatshirt.

She stepped toward her and squinted at the crescent-shaped moon pendant that rested in the hollow of her throat.

"That's cute."

"Thank you." Her mom nodded. "What's going on?"

"I just." Karrie shrugged. "I don't know, Mom. I came home to help Leigh. I need to do something."

"And she asked you to wash her windows?" Her mom shook her head. She rested her fingers on the counter to her right. "Really?"

"No." Karrie's sigh turned into a long-drawn-out groan. "No. She hasn't asked me to do anything. She won't tell me anything—"

"What's there to tell? Brad was in an accident. He's in critical condition, Karrie. How can she elaborate on that? What isn't she—"

"I don't know, Mom," Karrie mumbled. She dropped into a kitchen chair and hunched over her knees. "I don't know. But I feel horrible that I had no idea this accident was so bad. So I came home to do something. To help with the house or the kids. And she's not letting me do anything. She's not talking to me. I'm climbing the walls here. I could be at work—"

"You miss Dom."

"What?" Karrie looked up at her mom, shocked to

find that knowing smile on her face. "No. It's nothing to do with Dom."

Okay, maybe it was the fact that she had hoped to come home and throw herself into Leigh's life and forget her own. Maybe she had hoped to get so involved here with Leigh and the kids that her heart would scar a bit, and she could go home and look at Dom and not cave and slide right back into the no-win, go-nowhere love affair they had carried on for nearly two years.

"No?"

"I want to help."

She sniffled and looked away from her mom's curious stare. She didn't want to cry. Yes, she was hurt that Leigh had pushed her away again, but this wasn't about her. She didn't want to make anything about this visit about her. She wanted to be useful to her sister.

"Maybe she's hurting, Karrie," her mom reminded her.

Karrie nodded and swallowed hard. "I know that." She rubbed her fingertips under her eyes. "And before, she would have let me in."

"Before what?"

"I don't know." Karrie licked her lips. "That's what I'm trying to tell you. I don't know what's going on."

She stood up again and turned to the door. "I've got two weeks. I'm wasting time. If she doesn't want to talk, I'm going to do what I can to help before I have to go back."

Her mom pulled a kitchen chair out and sat down. "Leigh said you've been running at night."

Karrie nodded. "I washed Gino's windows. And the…room she has set up for Brad."

When her mom remained quiet, Karrie glanced at her over her shoulder.

"Her life has changed. Drastically." Her mom stared at the table, a thoughtful expression on her face. "Imagine what it'll be like when she brings him home, Kare."

Karrie considered reminding her mother of what she did for a living, but she thought better of it.

"I know."

"Maybe you could get her to run with you."

"No."

"What?" her mom asked quickly. "Why not?"

She needed that time to herself. To decompress. The lingering stress from work from the ER horror stories she witnessed and starred in seemed easier to think about, to deal with, when she had that quiet time. When she could physically work her body to exhaustion. And besides, if Leigh was with her, she couldn't go to the school.

"Um." Karrie cleared her throat. Well, she couldn't say *that*. Sure, the run itself was good for Karrie, and it *would* be good for Leigh. But Karrie had caught herself thinking about Dax a few times today. She didn't like the thought of sharing him with Leigh.

Sharing him. Seriously, Karrie?

"Leigh used to be in excellent shape," her mom reminded her.

"I know," Karrie agreed. "I know. I do. But she just… refuses. She won't do anything with me. The kids don't want to do anything with me."

"Maybe it's too soon."

"Too soon." Karrie dropped her hand to her side and looked at her mom with exasperation. "God, Mom, they can't stop living. Brad's gonna need them all completely ready for him, for his recovery."

"Sweetheart, I don't know that there'll *be* a recovery. That's what I'm trying to tell you."

Karrie huffed out a breath and winced when she felt a stab of pain under her ribs.

"He's not gonna make it?"

Her mom looked at her with big, innocent eyes and shrugged. "I don't know. But it doesn't look good."

"Why won't she talk to me?"

"Just be patient."

The door banged open, and Gino rushed into the room.

"Hi, Gramma." He flashed her mom a quick grin and dropped his backpack by her chair.

"Dude. I just cleaned the kitchen for your mom." Karrie pointed at his bag. "Put it in your room."

"I need a snack."

"Okay. Put the bag in your room, and I'll get you a snack."

Gino blinked at Karrie as if she was speaking a foreign language. He snuck a peek at her mom as he leaned over to snag one of the straps.

"Where's Hazel?" Karrie's mom asked.

"She probably went to the open gym—"

"She doesn't do that anymore," her mom argued. "She quit basketball."

"She's not quitting basketball." Karrie shook her head as the door banged open again and Hazel trudged inside.

"Yeah, I did," Hazel mumbled. Leigh stepped inside right behind her and looked from their mom at the kitchen table to the bucket of soapy water and finally at Karrie. "There's no one to coach us, and I suck anyway."

Karrie felt like Hazel had just plunged a shiv into her gut. She flinched, started to argue with Hazel, but stopped when she saw Leigh give her a short head shake.

"You don't suck," Karrie insisted. "You just need practice."

"Yeah? For what?" Hazel asked again. "No one's coaching us. Dad's never gonna walk again—"

Karrie met Leigh's eyes. She sucked in a sharp breath when Leigh looked away.

"I'll coach you." Karrie glanced at Hazel and then looked from her mom to Leigh.

"What?" Her mom frowned and narrowed her eyes at her.

"No." Leigh put her purse down on the table. "What are you even doing?"

"Why not?" Karrie asked Leigh. She stared her down, waiting for an answer, aware that even though her niece had proclaimed she wasn't going to play anymore, she was watching her now with interest. Trying to hide it, sure, but Karrie recognized that little spark of hope on her face.

"Because she doesn't want to play," Leigh answered quietly. "It's not her thing. Why push her if she's not interested? And because I can't pay you. The school won't pay you—"

"It's not about getting paid." Karrie stepped around Leigh and tossed the wad of paper towels in the trashcan. "It's about a team of kids who need a coach."

"Karrie, you do need to eat." Her mom stood slowly. "What about your job?"

She waved her mom's question off and looked at Leigh again. "What's wrong with you? You're not yourself. You would never have discouraged your kids from—"

"Things change, Karrie," Leigh said quietly.

"So let me help." Karrie shrugged and tossed her hands out in offering.

"You can't help. You have a life. You have a job. You have someone waiting—"

Karrie blinked at Leigh silently.

"Mom, can I have a snack?" Gino bounced back into the room. "Aunt Karrie said she would—"

"Maybe Aunt Karrie needs to butt out," Leigh snapped.

"Butt—?" Karrie yelped. "What? Leigh, what the hell is going on? I came home to do something for you. Let me—"

"I didn't ask you to come home!" Leigh roared. "Did I? Did I ever once in that conversation ask you to come back? Did I ever say I needed you?"

Shocked, Karrie's mouth gaped open, and she stared at her sister silently.

"Let's go get a snack," her mom suggested. Karrie's stomach turned at the thought of eating anything. She glanced at her mom, relieved to realize she was talking to the kids. Still, her stomach knotted as she stood on trembling legs and waited for her mom to usher the kids out and leave her and Leigh alone to duke it out.

"I didn't tell you how bad it was, because I didn't want you here."

Leigh's voice hung in the air between them once they were alone. Karrie heard her mom teasing the kids, probably trying to make them forget what was going on in the house. She heard a car door close and then another and then the car started.

"Why?" she whispered when the sounds faded, and she found her voice. "Why don't you want me here?"

Leigh licked her lips. Karrie saw the tears on her sister's face, knew they matched her own.

"There's nothing you can do." Leigh threw her hands up in defeat.

"Look, I don't know what's going on. I don't know how bad it is, because you won't tell me. You won't let me see him. The hospital won't let me see him without your permission—"

"You—? You tried to visit him?" Leigh cleared her throat.

"Yeah." Karrie nodded. She lifted her hand and tucked her hair behind her ear. "I drove an hour and a half to see him, but there was a specialist with him at the time. And then the nurse at the desk asked who I was. And said I wasn't on an approved list to see him."

"He needs to rest—"

"I know what he needs." Karrie rolled her eyes. "C'mon, Leigh. I wasn't going to go sing to him or yell at him to get up and get off his ass. I wanna know what's going on."

Leigh turned her back to Karrie.

"He's in a coma, Karrie." Leigh sighed. Karrie waited for her to go on, but when Leigh didn't seem inclined to continue, she stepped forward as if to grab her and shake answers from her.

"Yeah? And?"

"And?" Leigh pinched the bridge of her nose and then rubbed her fingers into the corners of her eyes. "And? Isn't that enough?"

Karrie moved her mouth when Leigh dropped her hand to her side and looked at her. But she couldn't find her voice or words to express her bafflement at Leigh's attitude.

"There was too much swelling on his spine for a long time for the doctors to even know how severe the injuries were. He's got…" Leigh shook her head and shrugged. "Fractures in his spinal column. Broken right leg. Ankle. Bones in both arms. Broken neck. He's on a vent. Lacerated spleen and liver. They have no idea what's going on with his brain, but they're preparing me for the worst."

Karrie nodded. Yep, sounded like that was necessary, because it did not sound good for her brother-in-law. But that still didn't explain Leigh's aloof recitation of Brad's injuries. As if she were catching Karrie up on a guy they went to school with rather than her husband.

"They think he swerved to miss a deer. Lost control."

"Have the kids seen him?" she asked, but her words were so small she wasn't sure Leigh even heard her. When her sister moved to walk out of the room, Karrie assumed she hadn't. She wasn't sure if she wanted to ask again. She was afraid of the answer. She wasn't sure what to say at all, because she was afraid of this cold woman in the room with her.

"Hazel saw him," Leigh finally mumbled as she walked out of the room.

Karrie stared after her for a long moment before sinking down to sit on the edge of the kitchen chair again. For whatever reason, Leigh didn't want her around. Maybe it was just the shock of the situation. Karrie had seen families torn apart by injuries less devastating than this. But she'd thought they were all closer than that. She'd thought Leigh trusted her and would want her around to lean on, if for no other reason.

Then again, it had taken Leigh several days after the accident to even call Karrie about it. And another few weeks to admit to Karrie that it was serious. Karrie sighed and stretched. She eyed the bucket of soapy water and then looked up at the glass door. The sun glinted through the pane. Even in her shorts and t-shirt, the kitchen had grown uncomfortably warm. She would dump the water and go for a run. Not toward the school. Because now that she thought about it, Leigh *hadn't* asked her to come home. Not once since she told Karrie Brad was injured in a bike accident had Leigh asked for her help. So maybe she wouldn't be staying. No point in looking for Dax again if she was going to pack her bags and head out within the next day or two.

The bucket of water felt heavier now. Karrie slid the glass door open and stepped out on the deck. No wonder it felt warmer in the kitchen; the afternoon sun had warmed the day to perfect. Rather than just pitch the water over the rail of the deck, she crossed the wooden floor, stepped off the deck, and dumped the bucket in the far corner of the yard.

The thought of leaving, of going back to her life in Phoenix, slowed her steps as she went back inside. There was a part of her—not as small a part as she would like—that wanted to get the hell out of here and run to Dom. She wanted to throw herself into his arms and feel like she belonged there. The hell of it was, she didn't. She never had.

Fifteen

DAX WATCHED AS THE DOOR OF THE BUS CLOSED. From where he stood at the back door of the gym, he could see the guys filing down the aisle, knuckling each other and laughing as they dropped into their seats. He had never been a soccer player, but he had several friends on the team when he was in school. And some of those boys on the current soccer team were also some of his basketball players. He huffed out a sigh as the bus pulled away from the spot where it had hovered for the past forty-five minutes. He didn't want to wish time away, but he was ready for basketball season. Ready for the fun, full afternoon practices and the games. It was busy; in fact, there were times when it was crazy busy, but he liked it that way. Less time to think. To dwell on the past.

He tucked his hands in the pockets of his khakis and moseyed across the parking lot. From inside the gym, he heard Marti Yancey, the varsity volleyball coach, yelling at someone to get up. Figured the girls were running a few drills before their big match tonight. There were still a few student cars in the lot, though the final bell had rung almost twenty-five minutes ago now. He heard the strains of a hard rock song somewhere close by, but he didn't look for the source.

He wasn't in the mood to talk to anyone now, anyway. That phone call from Emily last night was still nagging at him. In fact, it felt a lot like Emily had her nails stuck in the skin at the back of his neck, and not in a good way. Seeing Leigh's sister at St. Anne's open gym yesterday hadn't helped.

She hadn't come back. Three nights ago, they had a conversation—well. Maybe that was stretching it. They talked a bit; she had done some fancy footwork on the court. Shown her true colors, and he realized he had been fantasizing about Leigh's little sister, and that had been the end of it. She hadn't been pleased that he recognized her, or maybe, more to the point, she hadn't been happy to be called Leigh's little sister. As far as he knew, Leigh and Karrie had gotten along okay when they were kids. But he didn't know either of them that well—especially now. Leigh didn't mention Karrie a lot these days, and a lot could change between high school years and real life.

And maybe it was just as simple as Dax reminding Karrie that there were bigger and more important things going on in her world than a one-on-one basketball game that meant nothing.

Still. It rankled that she just vanished. He had waited around school the last two nights, half expecting her to show up. He hovered in his office, listening for the sound of her dribbling, only to leave disappointed. He supposed he could call her. Drive by Leigh's house. But that felt a little desperate. And odds were, he wouldn't be welcome. The last time he saw Leigh, he ran into her at the grocery store. He had heard about Brad's accident and offered Leigh his concern. Normally vibrant and pretty, she had been haggard and tired, and she simply nodded to acknowledge his words, tried to speak, and finally shook her head and slipped by him to the self-checkout lane.

Brad Avery might never come home the man he was before the accident. Rumor had it, Brad Avery would never come home.

Karrie had offered him a reluctant smile at the grade school open gym. But she had remained on the far end of the court, and as far as he could tell, after that initial smile, she hadn't so much as glanced at him. He snuck a peek her way a time or two. He wanted to look at her again; her body was starring in some pleasant dreams, and he looked his fill in the minute he had. But he also found her interactions with Hazel interesting. Hazel was still that washed out, timid version of herself. The one that her dad's accident had caused.

But Karrie. The scowl was gone from her face. Probably because no one at the grade school gym had commented on her ass, though Dax knew there were probably a few boys there who had taken a second look at her. She was still all over the floor with the beautiful ball-handling and the jump shots. But she was laughing. She was working with Hazel; she was trying to teach her niece the skills for the sport.

The sound of their laughter—Dax had noticed when Hazel's voice chimed in—had touched something inside him. He and Emily didn't have children. Most people assumed he chose to come back home and coach basketball either because he failed at his IT job in Chicago or because he was a washed-up has-been, and he wanted to feed his ego through the high school boys.

Maybe both were true, but it was so much more than that.

Dax gritted his teeth now and rubbed his hand over his chest. The chilidog lunch had tasted good enough going down, but he was paying for it now. He watched the defensive linemen run a drill out on the football field in front of him, but in his mind, he was searching his desk drawer, wondering if he had any antacid tablets.

He had wanted to talk to her, and when it had become obvious yesterday that she wasn't going to give him the time of the day there, he left without bothering her. But he came back here, thinking maybe she would show up. She hadn't, and that was fine. They had simply shot a few baskets together; there was nothing between them. But the fact that he had locked up and gone home with the weight of disappointment heavy on his shoulders had irritated him. He had never been the guy to get hung up on a woman. He didn't want to be that guy now.

A cool breeze nipped at his neck and feathered through his hair, reminding him that he needed to get in for a trim. Throat still burning with the dregs of that chilidog, he stuck his hand back in his pocket and took a deep breath. He would go home. There was nothing pressing he had to do here. Not even an email to send, and that was okay. Jim Lewis, the Quad City coach, had gotten back to him about rescheduling the game, and that worked out well.

Girls in long-sleeved maroon jerseys and little black booty shorts milled about inside the gym. He glanced at them, wondered who had decided the booty shorts were a good idea, and turned to head upstairs toward his office. Then again, the little shorts probably made their movement easier. He would turn his computer off, lock up, and head home. He greeted Jed as he moved past him down the corridor. Tried to remember what might be in his refrigerator that he could have for dinner. And damned near mowed her down just outside his office.

"Hey." She looked at him with wide eyes as she rushed to step out of his way.

Embarrassed to have nearly taken her out and embarrassed to be caught in his thoughts, and yep, let's be honest, embarrassed to have spent the last few nights mooning over her when he barely knew her, Dax gave her a quick once over and stepped past her into his office. Dressed in skinny jeans and a bright red blouse, she obviously wasn't here to shoot baskets with him. Still. She looked so damned good in that quick peek, he wanted to look again. The way those jeans molded her thighs, he desperately wanted to check out what they did to her ass.

But he couldn't. Not without being obvious about it and look where that had gotten him a few days ago.

"Hey." He sidled up to his desk, shot her a look over his shoulder, and then moved around to stand with the desk between them.

"No basketball tonight, huh?"

Her voice was thick and soft, and Dax felt it whip through him like a drug. Leaning over the desk, he lifted only his eyes to look at her. She watched him with big eyes—she had done something fancy with her makeup to make them pop—and when he didn't respond immediately, she shifted uncertainly from one foot to the other.

"No." He shrugged his eyebrows at her, because it didn't matter how beautiful or sexy he might think she was, they most definitely could not shoot baskets out there tonight.

"Do you..." She cleared her throat. Dax moved his mouse over his desk, clicked on the icon to shut the computer down, and stood up straight. He wondered what she wanted and why she seemed nervous about being there.

"Do I what?"

"Do you…" She drew in a deep breath and shrugged. With a sharp little jolt of laughter, she met his gaze again. "Do you have to be somewhere? Now?"

"Are you asking me out?"

She grinned, revealing perfect teeth and a dimple below her smile that hit him like an arrow in the heart. Could she get any cuter?

Well. Maybe if he could unbutton her blouse. Slide it off her shoulders. Okay. Not *cuter*. Definitely *not* the word he had in mind for what she might look like under those clothes. Under the sports bras and shorts he had seen her in previously.

"No." She shook her head, but he was pretty sure she was thinking about smiling. When he only stared at her, her lips finally tipped up in a ghost of a smile. "I'm not asking you out."

He nodded as he stepped out from behind the desk. He glanced around his office as he neared her, because she was the best site in the room and after the dumbass comment he made the first night he had seen her, he didn't think staring at her was a good idea. What if he drooled?

"Okay."

She moved, stepped out of the office to get out of his way. Dax pulled his door shut as he followed her into the corridor.

"If you're not asking me out, why are you asking if I'm busy?" He stuck the key in the lock and turned it.

"Um."

When he turned to her and dropped his keys in his pocket, she was working her lip with her teeth.

"I thought you might buy me a drink."

"You did, huh?" He laughed. "But you're not asking me out."

"No. I'm not." She shook her head.

"Okay. I could probably buy you a drink," he agreed. They walked side by side down the hall. Both of them hesitated and then stopped to watch the volleyball teams warming up on the court below them. Dax recognized the girls in the white jerseys; he saw most of them on a daily basis. He searched out Marti at the side of the court, involved in an energetic conversation with her assistant coach.

When Karrie groaned softly beside him, he turned his gaze to her.

"You okay?"

She nodded and turned to him, the flash of longing there and gone so quickly he decided he imagined it. After all, she told him the other night she liked basketball better.

"Did you see her? Number ten just landed in the net on a spike."

"Mm." He wrapped his fingers around the railing and leaned a bit, eyes back on the girls. "You wanna stay and watch the game?"

"Can I get a longneck here?"

He laughed and lifted his chin to look at her. Caught her staring at his hands.

"Sadly, no." He sighed. "Though there are days when it sounds like a good idea."

She flashed that grin at him, the one that had lit him on fire moments ago in his office.

"There are," she agreed. "And today was one of them. And yesterday, too, for that matter."

With a nod, he stood up straight and followed her out of the gymnasium. The lobby of the school was much quieter. Dax beat her to the entrance and pushed the door open for her. She was careful not to bump into him as she stepped outside, but he caught the scent of her perfume and drew in a deep breath. Definitely a hint of orange, but tonight there was something rich and heavy in the air. Dax followed her out, mesmerized by how good she smelled.

But not so much so that he didn't notice her tight, firm ass in the form-fitting, dark wash denim.

"Are you seriously looking at my ass again, Law?" she called to him over her shoulder.

"You know it, Blondie."

He expected her to chastise him. Give him hell for the sexist comment. Instead, she cut loose with a peal of laughter. He dragged his eyes away and decided he liked the sound.

"So." He glanced at her as they walked to the parking lot. "On this non-date drink that I'm buying you, are we taking separate cars? Or are you going to brave it and ride with me?"

"Brave it," she repeated with a frown. "Brave it? You think I'm afraid of you?"

He grinned. "Lot of man right here."

Again with the laugh. Didn't matter that she was laughing at him. In fact, he said it just to provoke that happy sound again.

"I think I'll take my chances," she decided.

"Good choice."

"I thought you moved away." Her tone slid back to neutral, and she turned her eyes back to the parking lot. Dax led her down the main sidewalk to his black pickup and stopped at the front bumper.

"I did," he answered. "This okay?"

She skirted her eyes over him and then over his truck.

"As opposed to your team of horses?" She arched an eyebrow at him.

He grinned. "It's a big step up."

She rolled her eyes and waved him off as she turned to the passenger door. He watched her yank it open and then smoothly hoist herself up into the seat. Odds were nothing would come of this night. It wasn't a date. She had told him that in no uncertain terms. She was in town visiting her sister. Keyword *visiting*.

Still. Might as well enjoy the night. The beer. The woman.

"What about you? Where did you move to?" he asked as he climbed up into the driver's seat.

"Phoenix." She spoke softly, her gaze trained on something in front of them, out the windshield. Lost in thought, she looked just a little sad, so Dax decided to tease her.

"It's a dry heat, right?"

She shook the look away and turned to him with a grin and a nod.

"You know it."

Sixteen

KARRIE WASN'T SURE WHAT SHE WAS DOING. SHE HAD spent the last couple of days avoiding him—well, okay, so she drove by the school both nights, but she had been late enough that she had known he would be gone—and today, after another disagreement with Leigh, she had gone looking for him. On purpose. With the idea that rather than shoot baskets, she wanted to sit and have a drink. And maybe normal conversation. Because she sure as hell wasn't getting that at her sister's house.

But now that she was sitting across a two-top from him at Captain's, which appeared to be a popular neighborhood tavern, she had no idea what to say to him. She couldn't get into Leigh and Brad's business. And she couldn't admit to being bummed out about her niece and nephew not being excited to see her or do anything with her, because that would only lead into questions about Leigh and Brad. She had no intention of telling him that she talked to Dom last night, and that even though she had made up her mind when she left Phoenix that she was done with their affair, she missed him.

She couldn't tell Dax that there was no reason for her to stick around here since Leigh didn't want her here, and she couldn't tell him that she didn't want to go back to Phoenix, because she didn't want to cave and settle right back into the status quo with Dom.

"What do you do?" He took a long pull from his beer and then cradled the bottom of the bottle in his hands as he waited for her answer. Karrie had been about to ask him if he came to the tavern a lot, and if so, was that because it was in his neighborhood. They were in the heart of town. Lots of bungalows and parks and mom and pop restaurants around.

Karrie drew in a deep breath and then swallowed before answering him. Because suddenly the appeal of the small-town neighborhood and family life was overwhelming, and she wasn't sure if it was simply that she had finally come to realize that wasn't going to happen with Dom. Or because she had expected to come home to that feeling at Leigh's house, and instead, she felt empty and more alone than before.

"I'm a nurse." She met his eyes. Saw the flicker of surprise and respect in his eyes, but she wasn't sure what to make of it.

"Pediatrics," he guessed.

She winced and gave him a tiny shake of her no. "E.R." She took a drink. Rolled her head on her neck and finally gave in and met his eyes again.

"That's…" He cringed and nodded his head back and forth.

"It's hard," she answered with a nod. "It used to be when I was asked, I could say rewarding. Because now and then, it is." She pursed her lips and considered her bottle, memories of the patients they lost—specifically the last young girl—making her frown. The headache was sudden and unwanted.

"How long?"

"Four years."

He took another drink and looked around the bar.

"Do you come here often?" she asked, happy to change the subject.

"Not often." He shrugged his eyebrows. "Now and then."

She couldn't ask if he lived in the area. She didn't need to know. And asking might imply an interest she wasn't sure was there. And if it was, it didn't matter, anyway.

"If you're a trauma nurse—"

She shook her head. "E.R. There's a difference."

"But you treat trauma patients."

"I do."

"Then you've seen something like…If you've done it for four years, you've treated someone in Brad's situation."

Karrie winced and turned her head away from him. She had finally talked Leigh into letting her see him. Just a five-minute visit. She hadn't recognized the man in the bed. She hadn't really *seen* him. Gauze bandages and casts and IVs and machines. And bruises. And the shell of what Leigh and the doctor and nurses said was Brad Avery. For the first time since she had become a nurse, the familiar life-saving equipment hadn't comforted her. It had scared the absolute hell out of her.

"Is he gonna—"

It had killed Karrie to argue with Leigh again. The soulless recitation of his injuries in Leigh's monotone had exhausted her. Even though she had seen patients who had probably looked much the same as Brad had when he had been wheeled in by the EMT, seeing him—hell, she hadn't even tried to sneak a peek at his charts over the nurse's shoulders—had been a blow.

Leaving Leigh there to sit at his bedside had torn her up. Leigh, who hadn't laid a hand on him the entire time they were there. Karrie had expected her sister to fall apart, to sob, to touch him, stroke any areas of skin that she could. Both in desperation for herself and to let him know she was there. That Leigh had remained stoic and apart had rocked Karrie to the core.

Devastated and confused. The mix was volatile. Obviously. Or she wouldn't have ended up trying to score a drink with the charmer who had commented on her ass on day one.

"Please." She pressed her lips together and shook her head. "Don't ask me that."

When she braved it and looked at him again, he answered with a solemn nod.

"How's your knee?"

Karrie blinked at him. She took a quick drink and glanced at her legs before looking at him again.

"What?"

"You said you tore your ACL."

She nodded uncertainly. "About ten years ago."

He shrugged. "Does it ever give you trouble now?"

"Mm." She sighed. "No. Not really. But then I don't take the time to do much, either. I'm lucky to get a run in most days."

"Adam blew his out a few years ago. Just a pick-up football game."

"Ouch." Karrie nibbled on her lip. "How's he doing? Where's he at now?"

"He's a cop. Lives in a small town near Joplin, Missouri."

"A cop, huh?" She considered that.

"He's married. Has four kids."

"Four kids? Are you kidding me?"

"Triplets. And a new baby."

"Oooh." Karrie laughed. "Ouch. Wow. He's busy."

"Yes, he is." Dax grinned. "The triplets are girls. They're four. Two of them are total tomboys. Lily has a good arm on her. Arielle is into dragons. And the other one—Violet—wears a pink tutu everywhere she goes."

Karrie pulled her bottle away from her mouth and snorted with laughter.

"The new baby is a boy. Violet says she's going to teach him dance."

"I love it," Karrie said sincerely. "That's so awesome."

Dax nodded. "Can I ask you something?"

Karrie assumed he would ask if she was married. If she had kids. She hated to be asked either question, because both made her feel naïve. Because yes, at one time, she had been stupid enough to believe Dom was going to leave Amy and settle down with her, and maybe even make a baby with her.

"What?" She drew in a deep breath to prepare herself. All she had to say was no. No explanation necessary.

"Did you sleep with Adam?"

Stunned by what he asked, Karrie stared at Dax in silence. Aware that her mouth was hanging open, she finally snapped out of the shock, closed her mouth, and shook her head.

"No."

"You didn't?"

"Adam and I were good friends," she said softly.

Dax nodded. The eye contact was a little intense, but Dax broke it first and glanced at the bar. "Want another?"

"Well, yeah, after a question like that, I might need another beer."

He grinned at her as he stood. She handed him her empty and watched him move across the scarred wooden floor to the bar. When he elbowed his way closer to get their beers, Karrie inspected his backside. Whole new view, especially with the snug-fitting khakis and the white button-down shirt.

She liked it. Especially his ass, no denying it.

Because she didn't want to be caught checking him out, she dragged her eyes away and watched two guys shoot pool. If the table was empty, she might suggest a game to Dax. Odds were he would beat her, though. She could handle him on a basketball court, but she wasn't a great shot when it came to pool. She considered checking her phone and decided she didn't want to. It was doubtful Leigh had a change of heart and called her. And even if Dom had, she didn't want to know. The conversation last night had been normal; Dom had shared a story about a cardiac patient. He told her that his son had scored a goal at his soccer game, and while that used to make her proud—back when she thought she might end up being a stepmom to his kids—now it made her wonder if Dom had sat by Amy at the game.

Dax appeared in her line of sight and leaned over to set her beer on the table.

"I slept with Jake Spencer," she announced as he sat down.

"You—?" Dax looked around the bar and then turned back to her. He blinked as he sat down again. "You —? When?"

"In school." She shrugged. She felt a grin tug at her lips, pleased to have surprised him with her revelation. "When I was with Adam and Jake all the time. Adam and I were friends. Jake and I were together."

Dax studied her face with a thoughtful frown. Karrie watched him ease back in the chair and cross his right ankle over his left knee. He took a long pull from his bottle and then lowered it to hold it in his lap.

"Why?" he finally asked. "That guy was a dick."

She snorted. She couldn't totally disagree with him, but she didn't want to sit here and trash old friends, either.

"It was a mistake," she admitted. "We both decided we were better as friends."

"What about Jake Spencer appealed to you, though?" He still wore the frown, but now he looked more confused than pensive.

"His arms."

"His—?" Dax laughed and rolled his eyes. "His arms. You did a guy in high school because you liked his arms."

She shrugged and nodded her confession.

"How's that different than me appreciating your ass the other day?"

"I didn't announce to the world that I was ogling his ass. I liked his arms. We were friends." She arched her eyebrows. "We got a little drunk one night, and things got out of hand."

"Was he your first?"

"Does it matter?"

"Was he?" Dax angled his head to the side and stared at her through narrowed eyes. Karrie felt a lick of heat low in her belly. She dragged her eyes from his and huffed out a quick breath.

"Yes."

He nodded and pursed his lips. "'kay. All I'm gonna say…is I hope you've found better since then."

Relaxed in her chair, Karrie hung her head back and barked a hearty laugh. She wasn't a serial dater, and she wasn't much into casual hookups. But she had been with a few guys, most of them at least a little more attentive to her than Jake Spencer had been. Dom, of course, had been her best lover back when she thought they were going places. When she loved him and thought he would eventually leave Amy and love her. Since she finally realized her mistake, even sex with him had become stale and uninspired. She had started faking orgasms a while back just to get those moments over with.

Staring at Dax Law's long, lean legs and picturing them in the loose-athletic shorts he wore on the court, looking into his dark eyes and seeing a flicker of interest there, reminded Karrie it had been a damned long time since she had enjoyed sex. Since she had enjoyed kissing someone, even.

"Well?" he finally tilted his head and wriggled his eyebrows.

"Oh my God. Really?" She leaned forward and covered her face with her hands when she felt the rush of heat in her face. Even hiding from him, she could feel that he was still watching her. Determined to act nonchalant, she laughed softly and lifted her head to look at him.

"I'm good."

"Oh, I have no doubt you are," he agreed.

The blush was fast and furious this time. No way to hide it. No point in trying.

"What about you?" She laughed softly and looked away. Thankfully, no one around them paid them any attention. Country music still churned at an okay decibel from the corner. The pool table was still occupied. The bar still crowded. Karrie dabbed at the corners of her eyes and took a drink of her beer.

"Oh. I'm good." He winked at her when she looked back at him.

"Dax!" Bottle at her lips, she turned away and lowered her hand. Nothing like snorting beer up her nose to create a scene.

"You asked."

"Are you married?"

"You already asked that, and if I remember correctly, you already decided I couldn't be married. Because I made a comment about your ass to Jed. Who I might add is very married and was looking at your ass with the same appreciation as I was."

"Right." She nodded and winked at him. "We'll go with that."

"I'm not married. And I never slept with Jake Spencer."

"Well, that's a relief," she mumbled. She took a deep

breath and puffed her cheeks up to let it out. "You dated Cynthia Hamm in high school."

Dax aimed a look of sheer surprise at her.

"You knew that?"

"Everyone knew that."

"Cynthia." He nodded and shrugged. "I did. We dated for a year."

"What happened?"

Karrie watched him lower his foot to the floor and shift in his chair. Now he leaned into the table, rested his elbow near his beer, and propped his chin in his hand. Much closer now. So close, in fact, she could see bits of gold in his dark brown eyes. Thick lashes framed those eyes and lent him a look of innocence, when Karrie knew damned well he had lost that years and years ago.

"Life," he said in a slow drawl. "I think we both knew we weren't forever."

"But you told her you loved her when you took her clothes off that first time."

"I did." He drummed his fingertips on the table. Held the intense eye contact with her. "Can't you love someone and still know it's not the forever kind of love your parents have?"

Karrie sighed. Sure you could. Not every love was meant to last a lifetime. Teen love especially. How many of her friends had been so over-the-moon in love when they were kids only to watch it fade away as life threw new experiences at them? Just because she had never felt that way for anyone at such a young age didn't mean it didn't happen. And just because Dax and Cynthia had gone their separate ways didn't mean they hadn't loved each other when they were dating.

"Okay." She nodded. "I'll give you that point. But."

Karrie pointed her bottle at him and arched her eyebrows. Recognizing the challenge to come, Dax grinned in anticipation.

"Did you love every girl you took to bed?"

"Oh, hell no." He rolled his eyes. "And not a lot of them made it to my bed, to be honest."

She laughed despite herself.

"So you don't do casual sex."

"Sure I do," she answered simply. "Just busting your balls."

Laughter lit up his face, and Karrie marveled at the way the years seemed to melt off him. His eyes were alive, and his shoulders shook with the laughter, and Karrie couldn't help but compare him to Dom.

When had she last seen Dom cut loose like this? *Had* she seen Dom relax and laugh as if the patient who had died of a gunshot wound earlier in the day wasn't possessing him and sucking his life out of him?

"My balls are pretty tough, Karrie Mallory."

His words were bold, and he was teasing her, but her eyes were drawn to his lips as he put them on his bottle again. Another streak of heat in her belly told her it was time to get out of there and away from Dax Law.

"I think we should probably not talk about your balls," she said softly. The comical way his eyebrows shot up over his forehead brought a smile to her lips, but she felt the flush of embarrassment creep up her neck again.

"You brought it up."

"Did I?" she mumbled.

Dax tried to swallow a mouthful of beer and nearly choked. Karrie laughed quietly as he turned away from her.

"You don't play fair," he told her a few seconds later, still sputtering and pounding his chest.

She took a deep breath and ran her fingers under her eyes.

"I think…" She pressed her lips together. "I think we should probably call it a night."

"Don't trust yourself around me?" He shot her a wicked grin. This time that flicker of heat shot straight through her core. No, no, maybe she didn't trust herself around him. Not that she would admit that to him.

"I didn't tell Leigh where I was going," she told him. A smile played at her lips, but she kept it cool. "I don't want her to worry."

He nodded and finished his beer.

"Then we should probably call it a night," he agreed.

Seventeen

"Were you serious?"

Karrie dipped the tip of her paintbrush in the can of white paint and then leaned closer to dab at the trim near the garage floor.

"Kare?"

The use of her nickname caught her off guard. Still, she was hurt by the way Leigh had blown her off since she had come home, and with only a week left here before she had to trek back across the country and return to real life, she was miffed enough to make Leigh wait. The cement floor was cold and hard on her bare knee, but still, she scooted closer to the overhead door and leaned even closer—her face was close enough to the doorframe that she could probably lick the metal rail if she wanted to—and took painstaking care to make the trim near the floor perfect.

"What?"

As she sat up straight, careful not to slide her nose up the metal rail and cut herself, she cleared her throat and looked at Leigh over her shoulder. At the other side of the garage door, her sister sat sprawled on her butt, paintbrush dangling from her fingers, half over her small can of paint and half over the garage floor. Karrie stifled a groan of frustration as white paint dribbled over the floor between Leigh's knees.

"Were you serious?"

"Was I serious about what?" Karrie asked. She dipped her brush again and looked back at the trim. Done. There was nothing more to touch up on her side. She sucked in a deep breath and noticed the change in the air. It was getting cooler. Felt a little more like fall. Karrie climbed to her feet, pretty graceful for a rehabilitated athlete pushing thirty—she thought—and crossed the garage to Leigh's side. She eyed the trim piece on this side and catalogued the chipped paint and even a spot where it appeared someone had crimped it with the side of a vehicle. Leigh had apparently been spaced out the entire time Karrie was painting. Either that, or she was good with the weathered look on the trim and was interested in a white scribble pattern—connected polka dots maybe —on the floor of the garage.

Karrie set her can and brush down by Leigh and moved back to her side of the garage to get the stepladder. She would start at the top and work down. Let Leigh sit there and moon about whatever was in her head a while longer. Chin ducked to her chest, Leigh didn't even look at her when she reached to pick up the paint can again.

"Coaching." The word was mumbled, and it took Karrie a moment to hear her and then another to process what Leigh had said. When she still didn't answer, Leigh looked up and let her eyes climb over Karrie's legs and torso and finally meet her gaze.

"Coaching," Karrie repeated.

"Apparently not." Leigh nodded and looked away. "'kay. Just thought I would—"

"Coaching Hazel?" Karrie clarified. "And her team?" She started to climb the ladder. Looked over her shoulder to Leigh and then turned her attention to the trim. She dunked the tip of the small, angled brush again and started dabbing at the wood.

"Never mind," Leigh whispered. "I wouldn't bother you with—"

"I've been here a week. I've washed your windows. Cleaned the garage out. Mopped the floors. Caught you up on laundry. And begged you to let me do more for you. Bother me, Leigh. It's why I'm here."

"You have to go back."

Karrie hesitated, brush on the wood. She took a deep breath and twisted around on the ladder to look at Leigh again. Careful not to drip paint everywhere, though at this point, one more splotch on the floor couldn't matter, she rested her elbows on the rung behind her and studied her sister.

"You're gonna fall," Leigh scolded her.

"Um." Karrie frowned and looked at her feet—safely tucked inside good running shoes—on the second rung of the ladder and shook her head. "Pretty sure I'm not, and if I did, it would be…like a two-inch drop. I'm good."

Leigh bent her knees and drew her legs to her chest. Karrie flinched, envisioning the paint can being bumped and knocked over. Paint all over the floor. Leigh's jeans. Before she could say anything, Leigh tipped her chin up to look at her again. Pain ripped through her—had to be her heart splitting—when she realized Leigh was crying. Big, silent tears, shoulders shaking, crying.

"Leigh," she gasped as she clambered to get off the ladder—wouldn't it be a hell of a note to trip and fall after being a smartass just ten seconds ago—and put the paint and brush down. She scooted both back on the tray of the ladder and then squatted in front of Leigh and rocked on her heels. "Oh, babe, God. I'm so sorry."

Leigh squeezed her eyes closed and shook her head. Karrie watched, helpless and frustrated, as Leigh covered her eyes with her hand and finally let loose with a soul-shattering sob.

"It's okay," Karrie whispered. She moved—not so graceful this time, because she was desperate to get closer and touch her sister, to comfort her—and dropped her butt to the floor. She reached out and put her arms around Leigh and pulled her huddled form close. "I've got you."

Leigh nodded against her shoulder, and for several long moments, the only sound was that of Leigh's quiet sobbing and hiccupping. Karrie let her own hot tears slide off her face, no intention of letting go of Leigh to wipe them away.

"She needs…" Leigh finally tried to speak again.

"Hazel needs you, hon," Karrie whispered.

Leigh shook her head as she drew away from Karrie. Outside the garage, neighborhood cars crept and zoomed past, most of them slowing and rolling through the stop sign at the corner. Karrie had been ticketed for exactly that not long after Leigh and Brad had moved in. Leigh rolled her lips inward and rubbed her nose with the sleeve of her sweatshirt. Face gaunt, her skin pale and splotchy from crying, she looked ten, and Karrie was overcome again with the need to protect her.

Face screwed into a frown of concentration, Leigh propped her elbow on her knee. "She needs the game. She needs…to be busy."

Well, Karrie couldn't argue with that. Not that Hazel didn't need Leigh, too.

"I can't do it." Leigh shook her head wildly, as if Karrie had suggested Leigh take on a team of junior-high-aged girls in her spare time. "I can't make myself get out of bed in the morning, much less..." She shook her head again and sniffled. "I shouldn't ask. You have to go back to work. I know that."

Karrie felt Leigh's stare like a punch in her belly. She gasped for air again and looked away. She had offered to do it. For a reason. The reason was still valid. Her niece needed her. Her sister needed her.

"Phoenix is...really, really hot." She cleared her throat.

Leigh tucked a flat chunk of hair behind her ear and licked her lips.

"Karrie."

"What?"

"Brad asked me for a divorce."

Karrie caught her breath as a chill slithered down her spine.

"What?"

"The night before..." Leigh's small voice faltered. She blinked at Karrie and unleashed another onslaught of tears. "Before the accident. He asked me for a divorce."

"Oh, Leigh." Karrie gritted her teeth and swallowed down a rush of emotion. Disbelief. Anger. Sorrow. "Oh, God. I'm so...I'm so sorry."

"We got in a huge fight." She closed her eyes and sniffled again. "I accused him of cheating. He swore there was no one else."

Karrie stared at Leigh silently and wondered if Leigh believed him. Wondered if Brad *had* been cheating on her. If Dom and Amy had really talked about divorce and agreed to an open marriage in the meantime, as he had claimed to Karrie when she hesitated to get involved with him.

"No one else *yet*." Leigh's big eyes climbed Karrie's face, and Karrie was again unprepared for the zing of pain and guilt that slammed into her and took her breath away. "But…he wanted…something. Someone new."

Karrie slid her right arm back from Leigh and pressed her fingers to her mouth.

"He was bored. And he didn't love me anymore."

"Oh, Leigh, I'm so sorry," she whispered past her fingertips. "Honey, I'm so sorry."

Leigh flinched and nodded. "No one knows."

"No one?"

The tiny shake of her head hurt Karrie as badly as if Leigh had slapped her.

"I was too embarrassed to tell anyone."

"Why would you be embarrassed?" Karrie reached for Leigh with the hand she had used to cover her mouth. "For God's sake, you didn't do anything wrong."

"Didn't I?" Leigh mumbled.

"Oh, God." Karrie ducked her head. It all made sense now. The way Leigh seemed so removed from what was happening. Karrie suspected a lot of that space was still shock, but she had assumed it was shock from the accident and the sudden precarious position her whole family was in. Now she knew there was so much more to it.

"You could've told *me*," she whispered. She looked up at Leigh and met her eyes. Lifted one shoulder in a cautious shrug.

"Yeah." Leigh nodded. "Sorry. Couldn't make myself confess my biggest disaster to my big-city sister."

"What?" Karrie shook her head. "What does that mean?"

"You did what I should have done." Leigh's voice was thick with emotion again. "You got out."

"Are you kidding me?" Karrie asked with a frown of disbelief. "Really?"

"You live in a place with perfect weather. You have a high-powered job. You've got this great guy—"

"I watch people die on my job," Karrie argued. "Days in a row, I watch people die. I wear other people's blood on my scrubs. I watch life just end, Leigh."

"You save people, too."

Karrie shrugged and looked away. "Not enough. I can't save enough, and some of them don't want to be saved. We just lost a girl before I came home. Drug overdose. We treated her six months ago for an overdose."

"At least you did something, though. You make a difference——"

"You have two beautiful kids in that house, Leigh." Karrie's voice throbbed with pain and need. "You've done something incredible there. You've given the world two incredible new people, and that? That is priceless. I would…"

Leigh stared at her boldly, waiting for her to continue.

"I would give anything…anything in my world…to have a child."

"So have a baby."

"Dom doesn't want babies, Leigh," Karrie argued. "I can't just go get pregnant if he's not on board."

"So find——"

Karrie squeezed her fingers tighter around Leigh's wrist.

"No. This isn't about me. I didn't mean to make it about me." She leaned closer to Leigh as if closer proximity could drive her point home. "I just wanted to remind you that you have done the most amazing thing a woman can do."

Leigh licked her lips again. Karrie flinched when she noticed how dry and chapped they were. Her sister had folded and curled into a ball to lick her wounds. Brad's leaving had done so much more damage than his accident. Karrie's body almost vibrated with the need to move, to fix things for her sister's family.

"Do you want me to stay?"

Leigh flicked her eyes away from Karrie sheepishly.

"I do." She nodded. Karrie watched her swipe at her nose and her eyes again and then shove her hair back from her face. "But I know you can't."

"It's okay—"

Leigh shook her head quickly. "No."

"Why?" Karrie drew back, stung by her sister's rejection yet again.

"I can't have you here for a week. Even a month. And then leave. I can't let Hazel need you when you come with a time limit." Leigh's nostrils flared when she drew in a deep breath. "Not now. She's too fragile, and if one more person walks away from her, she'll break."

"Do the kids know?" Karrie asked softly.

Leigh shook her head.

"No one."

"You've been carrying this around all by yourself for how long?" Karrie asked. When Leigh only stared at her, she groaned out loud and scrubbed her hands over her face. "I wanna help."

"You have." Leigh shook Karrie's desperation off.

"I wanna be *here*, Leigh. I want to help you and the kids—"

"But you can't." Leigh's firm tone invited no argument. "You can't do a damned thing for me, because the man I've loved over half my life doesn't love me back anymore. And you can't do anything for my kids, because their daddy is never going to be the same man he used to be."

Karrie drew in a quiet breath. She rubbed her eyes and then dragged her left hand up over Leigh's shoulder.

"Okay." She licked her lips and nodded when Leigh glanced at her. "I'll do what I can. While I'm here. And um…" She looked helplessly around the garage and tossed her hands up in defeat. "Go back next weekend. As planned."

Leigh's throat worked with emotion. Karrie waited for her to change her mind. To ask her to stay longer. She hadn't realized she was holding her breath until Leigh opened her mouth to say something, and Karrie went limp with relief.

"Where did you go?"

"What?"

"Last night." Leigh cleared her throat. "Where'd you go?"

Karrie stared at her sister for a long moment and wished she would have stayed here after college. Or that Leigh would have gone away for a while, just to gain some independence from Brad. She flinched when she remembered Hazel and Gino in the house. Because if anything with Leigh and Brad had worked out any differently, most likely, neither of them would exist.

"Um." Karrie blinked and lowered her gaze to the garage floor. "I met someone for a beer."

"An old friend?" Leigh suggested.

Karrie simply shook her head. She wished she were back at the bar across the table from Dax Law. Flirting. Instead of taking a beating for her sister's broken heart and her brother-in-law's selfish decision.

"New friend."

Eighteen

DAX HAD SPENT A LOT OF HIS DAY THINKING ABOUT Karrie Mallory. Far too many of those thoughts were centered around Karrie and Jake Spencer, though in his imagination he was picturing Karrie as a woman, not the gangly, tomboy athlete she was back in high school. Wasn't Karrie, thoughts of Karrie, that bothered him. In fact, he had gotten lost in those thoughts many times since he had taken her back to the school lot so she could retrieve her car and go home. He had been especially enthralled with the long column of her neck and her pulse there, the beat of her heart under her skin. He spent a little too much time fantasizing about flicking the tip of his tongue over that pulse point. Trailing kisses down into the V of her blouse. None of that bothered him, other than the fact that his dick had been on high alert for what felt like hours on end.

He could do without the Jake Spencer thing. What guy in his right mind wanted to imagine a woman like Karrie with any other man's hands on her? Spencer had been a pain-in-the-ass kid back in high school, and as ridiculous as it was, just the idea of Karrie being with him pissed him off.

He was jealous.

Dax slowed his pace to a crawl and looked around the long corridor, relieved to find it almost empty. Two freshmen turned the corner toward the school lobby. Kelsey Deavers, all-star senior setter for the girls' volleyball team, stood at Marti Yancey's office door, shoulder propped on the wall. She glanced at him and tossed him a distracted wave. Dax was grateful she didn't want to talk. Good kid, blah blah blah. But he didn't want to talk to anyone right now, least of all a student.

The realization that he was jealous of a pain-in-the-ass kid from ten plus years ago rocked his world. Wasn't the same cocky jealousy he carried around when he was in high school, when he had done his best to bed all the cute girls. This was different. Damn straight he wanted to get his mouth and his hands on her, but Karrie Mallory intrigued him. Why after all these years had she appeared in his gym joint—*clever, Dax*—driven to put in some hard physical time? What was the shadow in her eyes that made her look haunted? Okay, odds were she was more than a little bit affected by her brother-in-law's accident and the aftermath. But Dax thought there was more. When he asked about her life, her real life, she was subdued and less than talkative.

When he heard Marti's voice and Kelsey's soft laughter behind him, he picked up the pace again and continued to his own office. A little at odds with what he was feeling—he wasn't sure he ever had a real relationship with a woman, because he wasn't sure he and Emily hadn't been a mistake from the word go, and when she announced she was leaving, rather than hurt, he had felt a huge weight lifted from his shoulders—he tossed the newspaper he had gone in search of down on his desk. No longer interested in the article about local sports teams gearing up for the winter seasons, he stood at his desk and pulled his phone from his pocket.

What if he just called her? Suggested they go for a drink? And make it obvious that this time, they would consider it a date. He pursed his lips as his thumb hovered over the screen.

Pointless, wasn't it? If she lived in Phoenix, it was pointless to start something. And as much as he desperately wanted his hands on that sweet little ass, and as much as he wanted to see if she tasted as sweet as she smelled, he didn't want something disposable.

Dax groaned out loud. Damn. He was in trouble if he was so attracted to her, the thought made his dick jump to life and he had no intention of remedying that situation because anything they had would be temporary. He was pretty sure he had never been referred to as a gentleman; in fact, Dax would bet that Karrie had called him an asshole ten ways from Sunday since that first night he commented on her ass.

Then again, she came looking for him last night. And suggested he might like to buy her a drink.

Dax rolled his eyes and snorted softly. "Doesn't mean she wants the bone, Law," he mumbled. Maybe she just wanted a friend. Someone to distract her from what was happening in her sister's family.

Okay. So he would call her and ask her to have dinner and drinks. As friends. And then he could go home and jerk off in the shower with her in mind, if it came to that. Certainly not what he wanted, but he wanted to see her again. He wanted to get lost in her eyes, and he wanted her thick voice to drip over him like honey—

Fuck all.

He didn't have her number.

Frustrated to be left waiting and wondering if he would see her again, he tossed his cell down on the desk and stalked behind it to sit down. Time to get busy. This wasn't high school. No time to sit around and fantasize about making love to Karrie. He had a job to do, and he would just have to deal with the fact that he and Karrie weren't going to be anything other than one-on-one opponents for a few days.

Dax spent the early part of the afternoon reviewing the team budget he prepared earlier in the year. The new uniforms had exceeded their allotment, and he had been working to crunch some figures down in other areas. They probably didn't need much in the way of new equipment, so he slashed most of that section from the sheet. Varsity families were always gung-ho on the new stuff: new uniforms, new warm-ups, new shoes, new balls. But the JV families and the freshmen families tended to gripe about money spent, because that tended to translate to fundraisers. No one loved fundraisers; Dax understood that. He didn't particularly love them, either. But he had been coaching a winning team for several years now; he wanted his boys to look as successful as they played.

He covered study hall during seventh hour. After the final bell, he lingered in the classroom to talk. Several of the students crowded around his desk and by the door, and finally, the crowd had drawn Joe Collins— the history teacher—to the room and conversation. Joe was retired military and always had a good story to share. Dax was a little surprised to find the halls empty when he headed back to his office. He pulled his phone from his pocket as he walked. He had lost over an hour talking first to the kids and then to Joe. Not that it mattered. The volleyball girls weren't at home tonight, but his team couldn't practice just yet anyway. It was against the high school association rules for him to organize team practices this early in the year. Completely okay if the boys wanted to hang out and shoot and even run some drills on their own. The majority of them—Dax knew his starting five had started—were running and lifting weights, again all without him being present. But they weren't doing much in the way of shooting and drills yet, since the volleyball net was up more often than not.

He considered hanging around tonight to see if Karrie would show up. Decided it was pathetic that he had become the guy to putz around his office for hours when he was done with his workday and free to go home, all with the hopes of seeing a pretty girl again.

It bothered him that he had no idea when she planned to go back to Phoenix. They hadn't discussed it. They hadn't discussed a whole lot of anything, and Dax wanted to change that. But he hated the sinking feeling in his gut whenever he wondered if she would just vanish one of these days. If she would say goodbye to him before she left or if she ever even gave him a second thought when she wasn't here at the gym with him.

He slipped his laptop in his backpack and turned off the lights. Locked the door behind him and headed down the hall toward the gym. He could go on home. Throw something on the grill. He hadn't thawed anything out, but he could defrost chicken or pork chops in the microwave.

Or grab something on the way home.

He hated that. One thing he missed about the early days with Emily. They had been good at playing house, and they spent a lot of time in the kitchen.

Clothed and naked. Emily had taught him to cook, and for the first couple of years, they had eaten well. Now he hit fast food joints and pizza places far too often. Pretty soon it would start to show in his physique. There had been a time when he was cocky as hell, yes, but that had changed. At least he *thought* it had. Didn't mean he wanted to start sporting a pizza and beer belly, though. Not to mention the health risks he could end up creating.

Before he could decide if he was going to shoot a few baskets—i.e. hang around like a pathetic dope and hope that Karrie would show up—or head home and find something to eat, he heard the rhythmic pounding of the ball on the floor and knew without seeing the gym that it was her. Ignoring the swell of relief and even happiness in his chest, Dax hurried down the steps to the gym floor and swung his bag off his shoulder.

She wore black yoga pants in deference to the cold, he figured, and a hot pink work out tank. Dax noticed a gray pullover tossed on the bottom bleacher, but he looked back at her, hungry to drink her in. Hair in a ponytail, cheeks red with exertion, she was the prettiest site he had seen all day. Hard to decide if he liked this side of her—the disciplined, hardcore athlete—or the sexy feminine side he had seen last night better.

When she realized he was watching her, she shot a hard bounce pass at him. He knew without a word that it was her invitation to join her on the court. Luckily, he had read her intentions, and he caught the pass and put the ball down with his right hand as he lowered his bag to the floor with his left.

Without discussing it, he understood that they were going to resume their game of one-on-one from the other night. Didn't matter to him. He would run five miles with her right now if she broke out across the court. He took the ball to half court, mindful of the volleyball net, to set up his play. Karrie watched him as he moved, her gaze dark and intense. When he was set and ready to move, she sidled up closer to him to play defense. Up close, he saw a storm in her eyes and wondered what had happened today to piss her off.

She finally tossed her hands up. Dax watched her eyebrows slide up in question, as if she was asking him what the hell was taking him so long. Hard to reconcile this woman with the woman who had announced last night that she slept with Jake Spencer, but Dax had a feeling she might need the physical work out tonight more than ever, and maybe, just maybe, when they were done, she would talk to him.

And in the meantime, if the game got hot and sweaty and pushy, who was he to complain about it?

Nineteen

HE WAS CAREFUL AT FIRST, AND KARRIE WASN'T IN THE mood for careful. She was an athlete, and playing any sport *careful* was unacceptable. Not to mention that she needed to crash into something. She needed complete exertion and full contact, and she needed more than anything to leave everything on the court when she left later. She still hadn't told Leigh, but she had booked a flight to Phoenix for late tomorrow afternoon. She wasn't uncertain about her decision; she was anxious about how her sister would take it when she told her.

She was angry, too. She was angry with Brad for what he had done to Leigh, and she was angry with Leigh, too, for not confiding in her. And she was angry with herself for not realizing there was something going on. Okay, so, Brad had shocked Leigh when he had asked for a divorce, so Karrie couldn't have seen that coming. But she should have known there was something else going on with Leigh. She should have recognized Leigh's indifference to Brad's condition as something more than shock.

Needing to move, needing something physical, Karrie read Dax's intent to put up a shot when he pulled up at the free throw line and eyed the basket. She moved in closer and launched herself at him as he shot the ball in what would have been a beautiful arc, if she hadn't nailed him and smacked at his hands. She ignored the hard press of his body against hers and turned to block him out from the rebound, shoving her butt against his middle.

He groaned as he slid his hands up her arms—she hoped he didn't notice her shiver—to steady them both. Karrie kept her eyes on the ball as it banged off the rim and shot back to the court, several feet to the left.

"So, we're not calling fouls?" he asked as she lunged for the ball. She spared him a glance as she dribbled back to half court. When she looked back at the volleyball net, memories of high school games hit her in the heart. Leigh hadn't liked volleyball much more than she did, but she played, too. And Brad—the traitorous jerk—had come to all of Leigh's games and led the crowd—heavy on the sarcasm, because girls' sports, in general, and volleyball, in particular, hadn't ever drawn much of a crowd back then—in cheers. Karrie turned away from the net as another rush of anger hit her. She wasn't naïve. People divorced. Her own parents were divorced. But Brad and Leigh? How? Leigh hadn't seen it coming, so they weren't having problems in their relationship. How did you just wake up next to the love of your life and decide you were bored and ready to move on? How did you hurt someone like that?

Dax stood just in front of the free throw line. Karrie dribbled as he ducked his head to wipe sweat from his face. He wasn't watching her closely, so she moved suddenly and drove the basket. When he stepped left, she whipped the ball behind her back and cut the other way to put up a layup shot. Dax threw his hip at her as she got the shot off and sent her sprawling over the floor.

"Fuck." She groaned when her hip hit the floor. She had taken a lot of dives just like this when she was younger, but it had been a while. With another groan and a soft laugh, she rolled to her back. Dax approached her slowly. She eyed him in silence and wondered what he would say. If he apologized, she decided she would kick him. Maybe even sweep his feet out from under him and take him down.

He didn't, though. He simply held his hand out to help her up. Eyes never leaving his, she took a deep breath and placed her hand in his.

"I'd say we're even," he mumbled as he pulled her up from the floor.

"Even?" she repeated. "Are you nuts? I blocked a shot. You hip checked me."

Dax chased the ball down and dribbled it hard as he took it back to half court.

"What's the score, Mallory?" He raised his eyebrows.

Stunned by his callousness, Karrie opened her mouth to argue with him. He stared her down, still dribbling, knees bent and ready to take off. He was giving her what she wanted, maybe what she needed. No sympathy. No apologies. Dax was giving her game, a hard and physical game. She tilted her head at him, ignored the throbbing in her hip—that would feel good on the plane tomorrow—and moved into a defensive position, ready to go after him again.

Later—Karrie had no idea how much time had passed but they played to twenty-one—they stood under the basket, both with their hands planted on their bent knees, panting to breathe. He beat her by one lousy shot, and though it irked her, it did give her some satisfaction that he'd had to scrap and fight hard to beat her. His hair, wet with sweat, framed his red face, and his chest heaved with each breath he took, just as hers did.

Their eyes met as they both straightened to stand. Dax propped his hands on his hips, and Karrie raised her arms over her head, still struggling to breathe through the stitch in her side. She hated that she was so out of shape. If she was seriously going to quit her job and move back home to coach Hazel's basketball team, she was going to have to remedy that.

"Water?" she asked. Dax raised his eyebrows and nodded toward the steps, where she knew there was a water fountain. "Nice." She stepped around him, aware that he followed her.

"You okay?"

Okay, so she had needed him to play hard, and when he sent her crashing to the floor, she had needed him to push her and ignore that the fall had probably hurt. But it was nice that he was asking now if she was okay. He wasn't hovering; his voice wasn't heavy with concern. But he was checking to make sure she was okay.

She nodded as she leaned over the fountain to get a drink. Since she had grown up and especially since becoming a nurse, she hated using water fountains. But at the moment, this water was crisp and cold and just what she needed. She swallowed a mouthful, then a second. Rather than crowd her, Dax stood to the side of the fountain and leaned his back on the wall. His ragged breathing had slowed to something more normal, but when she backed away from the fountain and looked at him, she decided he still looked drained.

"I'm fine," she said quietly.

She squeezed the back of her neck and paced away from the fountain as he took a turn.

"I thought you were gonna beat me," he announced as he backed away and turned to look at her. She glanced at him in time to see him swipe the back of his hand over his mouth.

"I wanted to," she admitted with a grin.

"Oh, I know." His laugh strummed something low and primal in her belly. She dragged her eyes over his face and his shoulders and then sucked in a quick breath as she looked away. He was cute. Dax Law was hot—much more fun to look at now than when they were kids, even—but he was cute, too. Damned if she didn't see a little sparkle in his eyes, and that lopsided grin on his face told her he knew damned well she had wanted to beat him on the court and that she was irked that she hadn't.

"Thanks for not letting me win." She shrugged her lips and let them settle into a tired smile.

"Letting—? Letting you win? Are you kidding me?" He shook his head and sank back to lean on the wall again. "Not even an option."

It was her turn to laugh, because she knew he would never let her win. He had put his heart and soul into the game, same as she had. For a reason. She was good; he knew it. But he had wanted to beat her and show her that he was better.

She huffed out another deep breath and looked around for the pullover she had worn over her tank top. She didn't necessarily want it now, but it might be chilly outside. When she spotted it slung over the lowest bleacher further down the gym, she sighed and started after it.

A shiver climbed her spine when he touched her. Mouth suddenly dry, she tried to swallow as she looked down at his fingers wrapped around her wrist. He moved fast. When she looked up to meet his eyes, he stepped closer—much closer, close enough he might have felt her heart pounding against his chest—and pressed his lips to hers. Caught off guard by his bold move, Karrie gasped and then shivered again when he swept his tongue over her parted lips. Knees a little weak with excitement, she reached up to grab his arms. To hold on, or so she told herself, but when he kissed her again, when he rubbed the tip of his tongue over the center of her upper lip, she kissed him back.

Dax stepped closer, and Karrie felt his thigh hard against hers. She closed her eyes as he cupped the back of her head in his hand and deepened the kiss. The slide of his warm, velvety tongue over hers was like the slow burn of whiskey, thick and potent, leaving her mouth and a few other body parts hot and aching for more.

The sound of faraway voices brought her back to reality, even as Dax lifted his other hand to stroke her cheek. He shifted slightly so that his thigh and now his erection pressed against her. Karrie thought to protest, to back him up, but her hands weren't listening to her brain and suddenly, her fingers were around the back of his neck and in his hair. The fact that it was still damp with sweat from the game where they had wrecked each other on the court was suddenly very sexy. Karrie leaned in a bit and heard a soft moan when she pressed into him, her breasts resting now on his chest.

"Wait!"

He broke the kiss immediately, but he didn't move away from her. Part of her, the parts south of her brain and her mouth, wanted to weep with pent up frustration and need. How had that word finally come out of her mouth now? When things were really getting hot?

Well, because things were really getting hot, of course. They couldn't make out in the school gymnasium. Students caught doing exactly what she and Dax were doing ended up getting detentions. Teachers or coaches, like Dax, certainly couldn't get away with it. Could they?

The trouble was, he had obeyed her. He'd broken the kiss and pulled back just enough to look at her. If his eyes had sparkled before, when he teased her for wanting to win, they were on fire now, and they were still pressed body to body, so Karrie knew exactly what he wanted from her. She wanted it, too, and it finally dawned on her that she had stopped him for more than one reason.

This not-kissing pose was almost more intimate than kissing, though. She could feel his breath on her lips; his intense eyes watched her, moving constantly from her mouth to her eyes and back to her mouth.

"We can't do this." She shook her head to add a little force to her whispered words.

"Here," he added. "We can't do this here."

She shook her head again and took another step back. "No. We can't. Do this. We can't do this."

"Why not?" Rather than deter him, her words seemed to challenge him. The hand that had cradled her head now slid over her back and came to a rest on her hip, his fingers splayed possessively over her ass.

Karrie groaned softly when he rocked to his tiptoes and rubbed his middle against hers.

"Seems to me like we would be pretty good at doing this."

"Dax," she whispered. He kissed her again. A soft press of his lips to hers.

"Tell me why."

She sighed. Moved her hands. Slid them down over his shoulders—because if she was going to do the right thing by her married lover, she was going to steal one last chance to touch Dax Law's delicious shoulders—and rested her palms on his chest.

"I'm leaving tomorrow." Afraid to meet his eyes, she spoke to his chest.

"You're—?" He drew back as if she had hit him. "You're what?"

"Going back to Phoenix," she said quietly. She could tell him it would be a short trip. That she would be back. But it felt wrong. She was involved with Dominic Wolfe, and even though she had realized a while back that Dom was probably still intimate with his wife, she wouldn't do that to him. She would end things first. Tomorrow when she got back to Phoenix, she would talk to Dom—face-to-face—and tell him she couldn't do it anymore. He wouldn't care; she doubted he would wait a day before he recruited someone new to fuck around with on the side.

Still. She had to do things in order. Karrie was still reeling from Leigh's sorrow, and now that she was thinking about it again, she felt that guilt stomachache —she had taken Amy Wolfe's husband. She wasn't the first, and she wouldn't be the last, but that didn't excuse what she had done—and still, she wouldn't do this with someone else until she was completely single and not just in her head.

"Just. Just like that. You're just…" Dax finally stepped back, and Karrie sucked in a deep breath. A little lightheaded and still tingly in places that had hoped for Dax's touch, she crossed her arms over her chest and forced herself to look at him. To meet his eyes.

"Yeah."

His mouth froze in a grimace as he lifted his hands to link his fingers behind his neck.

"You might have mentioned it. Before now."

Karrie swallowed hard when his nostrils flared and his chest expanded with his deep breath. Was he angry? Frustrated, sure. She was, too. But had she given him the idea that she wanted to hook up while she was home?

"Kind of a spur of the moment decision," she admitted. She cleared her throat and met his eyes defiantly. "Would you have kissed me? If you had known I was leaving?"

"You bet your sweet little ass I would have," he answered simply. "I've been thinking about kissing that mouth since the first night I found you in my gym."

Karrie watched without a word as he dropped his hands to his sides and moved to pick up his backpack. He slung it over one shoulder and turned to walk away, never once looking back at her.

"Wow." She raised her eyebrows. Watched in disbelief as he walked away and disappeared on the steps.

Twenty

KARRIE TUGGED THE BILL OF HER HAT LOWER AND closed her eyes. The flight attendant was still talking; Karrie caught the word *federal* and figured he was at the part about no smoking on the airplane being a federal law. The guy was kind of cute, and people around her on the plane were smiling, but she didn't care to listen. Not today. She was still reeling over the confrontation with Leigh last night when she had come home from the gym.

And yes, the rest of her—specifically her nerves and all the girl parts—was still reeling from the kiss with Dax. From the implication that it had been more than a kiss. She had no misgivings; he wasn't interested in a romance. But he had made it loud and clear he wanted her. Karrie wasn't sure if she was still shaking inside over the fact that he kissed her, that he wanted to do the same wicked things to her body that she wanted him to do to her, or that if she hadn't had to worry about Dom, she would have gone home with Dax Law. She messed around some when she was younger, experimented like other kids had. And she had been involved with a few guys through the years before settling down with the one man who would never be free to love her and didn't care that he couldn't. But she wouldn't consider herself the girl to give it to just anybody, either.

Was he, though? Just anybody? Were they friends? Well, they weren't now, she was pretty sure of that. Should she have talked to him? Telling him that she had made a spur of the moment decision to fly to Arizona and get her life packed up to move back home would have invited questions. Questions she wasn't willing to answer, whether the answers pertained to herself or to Leigh.

She couldn't deny that she was attracted to him. Enough so that a one and done might have been acceptable. Except that if she was going to be living there, she didn't want that between them. She didn't want things to be awkward between them if they bumped into each other now and then.

Might be too late for that, though. He had kissed her. Having someone's tongue in her mouth was kind of a big deal to her. Having his hands in her hair and on her ass and his dick—hard and ready—pressed up against her was *something*. Something that would most definitely have led to something else and possibly something else, and Karrie wasn't sure she could make eye contact with him now.

Karrie blinked her eyes open as the flight attendant finished his spiel about changing air pressure and oxygen masks. Her thoughts bounced right back to Dax, the way he had moved so boldly into her space and the way his kiss made her feel lightheaded and weak in the knees.

She glanced at the woman to her right as she sighed and reached to adjust her earbud. No sense in dwelling on thoughts of Daxton Law. She wouldn't be gone long, but Karrie figured he would be hot and heavy with someone else by the time she did get back.

Five days. She had given herself five days to be in Phoenix and start the process of shutting that life down and transferring everything back home. Five days to speak to the director of the ER and give her notice. Five days to pack up more stuff and take it to Goodwill. Five days to track Dom down and get him alone to tell him she was leaving.

Leaving the ER was a major move, and it seemed extreme. Even Leigh had pointed that out when she found Karrie packing last night for the flight. Karrie loved the job; it was her nature to help people. It's why she chose nursing in the first place. She especially loved being part of the emergency team. Helping people at the absolute worst times in their lives. She was always able to remain calm and focused when others' lives depended on her. Always able to hold her emotions in check until she was alone, when sometimes the blood on her scrubs drove her to fits of tears and rage.

But she was starting to feel useless. Helping a patient injured in a car accident or a sports accident or treating a cardiac patient made her feel needed and sometimes, ten feet tall. But she wasn't lying to Leigh when she had said it was beginning to wear on her. Watching people bleed out from gunshot wounds or drunk driving accidents. Reviving attempted suicide patients. Shooting kids up with Narcan to combat heroin overdoses.

She squeezed her eyes closed and pressed her knuckles to her chest. That damned girl had looked her in the eyes six months ago and swore to her she would get help. That she would beat it. Karrie had worked tirelessly with the rest of the team to save her, and she had been physically and mentally spent for days after the girl had ended up in the ER. Karrie had followed up, checked in with her a few times, and she had been happy to see that she was working at a bookstore and living back at home with her grandmother.

It had nearly broken her to recognize that face again. To see the needle marks in her arms. To know that she had gone back to the drugs. The EMTs had given her Narcan on scene, and Dom had given her another dose in the ER, but they had all known she wasn't going to make it out of the exam room alive. They worked for two hours and thirty-seven minutes to bring her back, 157 heart wrenching minutes to save her, and only the haunted look in Dom's eyes when he called the time of death had reminded Karrie at the most inappropriate of times that he was a good man, a good doctor, even if he wasn't a good husband or father.

Leigh refused to understand Karrie's motivation. Then again, Karrie supposed burn out wasn't particularly a good reason to walk off a steady job and uproot a life and move back across the country. And she simply couldn't get into the rest of it. If she could help it, Leigh and her parents would never know she had spent the last year and a half involved with a married man. No way could she tell Leigh now, not after finding out that Brad had asked her for a divorce.

Karrie curled her fingers around her cell phone and opened her eyes. The woman beside her was reading a magazine article, so Karrie felt safe in opening her photo app. She wasn't in the mood for chatting with anyone, not even about her niece and nephew. But she needed to see them. She needed to remind herself, not that she was doing the right thing for herself, but that Leigh and her kids needed her. Because after Leigh's confession in the garage, she had gone back to that cool distance and when she found out that Karrie planned to come back permanently, and that Karrie did indeed plan to coach Hazel's team, she had been angry with Karrie.

Both for the rash decision to quit her job and for butting in. Even after she had broached the subject earlier in the day in the garage.

The picture on her phone was taken last year at Christmas; Hazel and Gino both wore big, happy grins. Gino's grin a little lopsided, his head tilted to the side and three big freckles stood out in stark relief on Hazel's nose. Both wore black and red checked pajamas, though they had both outgrown the footie pajama trend years ago. Karrie liked them; they made the kids look younger, and there were days when she called on those pictures and memories of innocence to get her through the rough times, the responsibilities her job demanded of her.

She had a boy in over the summer who had apparently crashed his bike. The blood all over his face was a bit startling; the kid's poor mom was completely unhinged when she came running through the automatic doors, the kid tucked under her arm like a football. Karrie had treated him and calmed the mom as she worked. She cleaned the blood from his face with gentle hands, and the mom's hiccupping sobs had died down when she saw one small cut on the kid's forehead. Bad enough, sure. No mom wanted her kid stitched back together in an ER. But head wounds bled so much that the kid had looked like he might not live through the night when Karrie had first approached him on the stretcher. His face had been red from crying, and he did have a little road burn on his left cheek. No doubt it had hurt. Throw in a broken wrist and a scraped-up knee, and the kid walked out with a cast to be signed, some stitches in his head, and bragging rights to boost his social status for at least a few days. He had reminded her of Gino, and Karrie had been warm inside watching the boy and his mom leave the ER together.

She groaned now, troubled not by the memory but with guilt. She was a good nurse. Certainly, quitting her job and hauling her ass and her possessions back home to hide from mistakes made in her personal life was a bit over the top. On the other hand, Karrie had every intention of working when she got settled. For one thing, she wouldn't live in Leigh's dungeon, even if Leigh let her stay. So she needed money. There was no money involved in coaching Hazel's basketball team. That would be a labor of love. And besides, she liked working. She loved nursing. She loved people.

Odds were, she would apply at the hospital back home, and she. would probably cross her fingers for an opening in the ER or maybe the cardiac unit. But what was the harm in walking away from Dom? Maybe he wasn't a toxic person, but their relationship wasn't going anywhere and never would. It was time to walk away from him, from her own ridiculous hopes, and get on with her life.

And most importantly to Karrie, Leigh needed her. Leigh and her kids needed her, and Karrie wanted to be there. To be back at home, where she could do the most good for her sister and her niece and nephew.

THE MEETING WITH THE DIRECTOR OF THE ER WENT about as Karrie expected. She liked the woman, had never had any issues with her. But they weren't close, and so Cheryl didn't get sentimental and try to talk her out of leaving. The goodbyes in the hallways were more difficult as Karrie had made friends with many on the hospital staff. She lost track of the number of times she alluded to Leigh's situation, though it was enough that she felt guilty for using her sister. Which was stupid, because Karrie had every intention of making good on her word to help once she moved back.

Naturally, Dom wasn't around when she went looking for him. She tried to be casual about it, though she figured there were plenty of people who knew the truth about their…situation. She refused to think of it as a relationship. Not anymore. When she had searched the corridors in the ER—even stuck her nose in the men's locker room—and still hadn't found him, she left. It was possible he was with a patient, but she wouldn't bother him at a time like that, anyway. Especially knowing that he would probably look at her with indifference, maybe boredom when she announced she couldn't carry on with what they were doing.

Instead, she cleaned out her locker and wondered if she was fortunate she had the vacation time saved up that she could use for her notice. She was in a hurry to get back home to Leigh and the kids. Okay, and if she were being honest, she would admit maybe part of her wanted to see Dax again, although she doubted that was going to go anywhere after the way she shut him down the other day. But was it a mistake to go rushing out of here like the place was on fire? She loved this job. She loved the people she worked with.

As she swung her locker door closed, she thought again of the girl they lost the night before she left. The desperation she had felt while she and her team had performed CPR, all the while knowing she was already gone. That wasn't the worst of it, though. Hard as it was, that wasn't what kept her up at night. It was the little thrill of hope, of happiness she had felt when she saw Jacinda, the young girl they had lost, six months before when she had been on the road to recovery.

That feeling. Got Karrie right in the heart, every damned time. She wasn't sure how much more of that she could take. And damned Leigh for not understanding that. Or maybe, it was more accurate to say that Leigh didn't want to understand the way Karrie felt. Who could blame her? She was reeling from the knowledge that her husband didn't love her anymore and that the man she still loved was fighting for his life. Torn between that awful, hurtful feeling of betrayal and the desperation for Brad to pull through and live.

If nothing else, he was the father of her children.

Her phone buzzed in her back pocket as she ducked her head and headed out the doors. She had said her goodbyes to her coworkers, and some of them hurt more than others. But she reminded herself with technology and social media, physical distance didn't have to mean that much anymore. With a sigh, she pulled her phone from her pocket and saw that she had missed a call from Leigh.

The sun was brutal as she crossed the visitor's lot and headed to the Mazda she rented at the airport. She had considered calling Sheena for a ride, but she had decided against it. Short notice meant that her roomie was probably busy. Not to mention that Karrie had wanted a moment or two to herself to get her thoughts in order before talking to anyone about her decision. Never mind the fact that she had the whole flight to think.

With her right hand, she unlocked the car and with her left, she bumbled her way through her phone screens until she got to missed calls. Tapped the top one and waited for Leigh to answer.

"So, what?" Leigh asked instead of the standard greeting. "You're avoiding my calls now?"

Karrie opened her mouth to argue, but she changed her mind and snapped it shut. She pulled the phone from her ear to look at it for a second and then stuck it back up beside her ear to listen.

"I was in the hospital," she said, proud of herself for sounding calm. After all, she had made the decision to leave, but she hadn't made it lightly, and she was still feeling a little off, a little sad. Not to mention, how the hell was she avoiding calls, if she had called Leigh back immediately? "Cell reception's not great in the ER area."

"Are you busy now?"

Karrie took a deep breath and raised her eyebrows. She might have liked Leigh to acknowledge what she just said. To just ask if she was okay, if she was sure she wanted to quit, to move back home. Of course, Leigh wouldn't. Karrie and her life didn't matter so much to Leigh right now, and honestly, she understood that. Leigh's whole life had spun out of her control recently, and on top of that breath-taking pain, she was alone. Completely alone in her grief, because only Karrie knew about Brad. Leigh had suffered too much of this completely on her own.

"No." Karrie rested her butt against the driver's door. At least she had found a tiny bit of shade to park in. Maybe she wouldn't melt for the duration of the phone call. "What's up?"

Leigh didn't answer immediately. Karrie watched an ambulance leave the parking lot and merge into traffic. She swung her gaze back over the lot to the building where she had spent most of her time for the past several years. She almost snapped at Leigh, asked her what she wanted because she was busy, but then she heard a sniffle. Maybe a small mewling sound.

Leigh was crying.

Karrie felt a chill climb her spine, even though her ass was on fire propped against the car door. She shivered and then stood up straight and rubbed her free hand over her arm, bent to hold her phone to her ear.

"Leigh?"

Her voice cracked, and though there was no one around, she cleared her throat and looked over her shoulder. She was surrounded by parked vehicles, but the nearest person was a good five rows of cars away from her.

"The team's coming in," Leigh whispered. Karrie dropped her head forward and rubbed her fingertips over her forehead. What was Leigh talking about? Team? Hazel's team? Why would that make her cry?

"What team?" Karrie reminded herself to go easy.

"The doctors."

Karrie straightened like someone shot steel through her spine. She dropped her hand to her side and took a deep breath. A team of neurosurgeons was coming to assess Brad's situation. To determine if he was brain-dead. She had known it would happen. Of course she'd known this was coming. She was a nurse who had spent most of her professional career in emergency medicine. She had seen her share of brain trauma and life support and brain-dead patients.

But this was *Brad Avery*. This was her sister's husband. Not a thirty something Caucasian male, victim of a motorcycle accident.

"When?"

Her voice sounded sideways and harsh, so she coughed to ease the emotion out of her throat and asked again. So, she was angry with Brad. Angry as hell with him, and to be honest, she had felt a rush of deep, dark hatred for him the other day when Leigh had admitted he wanted to divorce her.

But Karrie didn't want him dead. She was angry that he had hurt Leigh, but that didn't mean she wanted him to die.

"The day after tomorrow."

"Oh, Leigh." Karrie bit her lip and dropped her head back, wishing she could scream at the sky. She had to be there. Leigh couldn't ask a busy team of neurosurgeons to reschedule just so Karrie could get back to be with her, to hold her hand. And she had been adamant the other night, before Karrie left, that she wouldn't tell their parents the truth, so either Karrie found a way to get back home before the team of doctors came into assess Brad's injuries and prognosis, or Leigh suffered through what could possibly be a horrid situation and what couldn't be better than a really bad situation completely, utterly alone.

"I need you to come back, Karrie."

Twenty-One

"WHAT'RE YOU DOING HERE?"

Karrie stared blankly at Leigh, too stunned to answer and uncertain she would find her voice even if she tried. Over Leigh's shoulder, the living room was lit only by the flickering TV, though Karrie couldn't hear anything, so apparently the volume was muted. On the small front porch of Leigh's house, darkness enveloped her. Leigh hadn't bothered to flip a light on when she answered Karrie's knock.

Exhausted and more than a little bit blue, Karrie started to remind Leigh that she had just flown across the country and back within forty-eight hours, paid a fortune for the less than enjoyable experience, quit her job, and tried to break things off with her boyfriend (yeah, that was starting to hurt. Kind of a slow burn that had started low in her belly and finally reached her throat on the drive from the airport to Leigh's house) all to be here when Leigh faced the team of neurosurgeons tomorrow who would determine Brad's fate. She couldn't do it, though.

Leigh, with her arms crossed over her chest, her shoulders hunched inward, and a haunted look on her face, appeared small and alone, and Karrie didn't want to hurt her. Instead, she simply huffed out a quiet, frustrated sigh and cleared her throat.

"Can I come in?"

By Midwestern standards, it wasn't cold. But she had just come from Phoenix, and she had played phone tag with Dom while she was there, and she needed comfort, warmth. She wouldn't get either from Leigh right now, and she understood that, but she would like to come in from outside at least.

Leigh simply took a few steps back so Karrie could slip inside.

"Kids in bed?" she asked as she set a big duffle bag on the tile in front of the door.

"Yeah." Leigh shrugged when Karrie glanced at her.

Karrie straightened and looked around the room. She didn't wear a watch, not when she wasn't working, and her phone was tucked away in her purse. She had checked it a million times while she was at her apartment, packing things up to move her life a thousand miles back across the country. And she checked it another hundred as she boarded her flight. Maybe another when she landed. When there had been nothing beyond two missed phone calls from Dom for the duration of her short trip to Arizona, she had swallowed her hurt and wounded pride and stuffed the phone deep inside the middle zipper of her oversized bag.

She wasn't sure if she wanted a voicemail. A text message. She needed Dom's acknowledgment that she ended it. And she had. He had given her no choice in the short time she'd been there. So she had left him a voicemail and asked that he call her. Short and to the point, she couldn't be involved with him anymore, and then she ended it before he could hear her regret in her voice. Regret over walking away, yes, but also regret that she had ever been naïve enough to pursue him in the first place.

Maybe she *wanted* him to fight for her. To promise that he would leave Amy and proclaim that Karrie was his true love. But she *needed* him to acknowledge what she had said and walk away. She wished him well; she hoped that he would at least do the same for her.

"Any change?" Her whisper was gruff.

"No."

When their eyes met, Karrie saw Leigh's pain. She wanted to say something, to comfort her. But Leigh only gave her a curt nod and turned away.

"So you did it, huh? You just quit your job to come back home?"

"Yeah." Karrie drew in a deep breath, a little overcome with emotion. A wave of dizziness. What the hell had she done? Leigh didn't want her here. Sure, she needed someone around to help with the logistics of real life, but she didn't want *Karrie* here.

Her mom would be happy to have her closer, but she would demand an explanation for the sudden move. And Karrie couldn't tell her Leigh's truth, either.

"You're stupid." Leigh's voice lacked the venom necessary for such an announcement. Before Karrie could defend herself, Leigh shrugged and glanced at her over her shoulder. "Thank you."

Karrie sucked in a sharp breath when Leigh walked out of the room. Afraid to move, she waited to see if Leigh would return. When she heard a door close at the end of the hallway, she realized Leigh had dismissed her and gone to bed. Karrie doubted that her sister would sleep any better than she would, but she wouldn't bother her. Only so many kicks she wanted to take in her teeth.

She gave herself a mental shake and then reached to pick her duffle up again. The heavy bag in her right hand, she curled her fingers around the handle of the smaller carry-on luggage she brought in with her and moved through the living room. At the top of the steps, she stopped. Left her luggage there and went back to the living room to turn the TV off and lock the house up.

Would it be better for Leigh? If the doctors decided Brad was brain-dead? Would it be easier for her to move on, rather than letting this drag on forever? Sure, Leigh would have to move through the grieving process, made worse by the fact that only Karrie was aware that Brad had wanted to end their marriage. She would have to get her children through the loss of their father—Karrie felt a stab of pain in her chest—and judging from what she had seen already, Leigh wasn't going to handle that well at all.

But would it be better to have an end in sight? How long could Leigh go on as things were? Missing and loving Brad? Watching him cling to life and knowing that even if by some miracle he had a full recovery, he wanted to leave her?

She flipped the deadbolt and gave the door a gentle tug to test it. Satisfied that it was locked, Karrie slipped down the hall and peeked in first at Gino and then Hazel. Physically safe, just as she and Leigh were, but their hearts were already broken. What would tomorrow's news do to them?

Karrie listened to each of them breathe for a moment and hoped they were having good dreams. Afraid one of them would wake and catch her watching, she finally headed back down the hall and through the now dark living room. She hesitated at the top of the steps. The last thing she wanted to do was go back down and sleep in the dark, depressing basement room.

No. That wasn't true. The last thing she wanted to do was stand at her sister's side tomorrow and hear what the medical experts said about her brother-in-law. Maybe living in limbo as Leigh had been since the accident was preferable to knowing exactly where they stood.

KARRIE WASN'T SURE WHAT SHE EXPECTED WHEN SHE climbed the steps in the morning, but it definitely wasn't a well-dressed and groomed Leigh, sipping coffee while she leaned over Gino's shoulder reading something from what appeared to be a library book. Gino's giggle was music to her ears, and seeing her sister's fingers curled around his shoulder warmed her heart. Head still bent over the book, Leigh raised her eyes to look at Karrie and offered her a tentative smile.

"Hey." Karrie smiled uncertainly as she catalogued Leigh's fully made-up face and the small hoops that hung in her ears. "Did you leave me some coffee?"

"Of course." Leigh's answer sounded normal, like the Leigh Karrie had always known and loved. But rather than make her feel good, it filled her with dread. Leigh should be just about ready to buckle under the pressure. She needed to break. To rail and sob and cry. She needed to be angry, both about Brad wanting to leave and about the accident itself. Skipping any part of the process wasn't going to be good for her. In fact, it would lead to disaster at some point.

"When did you come back?" Gino asked her. The fingers of his right hand spread over the open book, he used his free hand to stuff a Pop-Tart in his mouth.

"Don't talk with your mouth full," Leigh admonished him as she straightened and backed away from him. Karrie moved around the table to stand where her sister had been just moments before. She read over Gino's shoulder, but she didn't recognize the story.

"I came back late last night," she told him. He pushed her hand away when she reached for his Pop-Tart.

"You snuck in?" He looked at her with wide eyes. "Like Santa?"

Karrie blinked. *Santa. Oh no. Christmas was coming.* Of course, Gino would be thinking about Christmas already. Hadn't she been the same when she was his age? She would start wishing for Christmas and snow as soon as the calendar rolled around to August or September. Christmas would tear Leigh apart this year.

"She knocked." Leigh handed Karrie a mug of coffee and stood side by side with her. "And I let her in."

Karrie took the coffee and stared at Leigh suspiciously for a moment. This was Leigh. This was the Leigh she had missed since she had come back home, but her appearance now—this morning—concerned Karrie. She wished for the hundredth time that she could tell their mom what was going on. It wasn't that she didn't want to help Leigh, but she wasn't sure she was up to the challenge, the responsibility of cradling Leigh's mental and emotional health until her sister was stable again. What if she wasn't enough? What if Leigh was permanently damaged from this?

When she realized Gino was still staring at her with those wide, innocent eyes, she turned a big grin on and raised her eyebrows.

"Dude, if I could sneak in and out of houses like Santa—"

"You wouldn't." Leigh cut her off. "You wouldn't sneak in and out of anywhere, like Santa, because that would be wrong. And creepy."

Gino rolled his eyes at Karrie and turned his attention back to the book.

"Where's Hazel?"

"She got a ride to school today."

"Why?" Karrie shook her head. She studied Leigh intently, wondering if she had some hidden agenda, a game plan that involved handing her kids off to anyone else in order for her to crawl in a hole and hide after she talked to Brad's doctors.

Leigh shrugged. "I dunno. Her friend called her last night, and they put this scheme together. You remember those days, don't you?"

Karrie laughed softly.

"Yep."

"Mom, could I ask Santa for a puppy this year?"

Karrie pressed her lips together and backed away from the two of them.

"Nope."

"Why not?"

"We don't need a puppy, Gino. We have our hands full."

Karrie looked from Leigh to Gino, amused when he held his hands up to look at them and then looked at Leigh with a curious frown.

"You know what I mean." Leigh dropped her hand on his head and tousled his hair. "It's been rough with Dad being gone. And when we get him back home, we all have to help him with his recovery."

Karrie felt the words like an icepick in her heart. First of all, she highly doubted Brad Avery would be coming home anytime soon, if ever. Second, if he did recover, would he come back here? Would Leigh sign on to take care of him if he had permanent brain damage? Paralysis? After he told her he wanted to leave? How the hell was that fair? And how the hell was it fair for Leigh to talk to Gino like Brad would be coming home and everything would eventually return to normal?

"If he was in a wheelchair, he could hold a puppy on his lap."

Karrie sipped her coffee and wished she were anywhere but here, preparing to do what she and Leigh had to do. Except maybe in an ER exam room fighting the clock on a drug-overdosed teen.

"Gino, Christmas is still several months away," Leigh reminded him. "And we're not getting a puppy."

"I'll just ask Santa for one," he mumbled.

"He won't—"

Uncomfortable with the conversation, Karrie slipped out the back door, coffee in hand. She was in no position to judge Leigh, but she wasn't sure her sister was doing the right thing with the kids and Brad. Hazel was certainly old enough to be told the truth—that he might not make a full recovery, if he ever made any progress from day one—but she wasn't sure Gino was. Sadly, he had the maturity to deal with it, and that was part of the problem. A kid his age shouldn't be mature enough to handle news like that about his dad.

She opened the garage door and wandered past Leigh's dented van to the drive. Her phone was in her purse; she left it there on purpose, because she was going to make herself crazy checking for a text from Dom. It was likely that she would never hear from him again, and it was time to move on. She didn't need his acknowledgement to do exactly that.

When she heard the squeal of the screen door behind her, she glanced over her shoulder to see Leigh follow her footsteps to stand beside her at the open overhead door.

"You think I'm doing this wrong." Leigh's voice was gruff. She avoided Karrie's eyes.

"I think I'm the last person who has the right to judge anything you do," Karrie said quietly.

Twenty-Two

KARRIE SNUCK WHAT SHE THOUGHT WERE SLY PEEKS at Leigh, checking on her from time to time while they waited. Bill, their stepdad, scrolled through his newsfeed on various apps—if the situation were different, Karrie would have been amused at the idea of Bill playing on his smartphone to pass the time—and their mom and Brad's mom both paced the waiting room and the hospital corridor, and two or three times, they slipped away to the cafeteria or coffee shop and returned with more caffeine than all of them combined needed. That would have made her nervous, but no one touched the coffees after the first sip or two.

She was worried about Leigh, though. Her sister had played at normal all morning, even after they dropped Gino at school. She had watched her son meander to the door and slip inside with a small smile on her face, and then as she eased her car out of the lot, turned the radio up a bit, and commented on a song playing. Karrie had assumed that once both kids were out of her sight, Leigh would shut down again. But she had talked as she navigated the highway for the hour and a half drive to the rehab hospital where Brad had been since the day after the accident.

Not about any impending divorce. Not about any fights she might have forgotten to mention. Not about how she had thrown in the towel and curled up in a ball after Brad's accident. Instead, she chattered nonstop about the old days. Fun times with her friends, fun times with the girls' basketball team. At first, Karrie had worried about how to respond to Leigh's stream of consciousness, but she closed her mouth when she realized Leigh didn't necessarily want Karrie to talk.

Now, though, Leigh sat as still as a statue. In fact, Karrie thought her skin looked white like alabaster, and a few times, she had been tempted to poke Leigh to make sure she moved. She was so still, Karrie wasn't sure she was breathing. She had to be a wreck inside, and Karrie wished she would get up and move around a bit. Walk off some of that fear. Instead, she simply sat in the chair in the waiting room, stiff as a board, staring at the floor. Karrie wondered what she was thinking about or if she was thinking at all. Maybe it took all her will, all her concentration, to hold herself and her life together, and if she moved the tiniest bit, everything would shatter to pieces.

"Mrs. Avery?"

Karrie felt a stab of ice-cold fear jab her. She lifted her eyes from the spot she had been studying on the floor to look at her sister. Leigh moved as if in slow motion. First, she tilted her chin up, and then she uncrossed her arms from her chest—Karrie imagined they might have popped, she had been sitting that way for so long—and finally she let her eyes zero in on the nurse at the door of the waiting room. Karrie noticed the tremor in her sister's lips and the sparkle in the wedding ring on her finger, and then Leigh blinked, and a tear slid from her eye.

She nodded, but she didn't speak. Karrie stood and looked around the small room for her parents. Brad's dad was propped in the doorway, pretending to watch the TV hanging in the corner of the room. Their moms stood arm in arm just out the other door of the waiting room and peered inside, as if they were afraid to come too close.

"The doctors would like to speak with you now," the nurse said quietly. Before Karrie could move to help her sister up, Brad's dad was at her side, offering her his hand. Karrie swallowed hard when Leigh slipped her fingers in his hand and stood. They moved slowly across the room. Leigh gave a halfhearted reach for Karrie's hand as she walked by. From the corner of her eye, Karrie saw Leigh ball her free hand into a fist, but she focused on the nurse leading them out of the room.

Pointless, and Karrie knew it. Only a doctor would deliver the sort of news they had all been waiting for. But Karrie found herself watching the girl for any telltale signs. For a tentative smile. For that haunted look that the nagging feeling of guilt and helplessness could paint on healthcare workers that failed to provide miracles when they were so desperately needed.

The nurse remained stoic and professional as she turned and led them down the corridor, past the pneumatic doors to the patient rooms and to a small conference room. Karrie's stomach clenched. Private conference rooms after an assessment such as Brad had just been through were part of the process. Certainly, a courtesy. Confidential. Not really comforting, though, as they were most often used to deliver bad news.

Karrie hung back, waited while Leigh sat down, and their parents gathered around her to sit at the long conference table. Part of her planned to drop into whatever chair was left empty. And part of her wanted to pace the room. But when Leigh turned and looked at her over her shoulder, she moved immediately to the empty chair at her sister's side. Leigh reached for her and closed her icy hand around hers in a fiercely tight grip. Karrie swallowed a knot of emotion when she realized how scared Leigh was, that she had put on a hell of an act of calm up until now.

She gave Leigh a small nod of encouragement and covered their entwined fingers with her other hand. Leigh turned back to the head of the table where a young blonde was sliding into the last remaining chair. Karrie thought the guy couldn't be any older than she was. She also knew he was qualified to do his job, or he wouldn't be here doing the job in the first place.

"Mrs. Avery." He took a deep breath. Karrie felt her body go cold. "I'm Dr. Maloney. We met when… when Brad was first transferred here."

Leigh responded with a quick nod.

"Mrs. Avery, unfortunately, Brad has not responded to any stimuli since the accident and—"

"What about…" Leigh hesitated. Karrie looked at her, noticed her struggle to speak, to remain in control. "What about when he moves? When I hold his hand? What about—"

Karrie was shocked to hear that Leigh had held his hand. From what she had seen since she'd been back, Leigh hadn't come within a foot of his bed. The thought of her sister holding his hand and remembering that he had wanted to leave her made her ache inside.

"It's all involuntary movement," he said quietly. "And it's important to note that there's been no movement whatsoever in the past week."

Leigh sniffled. Karrie dragged her chair closer to Leigh's and slid her arm around her.

"What are you saying, Dr. Maloney?" Brad's dad asked from behind Karrie.

The doctor took a moment longer to study Leigh and finally turned his compassionate gaze to Brad's parents. Karrie squeezed Leigh's hand and leaned her head on her shoulder.

"I'm so sorry, Mr. Avery." Dr. Maloney spoke reverently. "Your son is brain-dead. He's not going to come out of this. It's not a coma. He's not going to recover."

"The ventilator is the only thing keeping him alive," Karrie whispered before she realized she was going to speak. The doctor swung his gaze to her and nodded before turning his attention back to Brad's parents.

"How do you know that?" Brad's mom asked. "How can you know that for sure?"

"Mrs. Avery, your son sustained severe injuries in the accident. There was never a question of Brad making a full recovery. It was simply if he would wake up and how much brain damage there would be. I'm telling you that after repeated examinations, he does not respond to any external stimuli."

Leigh's mewling cry ripped through Karrie like a knife. She lifted her head from Leigh's shoulder to see her sister's face slide into a mask of horrified grief. Tears, blackened from mascara, slid over her cheeks and her lips. Karrie felt her body tremble under her arm.

"Damn you, Brad," she whispered. "Damn you for doing this to us."

Karrie doubted anyone else heard her, but she didn't particularly care, either.

"Mrs. Avery." Dr. Maloney sat back in his chair and studied Leigh intensely. "As his spouse, removing Brad from life support is your decision. But it is our position that he is brain-dead, and he will not wake up. There is no recovery."

"Leigh, you need to think—"

Karrie twisted her chair around and gathered her sister in her arms, maybe to shield her from her in-laws.

"You shouldn't—"

"What about Hazel? And Gino? You can't just—"

"Can you guys give her just a minute?" Karrie's voice was quiet but steady. She smoothed her hand over Leigh's back. "I know you all need to talk about this, but can you give her just a minute? Please?"

Leigh scrunched her face up and squeezed her eyes closed like a toddler having a temper tantrum. Karrie sat with her shoulders hunched, waiting to unleash the tension, the rage she felt, fueled by her own helplessness to fix things. The doctor stood first and slipped without a sound out of the room. Karrie held her breath until she heard the door swish open and closed a few times and then felt the stillness that told her she and Leigh were alone in the room.

THE GYM WAS SO COLD, SHE WAS SHAKING. EITHER that, or she was still shaking because the day had totally wrecked her. Maybe both. The temperature had dropped to an unseasonably cool forty degrees. Seemed a little chilly for October. She had turned the heat on high when she drove Leigh back home. Eventually, Karrie thought she might sweat to death, but Leigh rode the entire hour and a half with her gloved hands pressed between her thighs, shoulders hunched against the chill in the air.

They had tabled the discussion, of course. You didn't just pull the plug on life support the way you unplugged a phone charger. Leigh needed to think. She needed to talk with Brad's parents, with her parents, and yes, she needed to talk to Hazel and Gino. Maybe Gino didn't need the details, but he needed to know his dad probably wasn't going to ever come home.

Karrie dribbled hard and slammed a layup at the backboard. She needed that physical game she and Dax had played earlier in the week. She needed some bumps and bruises, the kinds you could see, because the internal ones were tricky and deep and hard to heal and hard to explain. But it was after eight, and she hadn't seen Dax Law since she had slipped into the school a half hour ago. There were lights on in the corridor with the AD's office; Karrie had considered going looking for him again. But she didn't.

Instead, she ran. Ten hard laps around the gymnasium. Left her sweaty and breathing hard but not hurting enough. Nothing was going to hurt enough to make today go away. She launched another shot at the board and watched the ball rattle around the rim and bounce back at her. No finesse. She felt heavy-handed, and she was throwing bricks, but the noise and the sloppy shots almost felt good.

She had looked at her phone when she settled into the driver's seat of Leigh's van. A missed call from Dom. No voicemail. No texts. She wasn't sure now what bothered her more. The fact that he hadn't left her a message or the little thrill his number on her screen had shot through her heart. If she had left him, if she was over him, that shouldn't be happening anymore, should it?

No idea how much time had passed since she'd first come inside, she drove for the basket again and put up another shot. Ready for the rebound, she slumped forward and propped her hands on her knees when the ball banked off the backboard and fell through the hoop. Sweat trickled down her back, as her eyes tracked the goosebumps on her bare legs. She was angry *with* Brad and *for* Brad, and she was sad for Leigh and worried about Leigh and her kids, and she was mad at Brad's parents for pushing Leigh to hold off, to wait and give Brad more time to recover when she knew damned well what the doctors had decided was correct. The mix of emotions played with her body, making her an uncomfortable mix of cold and hot and wired and exhausted.

Voices above her made her suck in one last deep breath and then straighten and let her hands hang at her side. A shiver climbed her spine—she was still sweating, but now her skin prickled—when she realized one of the voices belonged to Dax. Still breathing heavy, she ducked further under the overhang around the gymnasium and waited. It was stupid to hide, especially if she wanted him to know that she was here. But she had no desire to talk to anyone else, and it sounded like Dax was talking to Jed. As much as she had always liked Jed, she didn't want to get caught up in a normal conversation when she felt anything but normal.

Karrie propped herself against the wall next to the water fountain. Hand wrapped around the ball, which she held against her hip, she closed her eyes and listened to the voices fade. Disappointment welled inside, which only added to the restlessness. How in the hell could she be mooning over Dom and now feel disappointed that Dax wasn't going to notice her? And what if he did, anyway? What then?

On the other hand, if Dax didn't realize she was here, she might end up locked in the dark gym overnight. She almost laughed out loud at the thought. Wouldn't be the worst thing she was dealing with right now, but it might get chilly overnight.

With a resigned sigh—she would have to go home, go back to Leigh's and watch her sister fade away from life and pretend everything was normal at least until Leigh talked to the kids—she pushed away from the wall and started to move back toward the gym. She would put the ball back where it was—curious that it always seemed to be on the home bench now whenever she happened to come in—and grab her jacket and go. She was an adult, a nurse. Just because this tragedy was hitting much closer to home didn't mean she couldn't handle it the same as she handled so many others in her professional life.

She realized someone was coming when she heard the soft tap of rubber-soled shoes on the cement steps. Her luck it would be Jed instead of Dax. She wasn't sure she had the energy to attempt a normal conversation, but she willed herself to try. As she moved away from the water fountain, Dax rounded the bottom step and stopped abruptly right in front of her.

Karrie felt her mouth go dry. Restless again now that she was looking at Dax and not Jed, she gasped and then sunk her teeth into her lower lip.

"What're—"

Okay, so she still didn't want to talk. Dax watched her with a suspicious frown. Hungry for him, for all of him, she let her eyes roam over his thick dark hair, the thick eyebrows currently slanted over his deep, warm brown eyes, and finally his lips.

Karrie didn't realize she dropped the ball until she heard it bounce and then roll away out of sight. Dax was dressed for work, real work, not basketball practice. Karrie wanted to appreciate the button-down shirt and the khakis—a quick glance showed how well they fit his thighs—but her eyes had a mind of their own and kept returning to his lips.

He took a turn with the once over, and Karrie's whole body tensed under his inspection. She probably looked like hell. She had changed when they got home from the hospital from jeans to workout clothes, pulled her hair into a messy ponytail, and headed out without even bothering to check her makeup. Apparently, the lighting down here in the basement hall was bad or Dax simply didn't care, because he stepped toward her. His fingers brushed her hip, and that was all she needed.

She launched herself at him, arms over his shoulders, one hand in his hair and the other flat on his back, her breasts pressed hard against his chest. She didn't wait; her lips found his in a hungry, demanding kiss. His firm lips open against hers made her push into him harder, and the clash of their tongues sent a flame of desire straight to her core.

"Jesus, where—"

"Can we?" she whispered. "Can we do this here?"

"Karrie—"

Impatient with his questions, with his need to talk, she dropped her hands and pushed him away. Before he could protest, she reached for his belt. Her hands shook as she unbuckled it and then worked the button open.

"Fuck me." Her voice was hoarse with need. The look on his face—a mix of surprise and lust—made her whole body vibrate. "Dax?"

He reached for her, linked his fingers with hers and turned away from her. The sweat on her skin made her cold, and her knees were weak. She followed him when he ducked into the boys' locker room and reached again for his zipper when he pushed the door closed. He might have flipped the lock, but she wasn't sure, because he jumped and groaned out loud when she lowered the zipper and slipped her fingers inside his briefs to touch him.

Hands propped on either side of her now, Dax had her backed against the closed door. She cupped his long, thick cock in her hand and met his eyes.

"Sweet fuck," he moaned when she smoothed the pad of her thumb over the head of his cock. Karrie wrapped her fingers around him and applied a bit of pressure. Dax dropped his chin to his chest and sucked in a labored breath.

"Dax." She leaned forward and brushed her lips over his forehead. His thick hair was soft on her cheek. "I need you. Inside me."

She felt him thrust into her hand, and then he lifted his head to meet her gaze.

"Are you sure?"

"Yes." She nodded, because she had never been surer of anything in her life. He reached for his back pocket with one hand, covered hers at his groin with the other.

"If you want me inside you, you need to stop," he warned her. "I've been fucking you in my mind since that first day I found you here."

"And how is it?" Her whisper was thick and bold.

"Two seconds, and I'm gonna come in your hand, Karrie Mallory."

Turned on by his words, when she really had only wanted the rough, hard contact with him, she rested her head on the door and licked her lips. He pulled his wallet from his pocket. Karrie hooked her thumbs in the waistband of her yoga pants as he took a condom from his wallet. She eased her pants down and kicked out of them. Dax stood frozen, condom in hand and wallet discarded on the floor, as she repeated the motion with her panties.

"Fuck me," she said again. Slowing the pace had left room between them, room around her for the other stuff to creep in, and she desperately didn't want to think about any of it. She only wanted to feel Dax's hard body against her, his broad shoulders under her hands, and his long, thick erection pressing inside her.

Her body clenched as she watched him slide his khakis and briefs low on his hips. When he rolled the condom on, Karrie leaned again on the door and smoothed her hand down over her flat stomach and between her now quivering thighs. Dax muttered something when she touched herself, but suddenly, his hands were on her hips and lifting her toward him. Karrie threw her arms around him again as he drove into her, filling her, even stretching her body to fit him.

"Okay?"

She buried her face in his neck and nodded. "Hard, Dax. Fuck me. Fuck me hard."

Her nipples hardened and part of her wished just for a moment that they were naked and horizontal, and his mouth was on her skin. Part of her wanted to mold his ass cheeks in her hands as he pumped his hips, first slowly and finally—yes, finally—hard and fast, the way she needed him.

She came hard and fast, and again, for just a moment, she wished there could be more. Legs wrapped around his waist, she squeezed him as he continued to drive into her. Suddenly aware of the painful way her lower back banged the door, she ignored it and rode him until moments later, he gave a final powerful thrust and groaned out loud, called on God and then called her name, and eventually dropped his forehead to rest on her shoulder.

Tears burned her eyes. Humiliated, she turned her face away from him and took a deep breath.

"You okay?" he asked quietly.

"Yes."

"Karrie?"

"I'm fine."

"Fine?" he repeated. She felt him move, knew he had lifted his head to look at her. "Fine? That's it?"

Trapped, his cock still inside her and her legs wrapped around his waist, she rolled her head on the door to look at him.

"Are you crying?"

"No." She shook her head.

"You are."

"I'm fine."

"It happens? When you come?"

She shook her head again. No, she didn't usually cry when she reached orgasm. But then, she didn't usually fuck social acquaintances the same night she found out her brother-in-law was brain-dead, either.

"Did I hurt you?"

"No." She rested her hands on his chest and pushed at him gently.

"Ever done it in here before?" he asked with a quick look over his shoulder.

"Have I—? In the boys' locker room?"

He shrugged. "I have."

"No. I haven't." She cleared her throat and lowered her legs. "What number am I? In the locker room?"

"Only once before," he told her. She felt a wave of disgust roll over her as she reached for her panties.

"Great." She caught her nail in the purple lace. "Dammit."

Dax stepped back to give her room. She watched him toss the used condom in the trashcan next to the door.

"Are you crazy?"

"What am I gonna do with it? Put it in my pocket to take it home and throw it away?"

She sighed and rolled her eyes. Was she angry with him? Or herself? Or just the whole situation? He had fucked her in the boys' locker room. And she wasn't the first. On the other hand, she'd asked for it.

"What's going on?"

"What do you mean what's going on?" she asked as he tucked his cock away—Karrie felt a stab of regret;

he was still hard, and she wanted more—and zipped his pants again.

"Really? You shut me down cold a few days ago when I kissed you, and tonight you asked me to fuck you."

Frustrated with the scrap of lace she still hadn't been able to put on, she tossed them down and picked up her yoga pants. Dax watched with wide eyes as she slid them up over her legs.

"You're wet," he reminded her.

She shrugged. "What am I gonna do? Go home naked?"

His Adam's apple bobbed when she settled the Lycra material on her hips; his hungry eyes were zeroed in on the spot between her thighs.

"Come home with me," he told her.

"I can't." She shook her head. She couldn't. Really. The thought of taking her clothes off—all her clothes —the thought of Dax's mouth on her breasts, between her legs left her breathless and vibrating again. But she had to get back home to check on Leigh and the kids. Besides, the more she was with him, the more she might need him, and the last thing she wanted to do was get attached to someone. She had just left a relationship with a man who liked no strings attached locker room sex. Her heart wouldn't withstand that again.

"You gonna leave those here?" He arched his eyebrows at her and cocked his head. Karrie knew he was talking about her panties on the floor. Of course she couldn't leave them here. Even if no one knew they were hers, she would be mortified knowing the janitor or any of the high school boys had found them. But leaning over now to pick them up felt submissive and weak, and damned if she would let Dax Law make her feel weak.

Before she could move, Dax squatted down in front of her. Karrie held her breath as he picked the panties up, balled them in his fist, and stuffed them in his pocket.

"Really? This isn't high school—"

Rather than stand, he ran his hands up the backs of her legs and leaned in against her.

"Dax!" she sobbed when he opened his mouth and flicked his tongue between her legs. She felt his touch through the thin material, and her legs wobbled. To steady herself, she shot her hand out and plunged her fingers in his hair.

"There's more where this came from," he told her as he climbed slowly to stand in front of her. "Keep that in mind the next time you want me to fuck you."

Twenty-Three

"—ADD THE CALLAHAN COUNTY GAME?"

Dax heard Jed's voice in his ear, but he didn't process what was said. He stood in the door of the gym and watched the girls at the other end lined up for a layup drill. Jed started to repeat himself as Dax squinted as if it would help him see the far end of the gym clearer. The girls were lined up for drills, and there was most definitely an adult under the basket watching them.

Hazel Avery was in the line for rebounds. He recognized several other faces, but the one that got his attention looked a hell of a lot like Karrie Mallory. And he should know. He had been pretty fucking close to her body last night, *inside* her body last night, their faces pressed together. Lips locked. Tongues dancing.

Sparring, maybe, was more like it.

And if that hadn't been enough, he had gone home, guzzled not one but two beers, hit the shower—the cold water had killed his hard-on for the duration of the shower—and then gone to bed and dreamt about burying his face between her legs and tasting her.

"Dax? I need an answer. I gotta return the call—"

"Yes." He kept his eyes on the woman under the basket on the other end of the gym.

"Don't you need to check your schedule?" Jed asked him.

Dax squeezed his eyes closed and gave himself a mental shake. Which was it? Either Jed needed to know now, or he would have to give Dax time to check his schedule. Unfortunately for Jed and Callahan County, the add-on game for the JV team was the last damned thing on his mind.

"JV's good for that night," he told Jed.

"Callahan good?" Jed asked, apparently ready to move from the serious business of scheduling to conversation among friends. Dax took a step into the gym. Tracked the ball as a tiny little redhead drove the basket. He watched her lay up a sweet shot and follow through under the basket, turn toward the rebound line, and then let his eyes roam back to the woman under the basket. The woman who had most definitely asked him to fuck her last night.

"What? Yeah." Dax nodded and shrugged at the same time. "Don't know what record they finished with last year, but they're a bunch of scrappers."

"Farm boys," Jed suggested.

"Yep."

He stalked down the gym floor now, his loafers loud on the wooden floor. Karrie finally looked at him, but she only stared with the same aggressive look on her face that she had worn last night.

"Jed, I gotta go," he said into the cell at his ear, but his eyes were glued to hers.

"Yep. See ya."

The call ended, and Dax lowered the phone. He tucked it into his left hip pocket, the same one he had stuffed Karrie's lace underwear in last night after they had fucked like animals in the boys' locker room. He saw her eyes move from his gaze to his hip and back up. She looked rattled for a second, and then the cool control was back. The girls continued to run their drill, although a few of them watched him approach, Hazel included.

Thankfully, none of them seemed aware of the tension in the gym.

"What are you doing?" he asked by way of greeting.

Karrie, dressed in gray Nike joggers and a white Nike t-shirt, crossed her arms over her chest and shot him a look that suggested he was stupid.

"What's it look like I'm doing?" Her voice was cool, tone clipped. She didn't want him here.

"What the hell was last night about?"

He moved up to stand with her under the basket, and he spoke so quietly, there was no way anyone else heard him. But still, from the corner of his eye, he saw her bristle.

"Not now, Law," she returned calmly.

"Why are you here?"

"What the hell?" she snapped. Dropped her arms to her sides and moved so that she stood with her back to the girls. Her eyes were dark and angry, her brows slanted over them. "What do you mean why am I here?"

Irrationally angry that Karrie Mallory was here, apparently assuming the role of coach for these girls, that she hadn't mentioned it to him, that she had told him just a few days ago that she was leaving and obviously hadn't left, Dax answered with an exaggerated shrug.

"You told me you were leaving," he reminded her. "Remember that? Pretty good liar. I'm impressed."

She drew back as if he had slapped her. Point, Dax. He puffed up, nearly preened, proud that he landed an insult.

"Wasn't a lie," she answered.

"Uh huh?" He nodded. "Like you left and realized you couldn't go another day without my dick?"

"I didn't—you—Dax!" She sputtered.

Dax, two. Karrie, zip.

"Don't get me wrong." He shrugged again. The memory of the previous night, the feel of her tight body like a glove around his dick brought a smile to his face. "It was great. But we can do—"

"Not. Here."

"What?"

"Don't do this now." She tilted her head and smiled sweetly. "God, please don't do this in front of the girls."

Chastised, he bit his lip and hung his head.

"You used me." He scratched the back of his neck. "You used me for sex."

"Girls." Karrie stepped around him. Her voice was a little too chipper, a little brash with nerves. "How about you take a water break? Okay? When you come back in, we'll play a little three-on-three."

Dax watched over his shoulder—couldn't turn around just yet with his dick trying to bust through his zipper—as the girls skipped out the gym doors. Karrie stood with her back to him, hands on her hips, chin to her chest.

"You did!" He turned to her once they were alone. "You used me. For sex."

She took a deep breath and faced him. He felt her slow nod and shrug of admittance like a sucker punch.

"I guess I did," she mumbled.

"You're kidding me. Really? You showed up last night—"

"Yeah." She nodded and met his gaze. "I did. I came looking for you. For that."

"Son-of-a-bitch." He sighed.

"You're complaining?" she asked with a frown.

He shook his head, because what guy in his right mind would complain about a beautiful, sexy woman like Karrie showing up and reaching for his dick? Asking him to fuck her? That's the stuff dreams were made of. Wet dreams.

But there had to be more. Didn't there?

And he didn't just mean more skin. More sex. More licking and sucking and biting. Because fuck, yes, he wanted all the above. He wanted to be balls deep in her pussy again, and he wanted to taste her, and he wanted that throaty voice calling his name when he made her come. He wanted those luscious lips on his dick, and God, yes, he wanted his hands on her tits.

But there had to be more than that.

This time.

Sure as fuck felt like there could be more than that this time.

"Yes?" His voice came out sideways, and his dick throbbed in his pants again.

"God." She sighed again and rolled her eyes. "I stopped you the other day, and it pissed you off. I asked for it last night, and you're pissed—"

"Let's not forget that part in the middle where you lied to me," he reminded her.

"I didn't lie."

"And yet, here you are."

"Look, I'm sorry," she said quietly. "Next time I need something big and hard between my legs, I'll dig through my luggage and find my vibrator."

She started to turn away from him, but he moved faster and grabbed her by the upper arm.

"Oh, no." He shook his head. The way she lowered her gaze to his fingers on her arm and then returned it to look him in the eye shot through his dick like lightning. He wondered if she felt it, too. If she was wet right now, thinking about what they had done last night. If her nipples were hard. What it would feel like to flick the tip of his tongue over them. To lick around the globe of her breast.

"We're not done," he told her in a small, tight voice. A screech and the peal of laughter rolled through the cavernous room. No longer alone, Dax dropped her arm.

"Well, we're not gonna talk about it here," she told him pointedly.

"We're not just gonna talk, either," he promised her.

"Dax." She shook her head. A look of pain, sheer heartache, painted her face for a moment, and then it was gone. This time, he felt a twitch higher than his dick, but he wasn't sure if it was in his gut or his chest.

Karrie was hurting.

What if he had added to that when he fucked her last night? When he let her walk away? Should he have turned her away? As if. He almost laughed out loud.

"What time's your practice over?"

A few more girls appeared in the gym. Dax stepped closer to Karrie when one of them picked up a ball and dribbled it. The noise was a buffer between them and the girls, and yet, it kept a distance between the two of them. One he didn't want.

One it seemed Karrie preferred.

"Just." She licked her lips and shook her head again. "Can we just let it go? Forget it happened?"

"Forget—"

She stood up straight and tall and drew in a deep breath. "It didn't mean anything, Dax. It was rough and fast and just what the doctor ordered. Can we just let it go?"

Disgusted all over again, Dax bit off his angry reply. Karrie was right about one thing. They sure as hell couldn't get into this, into the heart of this conversation, right here, right now. Not with this audience.

"Sure." He nodded. "We'll let it go." He took a step backward. "For now."

Twenty-Four

LEIGH STARED AT KARRIE OVER THE TABLE. HER fisted hands rested together on the table; her wan face was unreadable, unwelcoming.

"What's going on?" Karrie's voice boomed through the silent house. As if in apology to Leigh and the stillness, she set her keys gingerly on the counter and then leaned a hip against it, waiting for Leigh to speak.

"How was practice?" Leigh's words were gruff and small, as if she didn't have the energy to speak.

Karrie had a flash of Dax Law striding over the floor to call her out for using him. She still couldn't say she regretted it, though she would change things if she could. For instance, she would have taken her all her clothes off, because while her thighs and her core still burned with the memory of his touch, the rest of her body was still a little too pristine, and she needed to feel bad all over to push everything else away right now.

Couldn't tell Leigh that, though.

"Good." She avoided her sister's eyes, though she wasn't sure Leigh was even processing the fact that she was in the room with her. "Why did you have me take Hazel to Mom's house?"

Leigh rolled her lips inward. Karrie watched a tear slide over her pale cheek.

"Where's Gino?"

"At Mom and Bill's," Leigh whispered.

"Okay. Why?"

"Because I needed to be alone."

Karrie raised her eyebrows and took a deep breath. "I could have just taken them out for pizza, Leigh."

Leigh shook her head almost violently.

"No?"

"I need to be alone. All night." Leigh looked around the room and then let her eyes skate over Karrie and then away again.

Karrie felt a spike of alarm. She straightened from the counter and moved slowly to the table.

"What do you have there?"

"What?" Leigh frowned and shook her head. Another tear tracked over her face.

"What's in your hands?"

Karrie lowered herself to sit in the chair across from Leigh.

"I just…" Leigh sniffled and swallowed hard. "He's gone, Karrie. And even if he wasn't…even if he did come home and live here forever, I would know it wasn't his choice. He didn't want to be here anymore."

Karrie bit her lip and waited a moment before she trusted her voice.

"You don't know that," she offered quietly. "You don't know that he wouldn't have changed his mind."

"Doesn't matter," Leigh argued. "It doesn't matter. It makes everything different once you know they don't love you the same anymore."

Karrie flinched. She supposed that was true, and it hurt her that she couldn't offer Leigh comfort.

"I need to talk to Hazel," Leigh continued. "I think she's old enough to know what's going on."

Karrie nodded, but her heart crowded her throat, and she felt a moment of panic. What if she wasn't? What if telling Hazel was a mistake? What if a year or five years down the road Hazel questioned Leigh? Accused her of moving too fast? Of killing Brad?

"I can't tell Gino." Leigh shook her head as if arguing with Karrie. "He's too young. He's—"

Karrie's eyes welled with tears. She nodded, because she agreed with Leigh, and she wanted her to stop. Stop talking.

"I just need…" Leigh swallowed hard.

"You're gonna do it?" Karrie's voice was gruff with pent-up emotion.

"What choice do I have, Karrie?" Leigh sounded angry now, though the look on her face remained the same. "What kind of life would it be for the kids? No dad in the house. Having to drive an hour and a half to a rehab hospital to visit his brain-dead body for holidays? As long as he's there, they'll think there's hope, and I can't give them false—"

"No." Karrie shook her head. She brushed at her tears. "I know you can't, Leigh. I know."

"I still love him." Leigh pressed her lips together again, as if she was trying to hold in something else. Another revelation. As if admitting she still loved her husband was shocking to Karrie. "I'm so mad at him. For leaving me. For getting on that goddamned bike. I'm so mad, Karrie. Sometimes I hate him for what he did to us."

Karrie wiped her eyes and covered her mouth with her hand. She nodded when she met Leigh's gaze.

"But I still love him."

"I know you do."

"And I just need—"

"What's in your hands?" Karrie asked again. Leigh wanted her to leave. She wanted to be alone. She had gone out of her way to get the kids out of the house, and now she was further inconvenienced because Karrie was here.

"What? I just need one night to myself." Leigh squeezed her fists so tight, her knuckles turned white.

"Okay." Karrie nodded, but she reached for Leigh's hands. "Just show me. Show me what you're hiding."

"I'm not hiding anything."

"I'm not gonna leave you alone until I know you're gonna be okay, Leigh."

"I'm not hiding anything, Karrie—"

"Then show me!" Karrie roared, out of patience. Her body was poised to grab it, whatever Leigh had. Pills. A razor blade. She would snatch it away and then throw her arms around her sister. Her muscles were coiled and ready to strike, and her heart pounded so hard, she thought she was having a heart attack.

Leigh loosened her fists, but she didn't open them. Her hands were cold and dry as Karrie pried her fingers open.

"Dammit." Karrie caved when she saw Leigh's wedding ring in her hand. "Oh, God."

"You think I'm that weak?" Leigh arched her eyebrows at her.

"I know you're hurting. I know you love him so much. He's your life—"

"I'm not that pathetic—"

"I'm not saying you're pathetic!" Karrie argued. "I'm not saying there's anything in the world wrong with the way you love him." She shook her head. "With the way he loved you."

Leigh sniffled again and swallowed. "Yeah, except there is, isn't there?"

"I'm scared for you."

"I'm not gonna kill myself."

"Leigh, hon, I'm so scared for you. For what you're facing. What you have to do."

"I would never, ever choose to walk away from my kids."

Karrie watched her for a long moment, and Leigh held her gaze, and the house was silent and dark around them.

"Are you telling me…" Karrie sighed and rubbed her throat to ease the tightness. "Are you telling me he said that? That he didn't want them—"

"Brad was a good father, Karrie." Leigh rolled her eyes.

"Yeah, I know," Karrie agreed. Jesus, she couldn't say anything right. "But you made it sound—"

"That's what you heard." Leigh pulled her hands away from Karrie and curled her fingers around the ring. "I'm telling you I'm not suicidal. I just need the night alone to figure out how the hell I'm going to tell Hazel that her dad is brain-dead."

"Don't."

"What?"

"Don't do it."

"Don't remove the ventilator?" Leigh's voice was tiny. A mask of confusion slid over her face.

"No. Don't tell the kids. Just tell them…he passed… tell them it was natural, Leigh."

"I can't lie to Hazel."

"You can't tell Hazel the truth and expect her to lie with you to Gino."

Leigh licked her lips.

"What if she comes back at you years from now and accuses you of giving up too soon?"

"It's not your decision." Leigh's voice was firm. Karrie watched her push her chair back from the table to stand. In the pale peach-colored silk robe, she looked ethereal and beautiful, and Karrie felt an ache in her chest. She coughed to ease the pain.

"And Karrie?" Leigh stopped at the doorway behind Karrie.

"What?" Karrie covered her face with her hands.

"No one knows."

"I know."

"No. I mean no one. No one will ever know that he was leaving me."

"Leigh—"

"No. One."

Karrie nodded, mumbled a choked *you can't do this* that apparently Leigh took as an agreement, because when Karrie finally looked over her shoulder, she was alone in the kitchen.

Twenty-Five

SHE HAD A PLACE TO STAY AT HER MOM'S HOUSE, BUT she refused to go there. For one thing, her mom would ask why she was there and not at Leigh's house. And Karrie wasn't sure she could lie for her sister after the conversation they just had. Leigh needed support, not secrets. Karrie wanted Brad's parents to know how selfless Leigh had been since the accident. They had seen a devastated Leigh at his bedside for days on end; something Karrie hadn't seen, had only heard them and her mom and stepdad discuss. But they had no idea how badly Leigh was hurting, and Karrie had a ridiculously childish need for them to know. She couldn't tell her parents, because if she opened up and said it even once, she might explode and then the whole damned world might know what was going on.

It didn't matter if Karrie thought she was protecting Leigh. Her sister would never forgive her if she told her secret.

She wouldn't go back to the school now, either. It was too late in the evening, anyway, as she had wasted a huge chunk of time driving aimlessly and then jogging in the dark in Winston Falls Park. Dangerous, but mostly because she could have tripped on just about anything in the dark. She wasn't worried that anyone would attack her here. Her sister's mood swings—

though justified—had done enough damage. And by quitting her job and moving back home, Karrie had voluntarily signed up for more.

Tired from the run, but still adamant about not going to her mom's house, she pointed her SUV in the direction of the bar she had gone to with Dax. Odds were he wouldn't be there. She couldn't face him now. Part of her wanted to cower in shame for what she had done. Part of her wanted to throw his ass down on the bench in the locker room and straddle him for round two. She had known she was in trouble when he kissed her. Throw in Brad's prognosis and Leigh's bleak future and the fact that Karrie had ended things with Dom and still hadn't spoken directly to him about it, and she was ready to explode. No wonder she had been desperate for him last night. Desperate to feel something inside, something to soothe her heartache and something to stroke the woman inside that Dom had left neglected far too long. Now she had messed things up so badly, she figured they would never even be friends.

And right now, she could sure use a friend.

At the bar, she climbed out of the SUV slowly. Pushed the door closed and leaned into it to make it latch. The parking lot was full; Karrie hesitated, uncertain that she was up for a tavern full of strangers. Then again, her other option was spending the rest of the evening and the night, even, in her car because Leigh wanted to be alone.

Was she roaming the house? Wailing and beating her breast in pain? Grief? Was she weeping quietly in the bed she had shared with Brad for all these years? Or was she trying to relive the passion she and Brad had once had? Karrie gave herself a mental shake. Whatever Leigh was doing was her business and perfectly acceptable, and it sure as hell wasn't Karrie's place to judge her.

Maybe she did need a bar full of strangers. Surely, the company of strangers would hurt less than that of her family right now, wouldn't it? She checked her joggers and running shoes and almost changed her mind. The door opened, and warm yellow light fell out across the sidewalk. Waylon Jennings' voice poured out for a moment. The song, "Luckenbach, Texas," made her wish she were there. Or anywhere but here.

She and Dom had planned a cruise once. They had even purchased their tickets, but Amy had come down with pneumonia, and Dom had stepped up with the kids, and Karrie had simply been out the money. When she admitted to him that she was sad they missed the trip, he asked her why she hadn't gone without him.

She should have known then that she would be the one hurt when their relationship ended. Now she wondered who he would take to his bed in her place. She considered the nurses in the ER and tried to picture each of them naked, lying in Dom's arms. It didn't hurt so much as annoy her. She had already given him too much of her time. Why was she dwelling on it now?

With one last deep breath to calm her nerves, she moved purposefully to the door and pulled it open. No one froze in their movements to watch her come in. No one called a greeting to her. No one told her joggers were inappropriate attire for a neighborhood bar. She crossed the floor easily and slipped between two groups of people at the bar to order a longneck.

Waylon's voice gave way to George Strait and on the TV in the far corner of the bar, an old black and white Western movie played. Different. Karrie shrugged. Settled on the barstool behind her when she heard the guys that had been standing there move away.

"Can I buy you a drink?"

She looked up a few moments later when she felt someone standing close to her. The guy looked friendly, kind of cute but she had no desire to flirt. Or talk, even, and so she shrugged apologetically and lifted her beer in a salute.

"I have one."

"I'm Billy."

"I'm not interested," she said softly. "Bad breakup."

"I'm married," he told her. "Happily married. She's at work, so I'm here with her sister and her husband

and a few friends, and the girls are all talking about some TV show, and I saw you as a rescue."

Karrie laughed in spite of herself. He nodded his head at a table near the west wall of the bar. She leaned around him and found herself waving at the curious people around the table.

"Let me guess. *Grey's Anatomy*?"

"No." He shook his head. "Some cop show."

"Hmm." She frowned.

"Wanna join us?" He tried again. "No strings." He held up his left hand to show her his wedding ring. "I have two kids. One's five and one's two."

"And where are they?"

"My niece is watching them. My wife's a doctor. She's on call. She was with us when we got here. But she got paged."

"What kind of doctor?" Karrie asked with genuine interest.

"OB. She's in delivery right now."

"That's gotta be fun." Karrie nodded.

"Join us. You look bored."

She waffled. Opened her mouth to say *yes, what the heck.* And then a heavy hand dropped on her shoulder and four fingers curled into her possessively.

"She's not bored."

His low, gruff voice stroked a spot low in her belly and left her body humming for attention.

"She's with me."

Billy—the married guy she wasn't entirely sure wasn't hitting on her—averted his eyes to look at Dax over her shoulder.

"You okay?" the guy seemed concerned about leaving her with Dax. Karrie almost laughed. "With him? Are you with him?"

She licked her lips and nodded. "I am."

"Bad breakup?"

She sucked in a quick breath when Dax tightened his grip on her shoulder.

"Not him," she said softly. The guy—Billy—eyed Dax suspiciously and then backed away from them. He watched Dax with heavy eyes until he was at the end of the bar where he turned and walked back to his table and the people there who had gone back to drinking and talking about their cop show.

"Well, thank you."

Karrie licked her lips again and sighed. She picked up her beer and took a drink. Finally turned to look at Dax.

"For what?"

"Assuring your friend you were safe with me."

She moved her eyes over his face, but she looked away skittishly when she met his gaze.

"What are you doing here?"

"What's it look like I'm doing here?" she asked quietly. Dax held a longneck, but his was almost empty. What would he do when he finished it? Order another? Or ask her to leave with him? Karrie's hands turned to ice just thinking about it.

"But why here?"

"Because I didn't know where else to go."

"This is the only bar you know of in town?"

"Am I encroaching on your territory?" She twisted the stool around to look at him. "Cramping your style?" She shrugged and looked around. "Someone here you have your eyes on? Because I don't care, Dax."

She did, though. And the realization hit her like a ton of bricks. Stole her breath away. She needed him to want her. No one else in the bar. Just her.

Rather than answer her, Dax moved quickly and cupped her chin in his hand. He leaned in to kiss her, but she tried to jerk away from him.

"Your friend's watching, Karrie," Dax told her. "You want him? Because kissing me like you did last night might turn him on."

Karrie closed her eyes, but she could still picture the two of them hot and heavy in the locker room.

"If you had showed a little tit last night, you could've been right out of a porno."

She let him kiss her. Mistake. Instead of the harsh clash of tongues like they had last night, Dax's lips brushed hers with tenderness. Before she could process the feeling, he slid his tongue over her lips and rubbed it slowly over hers.

Stunned when he pulled away from her, she blinked up at him. The gentle kiss still lingering between them, she remembered what he just said and slid off the edge of the stool.

"Well, that's what you wanted, right?" She shrugged. "From the beginning."

"It's not—"

"That's right. You wanted my ass. Would you be happier today if I would have asked you to fuck me there?"

She ducked under his arm and slipped through the crowd to get to the door. She had put cash on the counter when she ordered the beer, because she wasn't sure how long she would stay. Now she was glad so she could make a fast getaway.

The door closed behind her, and she was alone in the crisp fall night. Her cheeks burned with humiliation. No one had ever told her she looked like something out of a porn flick, and God knows, the things she and Dom had done together would qualify. But the words from Dax stung, and tears burned the back of her eyes.

She couldn't go home. Sure, she could probably sneak into the house without Leigh even knowing. But what if Leigh roamed the basement? What if she was digging through belongings, dusting off memories?

"Karrie."

The door opened and closed behind her. She dashed at her eyes before turning to look at him.

"Just leave me alone. Please."

"Karrie—"

"I didn't come here looking for you." Lie.

"Karrie—"

"I just needed a place to go."

Ignoring her protests, Dax stepped closer to her and backed her against the driver's door of the SUV. This time, she steeled herself for his kiss. She tensed her shoulders and her arms and her legs, and she promised herself she wouldn't react. She wouldn't like this kiss. She wouldn't kiss him back. She would stand there like a wooden pole and wait him out.

She didn't, though. This kiss was gentle but long and wet, and Karrie gave up trying to fight it. She fell into it, stroked her tongue over his repeatedly, drawn to his strength and the taste of the beer on his mouth.

"Come with me." He pressed the words to her lips.

"Where?" Eyes closed, she pretended he wasn't going to suggest they go back to his place to rip each other's clothes off and fuck each other senseless again.

"Anywhere." He shrugged. "Come to my place."

She had done it to herself, but it still hurt. Rather than look at him, she rested her forehead against his chin and nodded.

"Okay."

Twenty-Six

KARRIE WATCHED IN DISBELIEF AS DAX TWISTED THE top off a longneck. She took it from him when he handed it to her and waited for him to make his first move. Instead, he picked up the other bottle he had set on the counter and twisted the cap off it, too. She let her eyes slide over his face as he tipped the bottle up for a long drink. Down over the scruff on his chin to watch his Adam's apple bob when he swallowed.

"So."

When he spoke, she flicked her eyes back to his lips. Felt a tug in her belly when he licked them. She wanted his tongue on her lips, but she didn't want anything more. Not right now. As delicious as he tasted earlier when he had kissed her at the bar, as good as he looked right now in the form-fitting jeans and the long-sleeved green thermal tee, she wished they could erase what had happened and start over.

She stirred when she realized he was staring at her, and she hadn't answered him. Was she supposed to strip for him? In his kitchen? Would it be enough for her just to drop her clothes at her feet? Or did he expect a little tease and a wiggle of her hips and—

"Tell me."

Confused, she arched her eyebrows and tilted her head. She tightened her fingers on the cold bottle in her hand and tried to hide the deep breath she drew in through her nose.

"Tell you what?" She shrugged. His intense gaze made her fidgety; she cleared her throat and shifted her gaze to the microwave over his shoulder. He had flipped on can lights over the counter, but the turquoise numbers on the microwave clock still glowed bright in the dimly lit room.

"About your bad breakup."

Surprised by his question, Karrie snapped her gaze back to his.

"What?"

"Or was that another lie?"

She opened her mouth to argue, to tell him she hadn't lied to begin with, but the events of the past few days hit her again, suddenly. She sighed and shook her head.

"Dax, I'm beat," she mumbled as she covered her face with her free hand. "Can we just…"

"Just what?" He touched the back of her hand. Slid his fingers around her wrist and gently tugged her hand from her face.

What the hell? She sighed and set her beer on the counter, still without taking a drink.

"Get on with it."

He stared at her silently for a moment. Lifted his hand to her face again. Karrie shivered when he traced his thumb over her cheekbone. She held her breath when he stepped closer to her and rubbed his fingers on her lips.

"So, it was a lie?" His voice was quiet, but not gentle. She tried to swallow, but her mouth was dry.

"No."

He leaned into her and brushed his lips over hers. Karrie moved with him. Slid her hands up his arms, but he backed away rather than kiss her again.

"Dax."

"Tell me."

Desperate for something she couldn't even identify, Karrie ducked her head and leaned into him for a moment. She sighed with contentment when he wrapped his arms around her.

Scared of the moment, of the danger the safety of his arms posed, she pushed at him and turned away.

"It was more of a bad relationship than breakup," she said quietly. Behind her, she heard glass clink, and then suddenly, Dax linked his fingers with hers and led her out of the room. Startled by the movement, she threw a quick glance around, assuming he was leading her to his bedroom. She followed him down two steps into a screened-in back porch and eyed the patio furniture carefully.

"What does that mean?"

Dazed, she stood in the center of the room and watched him put the bottles on a big round table and then turn a small electric space heater on and direct it toward a chaise lounge and the small table beside it.

"Do you—can we not do it in your bed?"

Dax stood and turned to face her. She gulped down a wave of nerves when he cupped her face in his hands again. Watched him as he lowered his face to hers and finally let her eyes close when his lips touched hers. This kiss was different, still. His fingertips framed her face, and his mouth moved over hers with tenderness. He stroked his tongue in and out of her lips, against her tongue and the roof of her mouth. Heat pooled between Karrie's thighs because she was thinking of his body, his cock pressing and sliding out of her, even though he was careful that their bodies didn't touch now.

"I want to make love to you." He peppered her face with soft, sweet kisses. His words plucked that taut string between her belly and her core, and her knees went weak. "I will make love to you. I'll take you to my bed, and I'll worship every inch of your body with my mouth and my hands."

Unsteady on her feet, she reached for him. His hands still on her face, she gripped his wrists in her fingers.

"But I'm not gonna rush through anything," he added in a voice thick with lust.

"Dax." She licked her lips as he rubbed the back of his knuckles down the front of her neck. "We don't have—"

"You look like you could use a friend." He took her hand and brought it to his lips. Karrie's eyes filled when he kissed her fingers. "I would like to be that friend."

Overcome with emotion, with all the words she wished she could say, Karrie pulled away from him. She sucked in a harsh breath, propped her hands on her hips, and turned her back to him.

"Karrie?"

She held up a hand asking him to give her a minute. Her body was still wound, ready for his touch. Ready for him to make good on what he had said, his mouth and hands all over her. But her head hurt from all the things she was desperately trying to ignore, and her heart hurt because hadn't she just thought to herself an hour ago that she could use a friend?

"I didn't lie to you," she said when she decided she could talk past the emotion. She swallowed again and stood with her back to him a moment longer, breathing through the heartache the way she breathed through cramps and those damned stitches in her side back when she was a young athlete.

Funny. Didn't seem to help the way it had back then.

He didn't answer her, so she dropped her hands at her sides and turned to look at him.

"When you kissed me that night, and I told you I was leaving. It wasn't a lie."

Dax stepped up beside her, and a rush of heat rolled over. Her stomach quivered, and her nipples tightened at the thought of his lips tugging there. She rolled her eyes at herself and shook her head. Dax snagged his beer and then moved back to sit on the end of the chaise lounge.

"You also said we couldn't do it. Not that we couldn't do it then, just that we couldn't."

"Yeah."

"The relationship."

She answered with a curt nod.

"You're in love with him?"

A sarcastic laugh escaped her, and she shook her head. "It's a long story, Dax."

He shrugged and tipped his bottle at her.

"Ohhh. God." She sighed and reached to pull the elastic from her hair. When she lifted her eyes, Dax was watching her as she ran her fingers through the long, platinum blond curls.

"Promise me you'll do that again?" He wiggled his eyebrows above his lecherous grin, and despite herself, Karrie laughed softly. "When I have you naked in satin sheets."

"You sleep on satin sheets?" she asked doubtfully.

"No, but I'm gonna buy some now. Because you and that hair and satin sheets are going to blow my mind."

"You know, some women might take offense to being told they look like something out of a porn flick."

"Did you?" He cocked his head. His question seemed to be sincere curiosity, so she considered her answer before she spoke.

"Sort of."

"I can't help that you turn me on —"

She waved his explanation away and shook her head.

"I asked for it, I know."

"You did put your hand on my dick before I knew what the hell was going on."

She turned away as a hot blush flushed her face, but she laughed again.

"He was married," she said boldly, because maybe it was time to put the brakes on. She needed a way out of here tonight, and maybe Dax would be disgusted with her for being involved with a married man.

"And he promised he would leave her for you."

She shrugged her lips and shifted her feet.

"He did, but I knew better. I wasn't his first…affair."

"But you still wanted to be the one. The one he left her for."

Shamed by his words, she could only nod.

"C'mere."

"What?"

"Sit down." He patted the chair he sat on. "I'm not gonna wag my dick at you. Come sit down and talk to me."

She hesitated, because she did want him to kiss her again. To put his arms around her. And it wasn't a good idea.

"Karrie."

She ignored her beer and crossed the patio to sit by him. As she did, she pulled her phone from her pocket and peeked at the screen.

"Is he still calling you?"

"No." She shook her head. "Just making sure Leigh hasn't called."

"Mmm." He nodded. "How is she?"

Karrie bit down hard on her lip and offered Dax a lazy shrug.

"So you went home to break things off with him? Your married boyfriend?"

Karrie was grateful that Dax was going to let her non-answer pass, but she wasn't crazy about jumping into an in-depth conversation about Dom, either.

"I went home to quit my job," she finally told him. Her whispered words hung in the air between them for a long while before she spoke again. "Just...just before...I came home, we lost a kid. In the ER."

She skated her eyes over his face, enough to know he was watching her, his face a mix of curiosity and concern, and then lowered her gaze to the empty space on the chair between them. She had kicked her shoes off when she'd come inside his house earlier; now she pulled her feet up on the chair and stared at her black socks.

"Sixteen. We treated her last spring. Overdose." Karrie was surprised that her eyes remained dry, her voice steady. "CPR is...it's draining, Dax. Yeah, it's part of the job. It's an everyday thing, really. But it's... so huge. It's so fucking huge. You see it on TV. You see it on all the hospital dramas, and the staff crowds into the room, and the camera focuses on the resident's face or the patient's bloody face or the...the blood or the vomit on the floor. But what you don't see..."

She hesitated. Dax turned on the end of the chair to face her. He reached out as if to touch her, but his hand fell short of hers.

"You don't see the way the doctors and the nurses, the medical personnel there, are sweating. Shaking. Not from fear, although it's the scariest goddamned thing you'll ever feel. That's inside." She met his eyes. "That fear stays inside, because you can't let anyone there know how fucking scared you are. You can't even let yourself know how fucking scared you are."

He nodded when she stopped talking.

"You shake, because it's physically exhausting. It fucking drains you of everything. And sometimes, you win. Sometimes, you win, but then sometimes, you're only winning the battle, and you still lose the war."

This time, when he reached for her, he closed his fingers around her leg and pulled gently until she stretched her leg out toward him. She watched him as he eased her sock off and pressed his thumbs into her foot.

She moaned softly and closed her eyes.

"She cleaned up. She was living with her grandmother."

"It's not your fault."

She shrugged. "No, but that doesn't make it any easier." She shook her head and then rested it on the chair at her back. "The EMTs gave her the drug to counteract the heroin."

"Didn't work this time?"

"Dom gave her more Narcan, but…" She rubbed her face and then stayed frozen that way, with her hand over her eyes. "When you leave…when you walk out after a day like that, even if you bring someone back." She licked her lips. "It's not like your till didn't balance at the bank. It's you and your team. Being God."

Dax's big hand cupped the back of her other leg and tugged gently until she let him stretch it out and treat that foot with the same attention.

"You quit for Leigh."

Her laugh sounded like a sob.

"Yes." She nodded. "No."

"It's okay." His soft voice was soothing, and he continued to rub her feet. Part of her wanted to sink into the delicious feeling, but part of her wondered when he would slide his hands up inside her pant legs to touch her. Dom had never done anything for her without expecting something—sex or a blowjob—in return.

She blinked her eyes open and lowered her hand to find his gaze steady and intense on her face.

"She must be grateful you're here for her."

"She's not, though." Karrie frowned. Kind of hated herself for saying so, because Leigh had every right to act crazy right now. But if she were being honest, she had to admit Leigh's crazy had hurt her a hundred times over since she had first come home to help.

"Your married guy is a doctor."

Karrie nodded. "Yeah. We've been…together." She frowned and lifted a shoulder in question. "For about a year and a half. And I'm ashamed to admit it only recently hit me that I was hurting his wife."

"Why's that?"

"I mean, he gave me the song and dance about how she knew he wasn't faithful. That they had had an open marriage for a long time. For all I know, she has a boyfriend." Karrie watched his hands as he rubbed her feet.

"Why did it get to you recently?"

"And as much as I wanted to kiss you that night, I couldn't. I felt guilty, because I was in a relationship with him." Her laugh was bitter. "How messed up is that?"

"Was he upset? When you broke it off?"

"I dunno." She rolled her head back and forth on the chair. "I never saw him. I called. Texted. Finally had to leave a message."

"I wouldn't let you go that easily."

"You're not married," she answered simply. "And I'm no prize, Dax. I just told you I was involved with a married man. He has kids."

"And now you're not involved with him."

"I didn't lie to you."

He nodded. Karrie felt her heart break a little when he pushed her pant leg up and strummed his fingertips up over the back of her leg.

"I just…" She licked her lips and wiggled her toes. "I came onto you last night, and I'm sorry. But I need you to know I didn't lie."

"Don't be sorry about last night." He dragged his fingers back down to her foot, seemingly content to touch her there. "I'm not."

Of course he wasn't sorry about last night. He wasn't upset about last night. He was a guy. The sex was good, and she walked away with promises not to nag him. What wasn't to like?

The silence around them was charged with electricity, and yet, at the same time, Karrie almost felt like she belonged here. She could go to sleep if he kept at her feet, the pressure of his thumbs so intimate and so strong. Part of her yearned for his hands to touch her in other places. If his hands on her feet made her melt, what would it feel like if he rubbed those fingertips on her thighs and over her most sensitive spot? Then again, if she felt this relaxed with his hands on her feet, what would it feel like just to lie in his arms for a while?

In the beginning, for a week or two, Dom slept with her, tucked her against his chest and laid his arm over her possessively. But it hadn't been long before he stopped, before he stretched out comfortably in her bed and tucked his arm around his pillow instead and turned his face away from her to sleep. Karrie missed the warmth, the comfort of sleeping with someone who wanted to hold her. But that didn't mean Dax would be any different. Jumping from one relationship to another—if this even qualified as a relationship and usually hookups like last night didn't and never would—wasn't very bright, and Karrie still prided herself on being smart.

"Brad's brain-dead." The words gushed out of her mouth. She squeezed her eyes closed and prayed she hadn't said them out loud. But when Dax's hands stilled, his fingers wrapped around her foot, she blinked and met his stunned gaze.

"Oh, Karrie." His whisper was warm with concern, but Karrie's heart hammered in her chest. She just blurted out something her sister wouldn't want anyone to know, and she had blurted it out to someone she didn't know that well.

And she just patted herself on the back for being smart?

"Oh, shit." She covered her mouth and shook her head. "Oh, God. No. I didn't say that. Please tell me I didn't say that."

"Babe—"

Dax reached for her as she pulled her legs out of his grasp and swung them over the side of the chair. She jumped up as soon as they hit the floor and paced away from him. Her hands still covered her mouth, as if in some crazed effort to hold it in or maybe now, gobble the words back up.

"Oh, God. Oh, no." She shook her head and then drove her fingers back through her hair. "What the hell was I thinking?"

"Karrie."

Behind her, she heard him moving. He climbed off the chair. The clink of glass on iron told her he put his bottle down. When he touched her, gripped her by the upper arm, she jumped to stand straight, as if her spine were suddenly made of steel.

"I shouldn't have said that," she whispered as he spun her around to face him. "I shouldn't—dammit. Dax, I shouldn't—"

"Karrie." He spoke louder this time, and his firm tone shut her up. Tears burned her eyes, and before she could cry, she took a swipe at the tears.

"Leigh's handling this. She's trying to deal with all of

this on her own, and she will hate me when she finds out—"

"She's not gonna know you told me."

"It's just. It's a private thing. A family thing. And I shouldn't—"

"I'm not gonna say anything."

"Dax, we hardly know each other. You can't stand there and promise me you'll keep a secret like this."

"I would say we know each other pretty damned well." He shrugged his eyebrows. "I promise you, and I mean it. I'm not gonna repeat what you just said."

"We hooked up." She pushed her hair off her face and shook her head. "Dammit, Karrie, this is unforgiveable."

Well, what would be unforgiveable would be if she accidentally spilled the beans about Brad wanting to leave Leigh. After all, Brad's prognosis was factual. And if Leigh took him off life support, he would stop breathing, and he would die, and they would have a funeral, and the whole town would know.

But Leigh's struggle to come to terms with this, Leigh's decision to tell her kids or not, Leigh's discussions with Brad's parents, were personal, and Karrie had no right to divulge any of it to anyone, most especially a guy she sort of knew who still knew the town better than she did.

"I don't wanna be just some guy you hooked up with when you moved back home." He released her arm and raised his hand to stroke her cheek again. "But no matter what you think of me, no matter what you want from me, I won't repeat what you said."

Twenty-Seven

As many deaths as Karrie had witnessed in her line of work, she hadn't attended many funerals. Grandparents when she was younger. A great aunt when she was in college. Sad, but none had ever settled inside her and made her ache for days, the way some of those ER scenes had a way of doing. Maybe it was that bodies at funerals looked more at peace than when Karrie saw death in the ER.

Brad's funeral was different. So, she was angry with him, still, for leaving Leigh. For leaving Leigh with the memory of his leaving and then dying when she was alone. But she loved him. Leigh had known him all through school, and they started dating when they were young, and Karrie had always sort of just loved him as a brother. As the man who loved her sister, the man who made her sister happy. The man who had given her a niece and nephew to love forever.

She missed him. Leigh's broken heart couldn't just erase the fun times they all had as a family. The picnics and the ball games and the board games at holiday gatherings. They had doubled-dated once or twice, and mostly, those adventures had been more disastrous than anything. Karrie hadn't wanted to be seriously involved with anyone in high school; she wasn't like Leigh, and she had never apologized for that. But that meant most of her dates assumed she was okay with fast hands and maybe a blowjob, if they were lucky. Brad had been overprotective, and Leigh had been too judgmental, in Karrie's opinion. Karrie didn't do fast hands or blowjobs often— though she hadn't been innocent, either—but Leigh had pushed for Karrie to settle down and find a boyfriend.

Karrie missed Brad's stupid sense of humor and his quiet laugh. She missed the talks they had from time to time about kids and athletics, and she wondered what he would think of her coaching Hazel's team. Leigh had all but written Hazel's athletic career off, because the girl wasn't particularly gifted. But Karrie wondered what Brad had believed. Was he like Leigh? Had he just coached Hazel's team to get her through those awkward grade school years? Or had he, like Karrie, believed that hard work and hustle could make up for lack of talent? She would never know, and that saddened her beyond belief.

Leigh's grief was almost palpable, solid and ever present like another body in the pew with her and the kids during the service. Gino had cried big, heart wrenching sobs at the visitation the night before, and Hazel, though stoic and dry-eyed through the service, had come undone when they left the cemetery earlier.

Karrie called upon her training to get her through the day. It was one thing to let herself go and to experience the grief during the service. But at the community room at St. Anne's, Leigh and Brad's church, later in the day, she shoved all the pain back down her throat and greeted family and friends and Leigh and Brad's friends, and she watched over Leigh and the kids, and when Dax approached her as family and friends had started to leave the luncheon, she felt her heart jump and try to soar, and she squelched that, too.

He was dressed in a suit and tie, though he had loosened the knot by the time she realized he was there. The suit was charcoal gray, the shirt a lighter shade of gray, and the tie navy. His eyes were intense on her as he approached her and rather than speak— Karrie was so full of condolences, she hadn't been able to fit lunch in there besides—he simply reached for her. To her dismay, her body moved before her brain could stop it. Just outside the room where her family was gathered—where Leigh's grief was still raw and new—she stepped into his arms and rested her head on his chest.

His cologne was masculine and familiar, and it startled Karrie to realize that. When had she become so familiar with his scent that it comforted her? When they had a drink together that first time? When he had obliged her and given her the quick hard fuck in the locker room? Or when he invited her to his house and offered her warmth and friendship?

"Hard day." His voice near her ear was gravelly with

emotion. Overcome with tears, she only nodded. Slid her arms under his suit coat and up over his back.

It had been a hard day, but maybe not the hardest.

Maybe the hardest had been when Leigh and Brad's parents agreed it was time to let him go. Watching and waiting with Leigh while Brad's chest stopped moving, while the light went out in her sister's eyes.

"I'm sorry," Dax said now.

Karrie nodded again. She sniffled and stepped back from him. Dabbed at her eyes as Leigh and Hazel slipped out of the room and around them to head toward the ladies' room. Cold now, after he had held her, she shivered and rubbed her hands over her arms. She had worn a dress, and it had been so long since she had donned anything so feminine. Her legs hurt. Her feet hurt, and the memory of Dax rubbing her feet the other night made her want to cry again.

"She doing okay?"

Karrie licked her lips and shrugged helplessly. "I don't know. She's angry. At him. At the world. At me."

"Not you."

"It's okay," Karrie whispered. "It's not fair."

"So." He cleared his throat and lifted his chin to acknowledge Leigh when she and Hazel returned the way they'd just come. "This is why you're coaching Hazel's team."

Karrie watched her sister and niece make their way back to the table where they were sitting before she answered him.

"I just want to help," she mumbled. "And I…" She laughed softly and turned her eyes back to Dax. "I get it now. Quitting my job. Moving here to be with her, to help. It was stupid."

"It's not stupid."

"I can do anything. I can do everything for her. I've scrubbed every inch of her house until it shines. I've painted her trim work. I cook. Help the kids with homework. And none of it matters, because I'm not Brad. And I can't heal what…what this has done to her."

"Karrie—"

"I can't put Leigh back together, and I jumped at the chance to try for purely selfish reasons."

"You quit your job because you're selfish?"

Tears wet her face when she blinked. "Maybe it took that for me to break it off with Dom."

"You quit your job," Dax said again. "Not a retail position at the mall. You quit a job you love—"

"How do you love a job that involves so much death?"

"So much hope, too. You fight every day for someone's life. You told me that."

"It doesn't matter, Dax. She doesn't want me here. I'm in her way."

"Things will settle down. She probably just needs some time."

Karrie nodded and took a deep breath. "I guess."

"Call me. Later."

She shook her head. "I don't have your number."

"What?"

"We never got that far."

"Come by."

"What?"

"Later. Come to my house."

"For sex?"

Dax stepped closer to her and bent his knees to look at her eye to eye. "For whatever you need."

"And if I just need a friend again?"

"Come to my house."

"He's married."

Karrie froze in the act of slipping her shoe off. Leigh stood beside her, close enough to touch her.

Before they left the church, Karrie had forced herself to eat something. Now she wished she would have passed on the roast beef and mashed potatoes, because Leigh's words as a chaser were surely going to make her sick. Slowly, she lowered her foot to the floor, the gray pump dangling from her fingertips, as she straightened and turned to look her sister in the eye.

"What?"

Tears burned her eyes at the thought. Married. God. She had asked him, hadn't she? She asked him that the first damned day she had ducked into the gym and heard him make that comment about her ass. Yep, she asked, but had he given her a straight answer? He didn't wear a ring, but that didn't mean anything these days. He kissed her, but that didn't mean a damned thing, either, and she knew that from experience.

But the thought of Dax having a cute little wife tucked away at home while he stood there and let Karrie slide her hands inside his pants and cup his dick and ask for it—God, she had asked for it; she'd all but begged him. Of course he would oblige her— the thought burned her. Karrie swallowed hard and grimaced at the taste in her mouth.

"Wait." She frowned and shook her head. She had been at his house. It was possible he was married, and his wife had been gone from the house, but she doubted it. Granted, she had only seen the kitchen and the enclosed back porch, but she hadn't really noticed a woman's touch there.

But what did that mean? What would a woman's touch look like? It wasn't like there would be splashes of hot pink or pastels on the wall. No big signage anywhere that said Mrs. Dax Law lives here.

"What?"

"Your guy." Leigh shrugged, a smug satisfied look sliding over her face. Karrie opened her mouth to tell her it was unbecoming on her—the smirk—but she bit her tongue. Maybe it was preferable to the shattered look she had worn since the doctors had given them Brad's bleak prognosis and that whole scene had unfolded.

"What?"

She shook her head again. "Dax and I are just friends, Leigh," she said quietly. In the kitchen, their mom was busy getting Hazel a snack, and down the hall, Bill was hanging with Gino, probably trying in vain to get him to play a game or read a story. Anything to get his mind off how they spent the day.

Karrie hoped her cheeks weren't glowing. She and Dax might be playing at a friendship now, but they were no more just friends than Leigh and Brad had been. They shared something so intimate, it made Karrie blush now. They hadn't shared their hearts, and the fact that she begged him to put his cock inside her before knowing more about him shamed her and made her a little sad.

She wanted to know more about Dax Law. She wanted to go to him now and slide into his arms and breathe in that comforting scent she had remembered earlier. She wanted his hands on her feet and in her hair, and she wanted him to ask what she was thinking. To remind her that she wasn't a bad person, even though right now, she felt like the worst kind of person out there.

A little too promiscuous, a little bit stupid for wasting time with a married man, and incredibly sorry for her part in wrecking Dom and Amy's marriage, and stupid again, for suddenly needing to be closer to Dax.

It hit her then, with Leigh's cool gaze boring into her. She wasn't talking about Dax Law.

"Dom?"

"He's married," Leigh repeated.

Karrie shot a quick glance at the kitchen and looked back at Leigh with wide eyes.

"Oh my God." Leigh sighed. "Oh my God. You're sleeping with a married—"

"Leigh!" Karrie lunged for her, grabbed her hands and hobbled around the small, tiled entryway, still holding one shoe in her other hand. "Don't—"

"You had the nerve to cry to me about Dom not wanting kids?" Leigh narrowed her eyes at her. "Of course he wouldn't want you to have his—"

"I didn't!" Karrie squeezed her fingers. "I did not cry to you about it. I just reminded you that you have children, and I don't—"

"How—?" Leigh shook her head and stared at Karrie with cool hatred. "How could you do that? How could you look me in the eyes and pretend to be upset for me about Brad? When you're fucking someone who doesn't belong to you?"

"Leigh!" Karrie shifted on her feet, tried to hold Leigh in place when she moved around her. Leigh gave her a shove and knocked her back a few steps as she slipped away down the hall. She stared after her for a moment and fought to catch her breath. When she heard the unmistakable sound of her mother clearing her throat, Karrie gulped in a deep breath and turned to find her mom standing in the kitchen doorway watching her with a mix of curiosity and suspicion.

"Everything okay?"

Karrie opened her mouth to answer her, though she had no idea what to say. But when she saw Hazel sidle up behind her mom, she simply shook her head.

"Want a snack?"

"God, no," she mumbled. Intending to go downstairs and change clothes, she took a step forward and remembered she was still hobbling around in one shoe. She leaned over to pull it off and then stood with as much dignity as she could muster.

She deserved it. Every damned thing Leigh wanted to shovel her way, she deserved it.

Didn't mean she wanted to hear it, though.

"Excuse me." She avoided Hazel's eyes as she moved swiftly through the kitchen. Somehow, the thought of Hazel knowing what Karrie had been doing with her free time while she lived in Arizona was even worse than Leigh knowing.

"Aunt Karrie."

She froze on the steps and ducked her chin to her chest. Her whole body hurt with the poisonous emotions racing through her, but she took a deep breath and found a small smile before she lifted her head to look at Hazel.

"What, babe?"

"Do you wanna…"

She didn't. Whatever it was that Hazel was going to suggest, the answer was no. What she wanted was comfy clothes and shoes and Dax's warm body. Curled around hers. Inside hers. Covering hers. Invading hers.

"Shoot some baskets?" Hazel arched her eyebrows hopefully. Karrie felt a stab of pain in her chest, in her heart. Hazel was trying hard to be brave, but her eyes were glassy with tears. "Tomorrow?"

Karrie cleared her throat. "Tomorrow?"

Hazel nodded sheepishly. "I don't wanna do it right now."

"Oh, sweetie." Karrie turned on the staircase and climbed up the one step she had already taken and hurried through the kitchen to pull Hazel into a hug. Hazel had lost her fight with the tears, and now they streaked her face. She buried her face in Karrie's dress; the heat of her tears seeped through the thin material. "Tomorrow's fine. It's fine."

"I know you said I should practice every day," Hazel sobbed. Karrie cupped the back of her head in her hand as Hazel's fingers curled around her dress. Clawing for purchase. For safety. Karrie understood the desperation. "But I just—"

"Hazel, it's okay," she whispered. "This is different. I know that."

She met her mom's eyes, heard the creak of the floor in the hall and wondered who was there, just out of sight. Was it her stepdad with Gino, or Leigh, ready to take another shot at her?

"You won't be mad?"

"Of course I won't be mad," Karrie promised her. She rocked her niece and dropped a kiss on the top of her head. "I'll never be mad at you for how you feel, Hazel. I promise."

"Mom is."

"No, she's not," Karrie argued. "She's just sad because she can't help you. She's mad at herself because she can't help you feel better, sweetheart."

Hazel backed out of Karrie's embrace and covered her face with her hands.

"I just…"

"I know." Karrie nodded. Heart in her throat, every last splinter stuck there making it impossible to breathe, she watched Hazel turn and dart out of the room and head to the hall. When she heard her door close, she closed her eyes.

"I don't know why they don't outlaw those damned motorcycles," her mom muttered. Karrie stirred and saw that her mom had moved back to the counter, and she was filling the sink with hot, soapy water. Karrie didn't particularly like motorcycles, either, but then there was a lot more to the story that her mom didn't and wouldn't know.

Still holding her shoes, Karrie huffed out a sigh and danced around to slip them back on. Her mom looked back at her as she picked up her keys and her purse.

"What're you doing?"

"Going to see a friend," she answered as she hurried out the back door.

Twenty-Eight

DAX WASN'T SURE SHE WOULD EVEN SHOW UP, BUT HE
made sure to be ready for her. He had cleaned the
house a couple of days before, but he made a quick
run through after the funeral luncheon and picked up
an empty beer bottle from the night before and put
the book he was reading back on the stand beside his
bed. He stood for a moment and eyed the bed and
wondered if the satin sheets he had found and
purchased were too much. They were kind of sexy,
and adding a naked Karrie Mallory to the black satin
might kill him with lust. But it kind of seemed
desperate, and that was the last thing he wanted
Karrie to think.

At least he had foregone the candles. Not that he
wouldn't like the romantic atmosphere. Their first
time together had been memorable, and he would do
it all over again if she expressed interest. But the idea
of slowing it down and undressing her and laying her
down on the satin before making love to her made his
heartbeat quicken and his palms sweat.

He took another look at the satin sheets—he hadn't
actually pulled the comforter back, but even the
pillows in satin cases were inviting—and considered
changing them. Was it presumptuous of him to
think they would end up in here? After the way she

came on to him the other night in the locker room? Hell no. But what about the night he brought her here, and she ended up breaking, crying even though she had fought damned hard to hold herself together?

Before he could make up his mind—no woman had ever had him second-guessing himself like Karrie Mallory did—he heard the light tap on his back door. He was expecting the doorbell, so it took him a moment to make the connection and answer the door.

Still in the dress and the heels, hair still brushed and tamed into a sweet, modest look, she lifted sad, dry eyes to his.

"Hey." He fought for just a smidge of self-control, because he wanted to reach out and grab her. Grab her by the arm and yank her inside. He wanted to hold her. At the moment, he wasn't sure if she would welcome that or if she would flash her teeth at him. He liked her feisty; her feisty was sexy as hell. But he didn't want to dig under the hurt, the sorrow, just to feed on her sassy anger.

"Are you married?" she asked without a hello.

"What?"

She shrugged and raised her eyebrows. "Simple question, Dax. Are you married?"

"No?" He shook his head, still stunned by the question.

"No?" She repeated. She licked her lips and sniffled and stared him down. "No? Yes? Which is it?"

"I'm not married, Karrie," he told her.

"Then who's Emily Law?"

Dax blinked. Emily had been at the funeral. Hell, every damned person in town, every damned person who had graduated with or around the same time Brad had graduated, had been at the funeral.

"Emily's my ex-wife," he answered honestly. "Emily Franks."

Karrie's eyes lit with recognition. "You married Emily Franks?"

He almost chuckled. He and Emily had dated for a few weeks when they were sophomores. He broke up with her after one too many breakdowns after a mean girl fight. Emily was cute, and she was easy and willing, but she had also been a mean girl, and Dax got tired of the drama. They hooked up again after they started college. He had been fooled, thought she changed, and they did the whole big wedding event. She was still cute, and they had fun at times. But the flair for drama and her selfishness had driven him away again. She had refused to consider having children because she didn't want to gain weight or stretch marks or responsibility or simply, a child.

"Yes." He nodded. "I did. And after not quite two years, we got divorced," he said with a shrug. "We still talk now and then, though I wouldn't really say we're friends. Before you ask me, I haven't fucked her since maybe four months before the divorce was final, and I don't want to. But, yes, she was at the funeral. She called me when she saw Brad's obituary."

"You didn't tell her?" Karrie whispered.

"Tell her what?" Dax leaned on the doorframe and folded his arms over his chest.

"That Brad was…" She sighed and shook her head, unable to say the words again. Dax squeezed his eyes closed. He assumed she was asking if he had told his ex-wife that he and Karrie had sex in the boys' locker room. He hadn't told her *that*, either. Didn't plan to. Didn't plan to tell anyone about it, actually.

"No." He lifted his hands and rubbed his face, finally dragged his fingers back over his head. "I told you I wouldn't repeat what you said."

She nodded. Dax watched her chest and her shoulders lift when she took a deep breath.

"Do you want to come in?" he asked quietly. "Or are we going to spend the evening like this?"

The grin that flashed over her face was a little bit cute, a little sloppy, and pretty sad.

"I wanna sleep with you." She met his eyes. As if her words didn't go straight to his dick, the tip of her tongue darting out to wet her lips and then her pretty white teeth sinking into her full lower lip turned his dick to steel and nearly left him panting in anticipation.

He sensed that she had more to say, so he simply nodded. Tried hard not to stare at her lips or the way her breasts filled the front of her dress or the long, lean legs showcased between the dress and the little heels. God, but he wanted to slide that dress off her and see her in lace and heels.

"But I need more than that," she whispered the words, and before she said them all, she took a step backwards. As if she knew *more than that*, *more than sex*, was too much to ask. As if she thought he would turn her down. Before she could take another step, before she could get too far away, he moved. Leaned out the door and took her hand.

He had no idea what *more than that* might entail, but he was interested in anything she offered. Anything and everything. Body and soul.

Emily's rants and crying jags had never provoked a protective, comforting bone in his body. Karrie's struggle to control her emotions, her need to cave and talk the other night, had awakened some kind of hero thing inside him. Yes, he wanted to make love to her. He wanted to kiss away all the sadness inside her. But he wanted to hold her. He wanted to lie with her in his arms and press her body to his from head to toe, and he wanted to wake that same way in the morning.

To kiss her again. Worship her skin and her eyes and her breasts. He wanted to make her sob his name and then smile when he kissed her again. When he said he loved her.

Startled at first by his own thoughts, he pulled her inside and closed the door. Drew her into his arms and rested his chin on her head.

Did he love her?

Maybe. Too soon, sure. But, he could admit to himself that there was something happening between them.

He wanted more. More of her. More of everything with her. That was a start, wasn't it?

"You didn't sign up for this," she reminded him. "You eyed my ass, and you liked the rack. Pretty sure you weren't asking for the rest of this."

"Stop." He rubbed his chin over the side of her face and kissed her cheek. Just a soft press of his lips on her face.

"I want to be with you." She slid her arms around him and flattened her hands on his back. "I need you to drive all of this out of me, Dax. But that's just gonna make it harder to walk away—"

"For one thing." He kissed her again, his open mouth under her ear. He rubbed his tongue on her neck and felt her pulse flutter against his lips. "I never said anything about your rack. That was you."

He dragged a hand up over her side and traced his thumb under the curve of her breast.

"But I want to touch you there." He tugged at her earlobe with his teeth and then soothed the same spot with his tongue. "You have a beautiful ass, and it fits perfectly in my hands, but when I said that, I didn't mean I wanted anal sex."

"What do you want?" Her whisper was thick with heat and desire.

Of all the things he wanted from her, all the things he wanted to do to her body, the things he wanted her to do to him, he surprised himself with his answer.

"I want you to trust me."

He kissed her; this time he brushed his lips over hers and then drew back to look her in the eye. His heart hammered in his throat and his ears and his dick, and he held his breath as he waited for her to say something.

Lips parted, he felt her breath on his skin. Her tired eyes roamed over his face and stopped on his mouth. When she moved, he felt his heart shift a bit with disappointment. But she only reached to frame his face with her fingers.

"I'm scared to death of what we're doing," she said with a small laugh and cry, "but I wanna do it. With you. I wanna do all of this…with you."

She smoothed her thumbs over his lips and then met his gaze again.

"Why are you scared?"

"It's so fast."

Dax wasn't sure he heard her voice, but he read her lips, and it struck him that she felt the same way he did. A little uncertain where they were going but knowing that they were going fast and hard in that direction. Together.

"Doesn't mean it's wrong."

She nodded and licked her lips again. "I know." She leaned into him, and this time, she licked his lips. "I trust you, Dax."

The words, delivered in her soft, breathy voice, filled him inside and made him feel bulletproof. He pulled her against his chest again and smoothed his hands over her back. Possibly, he would have been content to stand there with her in his arms forever, but when she pulled back enough to lift her face to his and stare at him with those hungry eyes, his desire roared back to life immediately. Still with a tenderness he wasn't familiar with, he cupped her chin in his hand and kissed her.

Her lips and her tongue tasted a little like chocolate. Dax strummed his fingers over her cheek and then around the back of her neck and up into her hair. She sighed against his lips and wiggled closer to him.

Dax walked backwards, Karrie still in his arms, and eased his butt down to sit in a kitchen chair. Karrie met his eyes as he reached for her and slid his hands over her thighs. Her pulse throbbed in her neck, and Dax imagined he could see a flare of desire in her eyes when he eased her dress up over her ass and her hips. Karrie swayed before him as he dropped his gaze to feast on her pink lace panties.

"We don't have to hurry this time, do we?" His voice was gruff with need. Karrie answered with a tiny shake of her head. She gasped when he dragged his fingers down the inside of her thigh. From the corner of his eye, he saw her shiver, but he couldn't take his eyes from the scrap of lace that barely covered her.

"Dax." She swayed again on her feet when he stroked his thumb over the lace.

"Come here." He cupped her ass in his hands and tugged gently until she straddled him.

"I was kind of hoping to get out of the dress," she whispered.

"I think that sounds like a great idea."

He watched her as she let her small purse slide off her shoulder and hit the floor. His dick kicked in his pants when she gathered the bottom of the dress and slowly pulled it up and over her head. She watched him watch her as she tossed it to the floor on the other side of the chair. Her eyes hooded, she parted her lips and waited while he let his eyes roam over her shoulders.

The pink lace that covered her breasts didn't appear to be much bigger than the scrap between her legs. Her heavy breasts strained against the material, the ruby red centers lush and tempting.

Rather than divest her of the bra immediately and devour her—hell yes, he wanted to do exactly that—he scraped the backs of his knuckles up over her smooth stomach and pressed them under the curve of her right breast.

"Dax."

"As much as I want to take you right here on the table, I have a big empty bed just begging for this body to lie in it."

"Touch me." Thick with need, her whisper went straight to his dick. He caught her hand, though, when she reached for him. Linked his fingers with hers and then turned his other hand to cup her breast. He flicked his thumb over her nipple and felt his blood go hot when it puckered. Karrie moaned softly when he touched her again. Hungry for her reaction, he lifted his gaze to her face as he played with her breast, the lace a barrier between them. Her eyes were half closed, and her lips were parted, and as he watched, she darted her tongue out again to lick her lips.

The fly of his jeans was ridiculously tight. Painful, even. Dax sat up and dipped his head to press his open mouth against the curve of her breast, the creamy skin spilling over the top of the lace cup. Karrie closed her arms around his shoulders as he moved his hands up her back to find the hook of her bra.

"Dammit." She groaned and rested her forehead on the top of his head as he flicked the clasp and the elastic gave.

"What?"

"My phone's vibrating." She kissed his hair.

"Maybe it's just us."

She laughed softly. "Can I answer it? I'm so worried about Leigh."

"Of course."

The lace hung over her as she leaned to the side to pick up her purse. Dax marveled at her nonchalance. She didn't try to press the lace down to cover herself. In fact, she seemed at ease as she pulled her phone from her purse and tapped the screen to answer it.

Of course, he didn't mind that she wanted to make sure Leigh was okay. That didn't mean his dick was ready for a pause in the action. Her breasts—perfectly rounded globes that he knew already would be more than a handful—swayed as she moved. He wanted his tongue where the lace scraped her nipples, so he squeezed his eyes closed and forced himself to think about a new zone defense play he wanted to introduce to the boys when their season started.

Twenty-Nine

"I'm sorry."

Karrie sucked in a quick breath, a little surprised at her sister's greeting and all the more worried when she heard her tone.

"For what?"

Leigh cleared her throat, but when she spoke again her voice was still little more than a whisper.

"For what I said. About Dom."

"Leigh." Karrie sighed and closed her eyes. Dax smoothed his fingers over her belly and around her hip. Karrie covered them with hers, his touch comforting, rather than sexual. "It's okay—"

"It's not okay. It's not my business—"

"But you were right," Karrie said quietly. She wondered what Leigh would think of her if she knew exactly what she had interrupted when she called.

"Maybe. But I lashed out at you, because…"

"Because why?"

"I don't know. I just…" Leigh sniffled and then cleared her throat again. "I know you're with Dax, so I'll let you go."

"Leigh—" She groaned when the line went dead.

"You okay?"

She squeezed her hand over his and hung her head.

"Karrie."

"What?" She drew in a deep breath and lifted her head to look him in the eye.

"It's okay. We don't have to make love. We can—"

Karrie shook her head as she reached blindly behind her back to put her phone on the table. Dax drew his hands away from her as she slipped her bra off and tossed it to the floor with her dress. She leaned into him, pressed her breasts against his chest, and then skimmed her fingertips over his lips.

"Please?"

Maybe it wasn't fair of her to do this. Maybe the need to be with Dax was more about desperation to soothe her sorrow than attraction to him or whatever else she might be feeling. But at the moment, she needed him to possess her. Body and soul.

Rather than answer her, Dax closed his hands around her hips. She kissed him when he slid them lower to cup her butt, but when he stood with her in his arms, she squealed and looked around, heart in her throat.

"You don't have to carry me, Dax Law." She cocked her head and arched her eyebrows at him. "I have legs."

"You sure do," he agreed with a lecherous grin. "Delicious and long and lean." He moved down the hall toward what she could only assume was his bedroom. Karrie laughed softly and rested her forehead on his shoulder. "And I want you in my bed."

She lifted her head when he stepped into the room at the end of the hall. A streak of curiosity rolled over her, and she examined the décor for any signs of a woman's touch. She had felt sick after Leigh brought up the thing with Dom. And she worried that maybe Dax did have a wife or a girlfriend. She had seen the tall brunette talking to him at the funeral home, but she hadn't recognized her as Emily Franks. Even after she snuck a quick look at the guest book from the funeral home before she left the house and seen the name Emily Law, she hadn't recognized her and realized they were the same person.

The room was done in beige and crèmes and hints of darker browns. No pictures adorned the dresser or nightstands. No sexy lingerie hung from any doorknobs. No nightgown draped over the pillow—

"I would not have pictured you to be a satin sheets kind of guy." She blinked and did a double take. "Especially black satin sheets."

"Actually, I'm not," he answered. Standing now beside the bed, he slipped his fingers under the scrap of lace. "I found them after we were together and hoped that I would have an occasion to bring you here."

"That's pretty positive thinking." She offered him a playful grin when their eyes met.

"I'm pretty positive that you in my bed is going to be the sexiest thing I'll ever see."

"You haven't even looked," she reminded him.

"If I would have looked much closer, I would have shot my wad while you were talking to Leigh a minute ago."

Karrie slid her legs down his body until her feet hit the floor. She smoothed her hand over the buttons on his shirt and chuckled.

"Shot your wad," she repeated and rolled her eyes. "That's kind of high school, Dax."

He lifted his hand to play with her hair again. Karrie felt her skin flush with heat when he finally lowered his gaze to take in her nearly nude body.

"Maybe." He shrugged. "But there's nothing high school about you. I wanna bury myself in you, Karrie Mallory, but I wanna make you come first." He lifted his eyes to hers and grinned a bit sheepishly.

"Well, then I think you're a little overdressed," she said quietly. Slowly, hands trembling slightly, she worked the buttons on his shirt.

"Not yet." He took her hands and pulled them away. "You first."

"Me first?" She licked her lips and blinked at him in disbelief. Dom used to touch her first. He used to spend the time on her body to make her feel beautiful, but somewhere along the way, he started skipping that part. Rather than touch her beasts with his fingers, as if he were memorizing the feel of her skin, he would scoop them in his hands and squeeze them and pinch her nipples painfully hard, all the while pounding inside her. Forgetting what she liked. Taking what he wanted.

"You first," he said again.

Her mouth dry, a quiver of desire clenched low in her belly. She squeezed her fingers into fists as he dragged two fingers over her collarbone and skated them so ridiculously slowly over her chest, she cried out to urge him on. She tried to swallow as he turned his hand and rubbed the back of his knuckles over the curve of first one breast and then the other.

"Dax." The moan slipped from her lips when he stepped closer to her. She lifted her chin when he nuzzled her neck with his closed lips. "Please."

"You led the first time," he reminded her, and his warm breath over her skin made her gasp out loud. "This time, we do it my way."

"But don't you—"

He cut her off when he moved and dragged his lips over hers. Half-parted, she felt the heat of his breath again, but when she tried to kiss him back, he had already moved on. Pressed his open lips to the other side of her neck. Aware of her chest moving with the short, choppy breaths she took, she reached for him. To steady herself. Closed her fingers gently around his belt loop as he skimmed his right hand up the middle of her back.

"Dax."

The nibble of his teeth on the cords of her neck stole her breath away, but she turned her face to his and closed her eyes at the feel of his beard scruff on her skin. His hand no longer gentle on her back, he dropped it in a possessive stroke to cup her bottom again.

"Jesus," she groaned. "Touch me. Please. Touch me."

He flicked the tip of his tongue over the same spots where he had just nibbled, and then his warm breath caressed her when he moved to nip at her earlobe.

"Where?"

"Please."

She whimpered when he moved his hand from her bottom, but she lifted her face to his when he cupped her chin in the same hand. The attention he gave to her lower lip made her nipples painfully hard, and when he finally dipped his tongue inside her mouth to touch hers, she sobbed out loud and tugged at his hand.

He drew back the slightest bit to look at her. Moved closer to her to grind his hips against hers.

"You want this?"

"I just want," she whispered, wound so tightly, it hurt to stand there in his arms. "I want you."

His fingers, like feathers, traced a trail from her shoulders to her hands. Eyes locked with hers, he lifted her hands to his lips. Kissed her knuckles and then let go and let his eyes move again over her shoulders to her breasts.

"I'll do it," she warned him. Rather than touch her there, he stepped around her, letting his jeans and his oxford shirt rub over her bare skin. "Dax, I'll touch myself. You're kil—"

She gasped out loud when he pressed close behind her and wrapped his arms around her. His hands were hot, just a little bit rough. Karrie wiggled against him and threw her head back to rest on his shoulder.

"Now." She lifted her arm and reached back to cup his head in her hand. "Please."

Heavy hands disappeared, and again she sobbed in protest.

"I'm gonna touch you," he promised her, his voice tight and low. "I'm gonna touch you everywhere."

She cried out in pleasure mixed with pain and need when he pinched her nipples playfully.

"I want you naked in my bed every fucking night, Karrie." He curled his fingers around the curve of her breast, but with his other hand, he stroked the underside of her arm. She sobbed quietly as he played at her breast and finally gave the other his full attention. Pain, the promise of pleasure but for his denial, rolled over her.

His lips were in her hair; his erection pressed hard into her bottom. She moved, then. Slid her free hand over her stomach, intending to stroke herself. Dax caught her, though, his fingers wrapping tightly around her wrist.

"Are you wet?" he whispered.

She nodded and tangled her fingers in his hair. Dax rubbed both hands down over her stomach now and then slid his fingers inside her panties.

"You need to come, Karrie."

"Yes."

"Like this?"

She gasped when he stroked his finger over the sensitive skin begging for his touch.

"Yes."

He stroked her again, almost experimentally, and when she was ready to cry out again in frustration, he rubbed his fingers over her center and then further, until he was inside her.

Her arm tingled, and she dropped it to her side. Her legs trembled, and she entwined her arm through his to hold herself up.

"Touch your nipples." His voice was silky, and his breath on her ear was hot. Karrie gladly stroked herself, uncertain if she was doing it for him or for herself. The floor was uneven beneath her feet, and the edges of the room blurred. She rested her head on him again as the heat of her orgasm climbed slowly at first and then hit her with a rush. The room shattered around her, and she let her hands fall away from her breasts. Sweating and trembling, she hung on to him when he moved to take her in his arms.

"Ready for more?" he whispered.

Yes. No. Hell if she knew if she could even take more. Dom had never teased her as Dax had, and no one before had ever been that intent on pleasuring her. Karrie reached for him, framed his face in her hands and kissed him, hungry for his affection.

"There's more," he told her.

"Make love to me," she whispered.

Thirty

THE SHEETS WERE COOL AND SOFT ON HER SKIN, AND Dax's body on hers was hot and perfect. He made love to her with the same intensity he showed when pleasuring her, drawing her to the brink twice before he let go and exploded inside her. Pliant and struggling to right her breathing as she came down from the highs they had ridden together, Karrie was somewhat surprised when Dax pulled her close and urged her to rest her head on his chest. Eyes closed, she treasured the steady beat of his heart under her ear, the curl of his fingers around her waist, and the easy quiet in which they lay.

Horrified when the tears started, she smoothed her hand up over his chest and crossed her fingers that he wouldn't notice. They had said things earlier that had made her warm with hope, but they hadn't exchanged promises. Maybe if nothing else, the time she had given to Dom had taught her to be a bit more practical, if not cautious. She and Dax might have shared something sweet and special and yes, hot and satisfying. But that didn't mean they were an item. It didn't mean he wanted to lie here with her now and deal with her tears, her grief.

"Hey."

She squeezed her eyes closed when he moved his fingers from her hip up to play with her hair, and sniffled quietly, aware that an ugly cry wasn't particularly sexy. She lifted her chin, though, to look at him when he urged her to move. But when their eyes met, she ducked her head again and dashed at her tears.

"Don't." He stroked his fingers up over her arm.

Karrie took a deep breath and swallowed before she tried to speak.

"I'm sorry." The whisper sounded more like a croak, so she cleared her throat and tried again. "I know this isn't what you—"

"Don't hide from me." Her cut her off with a stern look and a gruff voice. "After what we just shared? Don't hide."

Karrie's eyes filled again. She blinked and then swept her fingers over her face.

"I'm sorry," she said again. "It's just…"

"Brad." Dax nodded. Karrie let her eyes roam over his face, his dark hair against the pillow. "Hard to believe."

"Yeah, it is," she whispered.

"He was just one of those guys everyone loves," Dax said quietly. "Hard to lose the good guys."

Karrie rested her arm on Dax's chest and propped her chin there to look at him. The words were in her mouth, and she almost said them. *Maybe Brad wasn't one of the good guys, though. Maybe Brad was cold and uncaring.* After all, he hurt Leigh. He had left the house that night on a motorcycle; who knows what his mindset was? What if he had been cheating? Why did his last conversation with Leigh have to be something that would hurt her for the rest of her life?

"Mmm." She nodded, but she pressed her lips together firmly to make sure she didn't say what she was thinking. There *might* be something here to pursue, something between her and Dax. But even if there was, wasn't it too soon to share something like that?

"What're you thinking?" Dax arched an eyebrow, the movement a little bit sexy and a little bit cute, and it tugged at something inside Karrie. All the girl parts, sure, but something more.

Well, she was thinking about Brad, but she wouldn't say so. She was wondering if Leigh was okay. She was thinking she wouldn't mind it if Dax wanted to slide into round two. Or that she would be happy if Dax just wanted to hold her, maybe kiss her into eternity. Probably she should get up and get moving. She should get back to Leigh's house. Check on her sister and the kids. And when Leigh kicked her in the teeth again, she should change her clothes and hit the streets and start looking for a place of her own. She wouldn't move in with her mom, but she couldn't stay at Leigh's indefinitely, either.

Still. Even the thought of being homeless didn't make her question her decision to come back. She would find an apartment. A duplex. Something. She would find a job. Maybe not exactly what she wanted, but she would find a job, and eventually, she would find the *right* job. And *maybe* she would keep seeing Dax.

She hoped so. She felt safe here. In his house. In his bed. In his arms.

"Just worried about Leigh and the kids." She realized she hadn't answered him, and because of the direction her thoughts had gone, she was careful not to look him in the eyes when she spoke. She was; she was sincerely worried about Leigh and the kids. The kids because they had lost their father. Leigh, because she had lost her husband before she lost the father of her children.

"What aren't you saying?" Dax's gravelly voice stroked Karrie's skin like a caress and caused her to shiver. "Are you cold?" He moved, shifted with her still pressed against him to pull the sheet and comforter up over them. Karrie took the opportunity to rub her eyes and swallow the tight feeling in her throat.

Cozy now with Dax's arm wrapped around her, her side pressed to his, and the comforter over them, she closed her eyes. She could sleep here with him. She *wanted* to sleep here with him. What would it hurt? Leigh didn't want her around, anyway.

She couldn't, though. What if her mom was still at the house? She would wonder where Karrie had taken off to. Sure, Karrie was an adult, but it would still be awkward facing her tomorrow, especially if her mom asked where she had spent the night.

"Karrie." His voice nudged her. She opened her eyes slowly and stared at him silently.

"Have you ever lost someone? To death?" She rubbed her fingers over his chest. Concentrated on the feel of tight, hard muscle under his warm, soft skin. Odds were, he had lost someone. By their age, most people had lost someone. "Someone you're supposed to love?"

Dax didn't answer her right away. She licked her lips as he traced the lines of her face with his fingertips.

"My grandfather. And a cousin, when I was younger."

She sniffled and nodded, unable to look away.

"Supposed to love?" he asked after a moment of silence. Karrie gasped when he dragged the pad of his thumb over her lower lip.

"I just." She frowned. Counted, aiming for ten but only made it to five. "I mean, he's been family for so long, Dax. Like...like a brother. And, and..." She swallowed, squinted her eyes to stop the tears. "I have my own memories with him. Ya know? Brad and me on clean-up after Christmas dinner. Brad and me against Leigh and my stepdad on summer nights after a cookout. He had this move. I don't know what it was, but he could pick every one of Leigh's passes off. Like he could read her mind." She shrugged one shoulder. "And I had the shot. I had the three pointers. We always won."

Dax, intense eyes still locked with hers, nodded. Maybe if he would have prodded her to keep talking, she would have stopped. Clammed up. But his patience, his concern for her, and the fact that they were skin-to-skin and had just made love, the fact that Karrie wanted him inside her again, to fill her again, kept her talking.

"That part hurts," she whispered. "Makes me sad."

He nodded, but he still didn't seem inclined to say anything. Maybe he thought she was just rattling, but he was listening, and Karrie wasn't sure when someone had last *listened* to her. She was heard at work; well-respected and trusted, her coworkers knew she was someone to be counted on. But she wasn't sure when someone had listened *to her*, on a personal level. Certainly not Dom. Maybe Leigh, but it had been a damned long time.

"He asked Leigh for a divorce." She bit her lip as she spoke and waited for the world to fall around them. She had promised her sister she wouldn't tell anyone, and she had caved. The world still standing, the walls of Dax's bedroom still around them, she felt guilt like a weight inside, pulling her down.

"Oh, Karrie." Dax flinched. "I'm so sorry."

Karrie nodded, arched her eyebrows. She was torn between the need to take a swing at Brad now that the secret was out and the need to take it back. To rewind. At the very least, to beg Dax not to repeat what she said.

"She must be wrecked."

"Yeah," Karrie agreed. "Sad. Angry." She shrugged.

"C'mere."

When Dax moved, Karrie willingly shifted to lie under him. She opened her legs for him to lie there, though he only kissed her. Deep, tender kisses that had nothing at all to do with Leigh and Brad, but everything in the world to do with making her feel better for a second.

"It's okay," he told her as he slid his mouth away from hers to lower his head and nibble at her neck.

"What's okay?" she asked, because if he was going to suggest they didn't need to make love again, she was going to hook her ankles together around his waist.

"That you're grieving for him." He licked a trail from her collarbone to a spot just below her ear. "And that you're angry with him."

"The kids don't know." She fitted the soles of her feet over his calves. "No one knows, Dax."

He nodded and switched his attention to the other side of her neck. He rocked his hips forward, and the feel of his cock pressed against her inner thigh elicited another soft moan from her lips.

"I told you before, I'm not going to repeat anything you tell me."

"You don't owe me anything," she reminded him. "I shouldn't be—"

"You said you trusted me." He locked his gaze with hers and then arched his eyebrows sharply.

"I did. I do," she whispered. She cupped his face in her hands. "But I also know that when we started playing around in your gym, you weren't looking for this."

"How do you know that? You have no idea what I was looking for, Karrie."

"What guy wants sex with a side of hot mess and tears?"

"I wanted you," he said simply. "Head to toe." He nodded. "Inside and out."

His gaze faltered when she took a deep breath. "Damn right I wanted my hands, my mouth, on you." He tossed the words out simply, without apology. "But there was more. I wanted to know everything about you. What makes you tick."

She laughed softly.

"You wanted more with me, right?"

She lifted her head from the pillow to flick his lip with her tongue. "Nope. Pretty much just wanted my hands on your shoulders and your package."

She grinned when she said it and laughed out loud at the look on his face.

"How the hell do you tame these when you're on the court?" He scooted down the bed, even as she groaned in protest. "Your girls look great out there on the court, but I wasn't expecting this."

She hissed out loud when he cupped her breasts in his hands and then lowered his head to lave her nipples with his tongue.

"Sports bras," she answered. "A woman's best friend."

"You're beautiful," he whispered.

Karrie caught her breath at his praise.

"When did he ask her?" Dax's voice was soft, reverent. Karrie threaded her fingers through his hair as he kissed and sucked at her skin, her breasts.

"The night before the accident."

"Damn." He nipped at her.

"Make love to me, Dax." She arched against him.

"Wait." He laughed and slipped back and away from her again.

"Why?"

"We need a condom," he reminded her. "We're having a moment, but we're not ready for babies."

She watched him stretch over the bed and reach to open the drawer on his nightstand.

"Yet."

She scooted off the pillow and dragged her fingers up the back of his thighs. Half sitting up, she took the tip of his cock between her lips and rubbed it with her tongue. Dax jumped and then cupped the back of her head with his free hand.

"Did you say yet?" she asked quietly.

"I did."

Karrie rubbed her fingers down the length of his cock and swirled her tongue over him again. Dax's groan was thick with desire, but he gave her hair a gentle tug.

"What?"

"I want my dick inside you," he told her.

"It's in my mouth," she pointed out with a wink and a smile.

"I wanna make love," he argued. "Slow and sweet and all night long."

Mouth dry and her stomach and things further south clenching with need, Karrie allowed him to ease her back to the bed. She watched as he tore the foil wrapper open with his teeth and then rolled the condom over his cock.

"They might have worked it out," he said softly.

Karrie shrugged impatiently. "Are you saying it's okay for someone to get bored and look for other things?"

"No." He drove into her hard. Karrie shifted under him and bent her knees to give him a better angle. "But sometimes love works."

Karrie moved with him, eased her hips from the bed to meet him thrust for thrust, and worked with him to bring them both toward the release they craved. Sometimes love broke, but sometimes it worked.

Maybe Leigh and Brad would have worked it out.

Right now, what she and Dax were doing worked.

Thirty-One

STILL SAD FOR HER SISTER, FOR HER FAMILY'S LOSS, Karrie found comfort in Dax's arms. They slept, though she didn't stay the night. As much as she wished she could, as much as she doubted Leigh wanted her around, she still slipped from Dax's bed to dress in the same clothes he removed from her body earlier. The same clothes she wore to her brother-in-law's funeral. Dax didn't complicate her decision to leave, though he didn't rush her out, either. He watched from his spot in his bed, arms pillowed under his head, as she stepped into her panties and then looked around helplessly for her bra and dress that had been tossed aside earlier.

When she remembered that she stripped both off in the kitchen, she looked at him sheepishly and ducked her head to hide her grin and the pink that flooded her cheeks. She swallowed hard and started to speak. Stumbled over her words and then cleared her throat and gestured to the hall. Mumbled that she could see herself out, but Dax was already moving. Tossing the comforter aside and sliding out of bed. Standing in only her lace underwear, she watched with growing hunger as the muscles of his back and his arms slid under his skin when he reached for his jeans.

Surprised to feel the clenching need low in her stomach, the embers of the fire he only recently quenched stir to life, she licked her lips. He pulled the jeans on; Karrie's eyes darted from his hands on his zipper to the briefs he left on the end of the bed.

He watched her with the same intensity when they reached the kitchen, and she finished dressing. The urge to run out and the wish for him to touch her again warred inside her, and when he sculpted her breasts in his hands after she hooked her bra but before she pulled her dress back over her head, she faltered. She wanted to stay. To lie in his arms and lock the rest of the world away.

But she couldn't. Not tonight.

Their eyes met when she pulled the silky dress on. Dax only stepped closer to her and pressed a sweet, lingering kiss on her lips.

"This is just the beginning." His words sounded like a promise, and she carried it with her minutes later when she walked out of his house. The last of the sun had been swallowed by the horizon, and she drove back to Leigh's by street and starlight. The fall air was chilly, but Karrie was warm with thoughts of Dax and what they shared, and she forgot to even turn the heat on.

Leigh's house was dark; only the living room was awake with lamplight. Karrie breathed a small sigh of relief when she saw that her mom's car was gone. Sure, she still had to skirt Leigh, but at least if she didn't, if there were more words to be exchanged, she wouldn't worry about an audience. Unless the kids were up.

Dear God, why hadn't she thought of that earlier? What if Hazel and Gino were both in the living room to watch her step into the house and try to explain her whereabouts to her sister? Okay, she didn't need to explain anything to Leigh, least of all where she had been or what she had been doing. But she would. She wasn't used to the hostility, and once upon a time, she and Leigh had been close, and she would have told her sister about what might be happening with Dax.

She parked at the curb, though she was doubtful Leigh had any intention of going to work tomorrow, so parking in the drive wouldn't have been a problem. But just in case, the street would do. She pulled her key from the ignition, shot another anxious glance at the living room window, half expecting to see the curtain move as if someone was spying on her. No one was, of course. Still. She flipped her sun visor down to examine the damage in her mirror. Sleep-tousled hair. Dreamy eyes. Lipstick kissed off; only the dark liner around her lips still somewhat evident. She looked like a woman thoroughly satisfied after hours of lovemaking, and she was, and for a moment, she simply stared at her reflection and wondered if Dom had ever made her feel or look this way. He had suggested recording themselves once, but Karrie had refused. What if Amy found something like that? It was one thing for his wife to know they were involved, quite another for her to actually have to see it.

She climbed from the SUV with a sigh and then swung the door closed and wobbled there in the street on her heels. Exhaustion crept in on her. Tightened her shoulders and her neck. Though the evening with Dax had been perfect, the grief she desperately wanted to outrun was still there.

At least she had been able to forget for a while. What about Leigh? Her husband had left her emotionally, and then she had lost him physically, and now she had two young children with a grieving mother and no father at all. Wasn't like *she* could get a break from *her* pain.

Reminded that nothing going on here was about her, Karrie took a deep breath and took the first step up the driveway. Dreading another confrontation with Leigh today, she slipped quietly in through the front door and turned to press it closed again. The garage door was closed, but this door was unlocked, so surely that meant Leigh was waiting to pounce. Karrie ducked her head and leaned into the door until she heard it click closed. Hands trembling, she flipped the lock and waited. The room, though bathed in the golden glow of the lamp, felt empty. She squeezed her eyes closed and finally lifted her head and turned toward the main part of the room.

Finding the couch and the recliner empty, she sagged in relief and curled her fingers around the doorknob. The TV was off. No hint of anyone around. No glasses or snack plates on the coffee table. No book propped open. Karrie wondered what time it was; surely the kids weren't in bed yet. Her phone was in her purse; she hadn't wanted any phone calls or texts from Leigh to harass her on the drive back. Seemed like the microwave clock in Dax's kitchen had said ten minutes after eight, if she remembered correctly.

Didn't seem likely that the kids would be in bed, but then again, they were probably exhausted. And maybe Leigh wanted them to sleep. Maybe living and grieving was too hard with the wide-eyed innocence of her children looking on. Whatever, Karrie would take the reprieve. She turned the lamp off and made her way through the room and into the kitchen. By the light of the clocks on the oven and the microwave, she grabbed a bottle of water from the refrigerator and slipped on down the stairs.

She showered, tempted to linger there under the hot spray until the aches and the demons in her muscles were washed out. Doubtful it could be that easy, she moved at a steady pace and then toweled off and dressed in long pajama pants and a tank. She wouldn't sleep; she knew that. Not after such a day. The funeral. The words she and Leigh had exchanged. Leigh's apology. Making love with Dax. Sleeping in his bed. By contrast, the bed—twin bed—

in Leigh's basement bedroom felt too big and cold. Karrie slid in between the sheets with a book in hand.

She wouldn't concentrate, either, but pretending that she would was better than simply staring at the ceiling for hours. Propped on her elbow, face turned toward the lamp on the nightstand, she stared at the book and thought about Brad and Leigh. Wondered if her brother-in-law had been in love with someone else or if he had been just flirting with the possibility. If, like Dax had suggested, things might have settled and been okay if not for the accident. Perhaps they would have fought. Raged. Screamed hateful things at each other. Maybe Leigh would have cried, and maybe Brad would have held her, and maybe they would have treated each other to the silent treatment. But maybe they would have stayed together. Maybe there wouldn't have been a divorce.

The buzz of her phone pulled her attention from the words swimming on the page in front of her. When she looked up to reach for it, her vision was blurred from tears she didn't realize had gathered in her eyes. She swiped at her face and then picked up her phone to find a text from Dax.

The words warmed her heart.

Sometimes it works.

She answered him immediately: *It sucks when it doesn't.*

When the three dots indicating he was texting back

appeared on her screen, she waited with bated breath for his reply.

But have you ever felt it when it does?

She started to answer. To say yes. But she paused, fingers hovering over the screen. Had she? Really? She had thought she loved Dom, but had she ever really believed he loved her? Sure, she had slept with him. Over and over again. She had gone along with him when he spouted off plans for when he left Amy and when they would be together, but she had known even then, it would never happen. She knew the first time he took her to bed that she was going to end up the clichéd younger woman involved with a coworker. Or more specifically, the clichéd younger nurse—capable, kickass, and sexy (she thought)—involved with a jaded, unattainable, sexy ER doctor. Except then, she had been too young, too exhilarated by her so-called power over him, to worry about the cliché. He hadn't loved her, but she thought she had something special he liked. It had taken only a few months for her to realize that she had the same thing between her legs every other woman did, and the only thing special she had offered him was access, no strings attached.

No.

She didn't feel the need to go into explanations. She had told Dax she was involved with a married man. No need to relive the mess. No need to say that she had dated before, and she had assumed love would come but never had.

But what about him?

Married and divorced, but had he been in love with Emily?

What about you?

She shifted. Let her arm slide up under her pillow and dropped her head to rest. The book, forgotten, flipped closed. Karrie held her phone in her hand and waited to see what he would say.

I doubted it existed.

Karrie swallowed hard.

Doubted?

And then I met you and decided it might. So I jumped.

Jumped?

His reply was slower to come this time. The three dots winked at her and then disappeared. After the third time, she sucked in a sharp breath and worried that she had pushed him too far.

Headfirst. Don't know what it feels like, but after a few weeks with you, I sure as hell want to find out.

"Can I ask you something?" Karrie held her coffee cup in front of her mouth, pretending to blow on it. Leigh knew her well enough to know she was simply hiding. The sun had yet to make an appearance, and though a slight breeze tossed the ends of her hair like a lover's fingers playing there, Karrie was comfortable on the deck with only her pajama pants and a fleece jacket pulled on over her tank.

Leigh, on the lounge chair, burrowed under a throw that Karrie happened to know belonged to Brad—the kids had given it to him for Father's Day a few years ago—gave no indication that she heard Karrie. She stared straight into the horizon. Rubbed one bare foot over the other and drew Karrie's attention to her chipped, stale pedicure. She had worn closed-toe shoes to the funeral, but Karrie knew she would have been given a pass, even if she showed the damaged nails off for everyone to see.

Still. It bothered her to see her sister anything less than perfect.

"Where are Hazel and Gino?" Karrie looked around the deck. She had come upstairs after eight. Still no sign of life, she made coffee and then came out to soak in the solitude. She had dreamt of Dax. Of the way he held her. The way his body had moved inside hers and the way his hands had molded her skin and stroked her body in long, delicious moves. He had claimed her. Marked her as his as surely as if he had tattooed his name over her heart.

Leigh's harsh laugh drew her attention away from the house and the kids. Karrie looked back at her and cocked an eyebrow in question.

"What's funny?"

"Is that your question?"

"What?" Karrie shook her head. "No. I just—where are they?"

"In my bed," Leigh answered quietly. Karrie waited for her to say more, but Leigh remained silent. Resting in the lounge, she held her coffee under the throw. Karrie could just make out Leigh's arms, her hands wrapped around her mug. She, too, wore pajamas, her breasts loose under the filmy pink t-shirt.

"Were you and Brad still making love?"

Part of Karrie hated to ask. True, they once had the sort of relationship that allowed—thrived on—these sorts of conversations. But it startled her to realize that had changed as they had grown up and become women. In Leigh's case, a wife and mother. In Karrie's, a professional home-wrecking whore.

Leigh's shoulders heaved and her nostrils flared with the deep breath she drew in, but she didn't rush to answer Karrie.

"Do you love him?"

Karrie kept her eyes on the throw—the one with the Chicago Bears' logo pattern—and fought her knee jerk reaction. She wanted to tell Leigh it wasn't her business. To argue that her own relationships didn't matter; she was asking because she was concerned about Leigh.

But to answer that way would shut down any conversation, and Karrie missed her sister. Sure, she wanted to offer Leigh hope. To suggest, as Dax had, that maybe if things had turned out differently, Brad and Leigh might have salvaged their marriage.

"No." Her voice was gruff. Eyes still on the throw, Karrie felt Leigh turn her head to look at her. She shook her head and repeated the word, quieter this time.

"Then why?"

Karrie took a drink. Wondered why Leigh was pushing this instead of answering her question. What if she did finally answer, and she said no? That she and Brad hadn't had sex in six months. That might make it kind of hard for Karrie to argue that maybe Brad had said he wanted a divorce, but maybe he didn't. Maybe his eyes and his mind had wandered, but that his heart was still there. Still in love.

"He was good—"

"Was?" Leigh's voice was sharp.

Karrie lifted her gaze and met Leigh's eyes, but she was quick to look away.

"Yeah."

"You're not seeing him anymore?"

Karrie's eyebrows shot up, but she only shook her head. "Just moved back home. Remember?"

"So, you used me as a reason to break up with your married lover?"

"Leigh." Karrie sighed. "Why are you doing this?"

Leigh's stare was heavy and harsh; Karrie felt the ice, though she refused to look at her sister. Finally, Leigh turned away. Karrie slumped her shoulders in relief as Leigh lifted her cup to drink.

"Thought I had the right to be a bitch right now," Leigh mumbled. "I don't get how you thought it was okay to fuck him when he's married."

Karrie's eyes filled, but she didn't speak. Nothing to say. She was in the wrong, and sitting here beside a woman whose husband had asked for a divorce made her squirm with guilt.

"I wasn't the first." When she finally answered, her whisper was thick with regret. "Won't be the last."

"And that makes it okay." Leigh shrugged.

"No." Karrie shook her head. Eyes closed, she felt

tears slide over her cheeks. "It's not okay. It was never okay."

"You didn't even love him?"

"I wanted to." Karrie sniffled. "I thought I did. I was naïve, Leigh."

Karrie's skin itched, but she wasn't sure if it was the tears on her face or Leigh's judgment—she was staring at her again.

"Hot shot doctor…older man. Interested in you."

Karrie flinched. Cliché with a capital c.

"Yeah."

"What did he say? When you told him you wouldn't see him again? That you were leaving?"

"I don't know." Karrie cleared her throat. She drank from her cup and then lifted her feet to rest on the rail of the deck. Her chair too far from the railing, she lowered them back to the floor and sighed. "You need another lounge chair out here."

"No, I don't," Leigh argued. "Because you don't live here."

Shocked and hurt by Leigh's cool tone, Karrie looked at her quickly. "Yeah." She nodded. "So you've said. You don't want me here—"

"Kare." Leigh reached for her. Covered her hand with

hers for a moment. "I didn't mean it that way. How long do you wanna live in my basement?"

"Until yesterday," Karrie mumbled. She swallowed the bitter taste of hurt feelings—again—and half stood to scoot her chair around to face Leigh.

"You can…" Leigh started and stopped. She stared at Karrie for a moment, blinked, and finally lowered her gaze to her lap. "Have the room…ready for—"

Karrie hoped Leigh didn't see the violent shiver that ripped through her. Doubtful, she lifted her feet and propped them on Leigh's chair.

"I'm cold," she said quietly.

"No, you're not. You don't want to sleep in the hospital room."

Karrie shrugged and shoved her feet under the throw. Pressed them against Leigh's leg.

"Damn!" Leigh jumped and pulled her leg away.

"Told you." Karrie cocked her head. "And no, I don't want to sleep in the room you had ready for Brad's recovery."

"Why are you afraid of it?"

"I don't know, Leigh. Losing a family member is different than…the death I see at work."

Leigh nodded pensively and then rested her head again on the chair and closed her eyes.

"Would you have done it?"

"Done what?"

"If Brad had lived, would you have brought him here and cared for him?"

"Yes." Leigh nodded.

"Even if he'd been…paralyzed…suffered brain damage? Would you have saddled yourself with that for the rest of your life?"

"Well, I can say anything now to make myself look good, but yes, Karrie, I would have." Leigh shrugged. "I loved him. I do love him. I would have done anything for him."

"Seems unfair."

"There's a line in wedding vows…in sickness and in health…Sound familiar?"

"Well, there's also the line until death do us part, right?"

Leigh rolled her head on the chair and opened her eyes wide to stare at Karrie. "And here we are."

Karrie sighed.

"And the answer is yes," Leigh added in a whisper.

"Yes, what?"

"We were still…intimate. We were together two nights before he asked for a divorce."

Karrie dragged her teeth over her lower lip and tilted her head in askance.

"No issues?"

"No." Leigh shook her head. "Nothing. We got up that morning, and we talked like we did every morning. Had coffee. He ate a muffin, and I griped at him for stealing the last one. He kissed me goodbye. Said he loved me….and then before dinner—I was fixing fajitas—he just said he'd been thinking, and he was bored, and he needed to move on. Asked me for a divorce."

Karrie winced and looked away. The pain in her sister's eyes was too much to witness. She tried to draw a deep breath, but that hurt, too. Leigh rubbed her eyes, but Karrie knew she was crying.

"Do you think…" Karrie narrowed her eyes and blinked rapidly, but she couldn't hold her own tears in. "You might have worked things out? If he…"

Leigh sobbed and shook her head. "I don't know. I don't know where he was going. If he would have come back home that night." She covered her eyes with her hand. Karrie watched the tears slide under her hand and over her lips. "I'm never gonna know, Karrie."

"If he would've come home," Karrie whispered, "would you have let him in? Slept beside him? Would you have wanted to make it work?"

"Yes."

Karrie felt the tightness in her chest ease a bit. She hung her head and squeezed her eyes closed. Breathed for just a moment.

"Then maybe love wins, Leigh," she whispered. "Because I believe with my whole heart and soul, he would have come back. And he would've said he was sorry."

Before Leigh could speak, the sliding door opened. Karrie looked up to see Hazel lingering there in the open doorway.

"Mom?"

"Right here, babe." Leigh rubbed her eyes and lifted her head to look back at Hazel. "C'mere."

Hazel, purple nightgown hanging askew on her awkward teenage frame, stepped out to the deck and closed the door. She eyed Karrie silently as she made her way to the lounge chair. Karrie felt something shift inside, something around her heart, when Leigh opened her arms and Hazel crawled onto the chair with her.

"I miss Daddy." Hazel pressed her face close to Leigh's neck.

"Me too, Hazel." Leigh curled her arm around Hazel and looked helplessly at Karrie.

The door crashed open this time, and Gino half ran and half tripped over the deck, leaving the door wide open. He threw himself over his mom and his sister, and Karrie felt her throat squeeze tight with emotion.

"Why don't you—" She was going to offer to take Leigh's cup, so she didn't end up spilling on the kids or herself. But before she could get the words out, Gino stood and backed up to climb into Karrie's lap.

"I thought you were all gone."

Karrie wrapped her arms around him and kissed the top of his head. She wanted to promise him none of them would leave him, but the words seemed empty the day after they buried his father.

Thirty-Two

LEIGH KEPT THE KIDS HOME FROM SCHOOL FOR A FEW days, but eventually, even she realized the need to push back to normal, at least for the kids. Karrie was relieved to see her interacting more with the kids again, even though her smiles were tired and strained and her eyes were often glassy and bloodshot. Maybe she had needed to push through to this part, to know that Brad was gone and wouldn't need her before she felt she could give her full attention to the kids.

Whatever it was, it broke Karrie's heart as badly to see the three of them fighting back to life as much as it made her happy to see her sister loving her kids openly and completely again. Karrie started her searches for a job and a place to live, though she kept both low-key because Gino had developed a fear of abandonment. It worried Karrie, because she couldn't stay there with them indefinitely, but she decided that for the time being she would spend as much time as possible with her nephew.

She and Gino bundled up every afternoon after school for a brisk walk. Fall painted the landscape with crisp, bold colors, but it also ushered in shorter, colder days. They talked about the change of season, and they talked about school, and Karrie prayed that while they were walking and talking, Leigh was doing something with Hazel. Probably not fun, because right now, there probably wasn't much fun to be had for any of them. But something. Leigh was back at work at the bank, but she was usually home by four, so Leigh and Hazel had time to be together, even if they just sat huddled together on the couch.

Basketball season rolled in fast and easy. The coach's meeting was a strange mix of sorrow over losing Brad, reminiscing about the good old days with Brad, and muted excitement over having one of the town's own back to get involved. Karrie had to roll her eyes at that comment—she wasn't sure who had said it—but it wasn't like she was coaching a high school team. She wasn't even sure her girls would be considered a feeder team for the high school program. Technically, yes, but none of them was particularly talented, and Karrie thought that at the time, maybe something fun was more appropriate.

Their progress surprised her, though. It appeared that some of the girls had been practicing since she started hanging out at the open gym sessions with them. Hazel certainly had. The kid had hit it hard, and Karrie wavered between being proud of her niece for the hard work and worrying about her because of her new obsession. Was she simply pouring her heart, soul, and energy into the game for the physical exertion? Karrie could certainly understand if that were the case. Or was she desperate to prove to her mom and her dad (even though he was gone) that she could do it, that she could play for the high school team in a few years if she wanted to?

"You guys might do well in the Snowflake, after all."

Eyes on the girls on the court, three-on-three, Karrie nodded absently. She had heard conversation in the hallway outside the gym before, but she hadn't bothered to see who it was. Likewise, when she heard the squeak of tennis shoes on the gym floor, she hadn't paid much attention. The six girls currently on the court were her top six, and she was pretty impressed with the play going on.

"How's Hazel doing?"

Irritated at the distraction, Karrie held her hand up to tell her chatty visitor she was busy. She watched Hazel lob a pass at her classmate directly under the basket. Karrie flinched, started to blow her whistle to call Hazel out on the lazy pass, but let it drop back to her chest. Marli Kasen intercepted the pass and dribbled the ball back to half court. Karrie felt a flutter of pain for Hazel when the girl hunched her shoulders and dropped her chin to her chest. But she reminded herself that out here she was Hazel's coach, not her aunt. Feeling sorry for her wasn't going to teach her anything.

From the corner of her eye, Karrie saw that it was Jed standing beside her. However, he was as into the ongoing battle as she was, and they both watched Marli sling a bounce pass to Cheyanne Morton at the top of the key. Much to Karrie's surprise, Cheyanne turned and put up a beautiful shot. The ball swished through the net, taking Cheyanne's team to the score of twenty-one.

Game over.

Karrie fiddled with her whistle again, but the girls continued play. She turned her attention to Jed, still somewhat embarrassed by what Dax had said to him that first night she had been at the gym. One thing for a guy like Dax to check out her ass. Completely different for him to say that to Jed, who had been a coach and teacher here when Karrie was younger.

She had been at the high school gym several nights a week since she and Dax had started seeing each other. They kept it friendly, if not professional now. No more salty, sweaty kisses in the halls and certainly no more hard, fast sex in the locker room.

The thought, the memory of sliding her fingers under the waistband of Dax's shorts that night, curling her fingers around his shaft, made her knees go weak. She looked back at the girls when heat flooded her face and wondered if Dax and Jed were close. Would he tell him something like that? Well, not *that*. No coach in his right mind would tell a school athletic director that he balled a chick against the wall in the locker room. But had he confided to Jed that they were together now? Mentioned her name in passing? Something about fixing dinner with her last night? Looking for houses with her?

"What?"

Snowflake. Had Jed said snowflake? What the hell?

Jed whooped and threw a fist in the air when Hazel drove the basket. What her shot lacked in finesse, it had in power. The ball banked off the board, rattled the rim, and fell through the net. Karrie grinned and nodded at Hazel when she saw her niece look at her from across the court.

"How's she doing?" Reluctantly, he dragged his eyes from Hazel and turned to give Karrie his attention.

"Coach?"

Still wondering what he meant when he mentioned snowflakes and no idea how Hazel was coping and uncertain it was her place to voice an opinion on her niece anyway, Karrie frowned at him and glanced toward the mess of girls gathered in the lane under the basket.

"Get a drink," she said with a nod. She and Jed watched the girls move—some jogged and some sprinted—toward the door to the hall. Still not sure if she should comment on Hazel and not sure what to say if she did, she flicked her gaze back to Jed. He wasn't technically her boss as her coaching position was a volunteer thing. Still, he was the head of the high school athletic department, and she was coaching girls who would go to school there and probably play ball there.

"Um." She shrugged. Shook her head. How was Hazel doing? Living second to second, really, just like Leigh and Gino. One second, she was Hazel with that sweet, timid grin on her face. The next, she was a mess of tears and hiccups, and she wanted her dad. Karrie couldn't measure that, and she couldn't rush it, and she couldn't judge any of them. Sure, Leigh had gone to pieces on her just this morning when she couldn't find her keys. She had been raging through the kitchen, tugging drawers open and digging through them, and Karrie blinked, and Leigh was on her knees, on the floor, chin tucked to her chest and shoulders heaving with the sobs. Even Karrie found herself battling the grief back at the most random times.

"I don't know, Jed," she said quietly. "I guess as well as can be expected."

He nodded thoughtfully. Looked around the empty gym again.

"Well. I guess it's just that much harder," he mumbled. Karrie frowned, ready to ask him what his comment meant, but Jed pushed on and flashed her an apologetic smile. "Your girls just might be contenders."

Karrie stared at him silently, frustrated when the girls began reappearing in the gym one and two at a time.

"Wait." She shook her head and reached toward him.

Jed shrugged when she touched the back of his hand. "What—"

"The Snowflake Tournament."

"The what?"

"Basketball tournament."

She shook her head. "For the high school teams?"

"Them, too, yeah. But seventh and eighth grade teams play, too. Brad didn't tell you?"

There was that stick of pain. Karrie flinched, but she reminded herself to breathe through it.

"No."

She and Brad had talked often, and they did talk about sports. But no, he never mentioned any basketball tournaments, especially not one in which Hazel's team would participate.

"It's fun. All evening on a Friday and then all day Saturday." He folded his arms over his chest. "Mid-November."

"Oh." She nodded. "Okay. That sounds kind of fun."

"It is. It's a kick-off to the season for the high school teams. And it's a fun thing for the junior high kids before the Snowflake Ball Saturday night."

Karrie laughed and arched her eyebrows.

"Sorry. I don't know what that is either."

"You've been gone for a while," he reminded her. "High school semi-formal."

"Really? They squeeze it in between homecoming and prom?"

"Yes." Jed acted like he agreed with her; it was a bit much. "But the kids do have fun. And it's girls ask boys."

"Oh." She pursed her lips. "Okay. And that's for the high school kids?"

"Freshmen and up."

"Hmm." She nodded. "Okay."

"Dax Law usually chaperones the dance."

Karrie laughed softly, but when Jed winked at her, she blushed.

"But you'll have to ask him if you want to go with him."

Mouth dry, curious again what Dax had told Jed about their relationship, she laughed softly and lowered her gaze.

"Listen, I'm really sorry about Brad and Leigh," Jed said quietly. "I hated to hear that. Must be terribly difficult for Leigh."

The girls were all back in the gym now, and the sounds of balls banging off the backboard and the girls giggling and talking as they practiced dribbling and shooting sort of drowned out Jed's words. Karrie heard him, though. Her stomach tightened like a belt cinched hard and fast. How in the hell did Jed know about Leigh and Brad?

Before she could say anything, before she could ask, Jed dropped a heavy hand on her shoulder and gave her a squeeze.

"You tell Leigh we're thinking about her, okay? Give her our love."

Stunned by what he said, Karrie nodded and watched him walk away. He waved at the girls as he left. Dressed in black yoga pants and a blue tank, Karrie had been hot only moments before, from running practice. Now she shivered as she watched Jed leave the gym.

Thirty-Three

DAX HAD ASSUMED THAT HE WOULD STOP WATCHING the clock every afternoon, counting down the hours and minutes until Karrie showed up either to shoot baskets or drag him out of the gym and go to dinner. He had assumed the excitement of seeing her would wear off, and that they would settle into a boring routine and maybe they would eventually exchange the L word. They had settled into a routine of sorts, but it was anything but boring. Mostly, it involved being together. She still spent a lot of time with her sister and the kids, and Dax was okay with that. She had brought him with her once when she ran back to Leigh's house because she forgot her purse. He had talked to Gino; the kid was hilarious. Sad, but resilient as kids were, and he had quietly explained the premise of a cartoon he was watching to Dax from his spot on the couch.

They had found a few houses that Karrie liked, and he had to admit they were nice houses. One of them was perfect for her, but Dax kept leaning toward apartments. If she were in an apartment, and her lease came up after a year, and they were still seeing each other…It was too soon to ask her now to move in with him, but he certainly had his eyes on that as a future goal. Still. Even mentioning it at the time seemed wrong, so he quietly leaned toward the apartments they looked at and urged Karrie to do the same.

He couldn't help much on the job front. He had put the word out to friends who worked in the medical field, but he wasn't sure what Karrie was interested in or what sort of salary she expected. So he discussed any options she mentioned without offering advice. And continued to hope that she would be happy back here at home and stay long after Leigh and the kids were back on their feet.

She hadn't come by between school and practice, which happened now and then. He missed her, though. Spent some of his practice time with her on his mind, though his boys would never question his dedication. Jed mentioned that he had seen her earlier in the day at the gym, that they talked about the snowflake tournament and the ball. Dax had to laugh at himself, because for the first time since he had graduated from high school, he was looking forward to a high school dance and hoping that the girl of his dreams would ask him to go.

When practice ended and he still hadn't heard from her, he decided she must be spending the evening with Leigh. He knew there had been a few nights when her mom and stepdad had taken the kids and she and Leigh had gone for pizza or nachos. He kind of loved that about her, that she loved her sister and wanted to be there for her, but also that she was taking care of his friend Leigh. Of his friend Brad's widow. They had all been close back in the day; he thought it would be nice to one day call Leigh family.

He tugged on his sweats before he headed out to the parking lot. The calendar declared the official start of winter a good month away, but the temperatures said otherwise. Cold wind tampered with the touch of moisture chased him to his truck. His hands too damned cold to text, he decided to wait until he was at home to text her or call her.

Hell, maybe she had taken her girls out for pizza. She'd done that once last week or the week before. Took the bunch of her basketball girls—nine of them, he thought—out for pizza and soda. Maybe she had done it for Hazel, but when she dropped by his place later, her eyes had sparkled as she told him about her night with the kids.

Made him wonder if she wanted one of her own.

They were intimately involved, and sometimes they made sweet love and sometimes, they fucked dirty and hard, and Dax loved it both ways with her. She never held back, and he loved the way she sank her fingernails into his skin when she moaned his name. He loved that she wasn't modest with him, that she would sip coffee in bed with him or at the kitchen table in nothing but her panties. He loved when she rode him and arched her back and put her beautiful breasts on display, and she had a hot, sassy mouth that felt damned good, too. Best of all, if they didn't strip down, she still loved to curl against him and sleep in his arms.

He noticed the light on in his house first. Then he saw Karrie's SUV parked in front of the garage. Happy like he had never been to come home to Emily, Dax parked beside her and nearly jumped out of his truck to hurry inside. Probably, his friends would revoke his man card if they knew how whipped he was. Hell, three months ago, he would have done the same. But then, those friends didn't know what an incredible woman Karrie Mallory was, and if he had any say about it, none of them would, because he intended to keep her for himself.

The door was unlocked. He found her in the living room; her face bathed in the orange light from the gas fireplace. The TV was off; she appeared to be sitting in silence. Dax looked around and wondered if she had been on the phone moments ago. But her phone was nowhere in sight.

"Hey." He offered her a smile as he shrugged out of his jacket and tossed it on the back of the rocker. "God, I love coming home to you, Karrie."

She looked at him then. She wasn't crying, but he knew her well enough now to know she wasn't happy.

"What?" He moved quickly. Sat close to her. Her sudden movement when she jumped back from him set off a silent alarm inside.

"I just wanna know one thing."

"What?" He shook his head and tossed his hands up helplessly. "Of course. What's going on?"

"How long did you wait to tell Jed that Brad asked Leigh for a divorce? Was the bed even cold? Was it the day after? Last week? Yesterday?"

"What?"

"Why would you do that?" she whispered.

"I didn't."

She stared at him coolly as she climbed to her feet and made her way around him.

"I trusted you, Dax. With my sister's heartache."

"I promise you I don't repeat—"

"Jed also hinted around that if I want to go to the Snowflake Ball, I needed to ask you."

Dax frowned and nodded. "I don't think the rules hold for chaperones, but I most definitely want you to be there with me."

"So he knows?" She shrugged innocently.

"What?"

"Jed. Jed knows? That you're fucking me?" Her voice broke, but that only seemed to feed her anger. "Did you tell him about the night in the locker room? That I came on to you?"

"No."

"No? Really?"

"Jed knows that we've been going out. No one knows we're sleeping together."

She stared at him for a beat of silence.

"Well. We aren't. Anymore." She said it simply, as if she were telling him they weren't scheduled to play a game that weekend. "I won't sleep with you if I can't trust you, Dax. The last thing I would ever do is hurt my sister."

"Karrie—"

"I didn't think you were the type," she whispered.

"Karrie, I didn't—"

"Then who did?" She snapped.

"I don't know."

"I am the only person Leigh confided in. And you are the only person I shared it with. Because it made me sick to think of her grieving for him, when she wasn't even sure he loved her. I needed…"

"I promise you I did not repeat it." He stood. Crossed the room cautiously, afraid she would run out. "I haven't shared anything that we've talked about. Anything we've done—"

"I thought you were different," she whispered. "From the rest. From the high school you. And you're not."

"Why would I do that? Why would I tell anyone about Leigh and Brad?"

She shrugged and ducked her head to wipe at her eyes.

"Don't." She licked her lips as she looked up at him again. "Don't call me, Dax. If this blows up, they're all gonna go through hell again."

"I would never hurt your sister or her kids. I wouldn't do that to you."

She shook her head again and backed away from him as he stepped toward her.

"Karrie, I love you—" he called as she yanked the door open. If she heard him, his words weren't enough to convince her. A gust of wind whipped the screen door back against the house and then he heard her close her car door.

He stood and watched her as she started the SUV and threw it in reverse. She looked up at him again as she backed out of the driveway.

"I'm in love with you," he said when their eyes met. She wouldn't hear him; she was in the car, and he was in the house. But still, he had to say the words, and he could have sworn for just a moment that she at least read his lips, because she hit the brakes and stayed there for a minute. Didn't move again until he stepped out on the stoop.

Who the hell had told Jed that Brad Avery had asked Leigh for a divorce? Because it sure as hell wasn't him. If he could figure out who had spilled the beans, maybe he could convince her he hadn't betrayed her trust.

Then again, he had done nothing to suggest he couldn't be trusted, that he would hurt her.

He slipped back inside and slammed the door closed.

Anger simmered in his head and his gut. How dare she accuse him of something when he flat out hadn't done anything of the sort?

He stalked to the kitchen and yanked the refrigerator door open to grab a beer.

He and Emily had fought, but he wasn't sure he had ever felt this sort of frustration seething in his body over anything she said or did. Then again, maybe that made sense, because while he wasn't a hundred percent certain what love was, he did know what it wasn't. And what he had with his first wife wasn't love.

Thirty-Four

"WHAT'RE YOU DOING?"

Karrie looked up when Leigh propped herself in the doorway of the basement bedroom. She had done her laundry, washed and folded and tucked it away in the dresser drawers in the room she was sleeping in. She had found a house; well, she and Dax had found the house together. It was perfect for her, and she hadn't admitted it to him, but she had both envisioned herself living there with him one day and imagined what it would be like if she announced to him that she was going to make an offer on the house and he talked her out of it. And asked her to move in with him.

Too soon. Obviously. Sadly, a few days ago, she had entertained those ridiculous thoughts, and had he asked, she might have said yes. Because fools rush in, and she had rushed this relationship with Dax, and she had been a fool to trust him. Kind of made her feel stupid that she thought she had learned from her relationship with Dom and yet, here she was a few months later, alone.

This time it hurt a hell of a lot more. The only time she and Dom had spent together was either at work or when they could steal a moment together for sex. Their romantic rendezvous had morphed into grabbing pick-up dinners on the way to her place, and finally even that had been too much work. By contrast, she and Dax had done everything together lately, and she was lonely now that she had told him to leave her alone.

"Reading." She closed her book with her finger holding her place. "You guys ready to go?"

Leigh had announced earlier in the week that she was taking the kids to dinner. Just the three of them. Pizza or tacos, or whatever the kids decided they wanted. Karrie had heard the desperation loud and clear. It wasn't that Leigh wanted to exclude her; she simply needed to share something a little bit normal with the kids.

"Yeah. Why are you home?" Leigh cleared her throat. She stepped into the room, and Karrie wondered if it was the first time she had come inside the room while she'd been here.

Karrie shrugged. She knew what Leigh was getting at, but she didn't want to talk about Dax. She didn't want to tell Leigh she wasn't seeing him anymore, because she didn't want to confess to Leigh that she had whispered her secret when she had been vulnerable in Dax's arms.

"I have a job interview next Tuesday after school."

Leigh nodded. "Hazel said you had to move practice around."

"It's at the hospital."

"Emergency room?"

"Cardiac unit," Karrie answered on a deep inhale. "But it's something. It'll work out eventually."

Leigh narrowed her eyes at her and tilted her head. "Will it?"

Again, Karrie knew Leigh was curious about Dax. She hadn't come right out and asked Karrie if she was sleeping with him, and Karrie sure hadn't told her. But they had been going out often, and Karrie was at his place often. Leigh might not know that, but she knew Karrie was gone a lot. Didn't take a math degree to put two and two together.

"Yep." She shrugged and offered Leigh a small smile. "Always does."

"You gonna be okay?"

"Of course," Karrie answered quietly. "I think I'm going to indulge in frozen pizza. And a glass of wine. And I might soak in the tub for a while."

Leigh nodded. She studied Karrie with serious eyes as she backed toward the doorway. Karrie let out a breath she hadn't realized she was holding when Leigh disappeared from the doorway. Her hands shook as she smoothed the pages of her book open again.

She missed him. Dammit, she missed him.

He had said he loved her, but she'd walked out. Because there was simply no other way Jed had found out about Brad and Leigh than Dax telling him. Karrie didn't want to be responsible for breaking Leigh all over again, and she didn't want to worry about the things she needed to talk about with a man who claimed to love her.

"Kare?"

She looked up when she heard Leigh's voice again. Said a silent prayer of thanks that she wasn't crying when she saw that Leigh had peeked into her room again.

"What?"

"You could go with us," Leigh suggested.

"No." Karrie shook her head and smiled. She waved Leigh away. "Go. You guys need this. And I could use a night at home."

Leigh stared at her curiously and then propped her shoulder in the doorway again.

"You're sleeping with him."

No idea what to say, Karrie simply returned the stare.

"You're sleeping with Dax Law."

Karrie took a deep breath and inflated her cheeks. She nodded as she let the air out slowly, dropped her gaze to her open book.

"I hope you're enjoying the hell out of that," Leigh said quietly. Karrie laughed softly and watched the doorway even minutes after Leigh was gone. She didn't rush upstairs when she heard them leave, but she didn't bother to open her book again, either. Instead, she sat quietly and wondered what was going on in Arizona right now. Who Dom was doing. What her friends were doing. If her friend Teena's son had started sending in his college applications. If Sheena had found a new roommate.

Not that she intended to go back. Maybe her affair with Dax had burned out quickly, but she belonged here now. With her sister and the kids. There might be someone else for her someday, and it would be tricky avoiding Dax with all the basketball stuff going on right now. But she would figure it out.

When enough time had passed that she was certain Leigh and the kids were long gone, she climbed off her bed and tossed her book back at the pillows. Made her way upstairs to dig through the freezer. Her choices for frozen pizza were limited. Cheese or four cheese. Assuming that the four cheese was higher in fat and calories and not taste, Karrie grabbed the regular cheese from the freezer and then turned the oven on to preheat.

She stood at the sliding glass door, arms crossed over her chest, as she waited. Since she had come back home, she'd been on the go constantly, and slowing down was hard. Especially because it made her miss

Dax that much more. She hated standing still, always had, which was probably just one characteristic that made her a good nurse. But alone with her own company tonight made her fidgety, and she might climb the walls before Leigh and the kids came home.

Speaking of walls. Karrie took a step back and looked up toward the ceiling. She could paint. Then again, if Leigh came home and found her kitchen torn to bits and Karrie up on a ladder painting just because she was fidgety, she might kick her out. Not to mention that the lighting wouldn't be favorable for such a project this late in the day.

She backed away from the door, chuckling at herself, as the oven beeped.

"Get a grip, Karrie," she told herself. She tore the bright orange and blue box open, pulled the frozen pizza out, and then tore into the plastic wrap. Okay, so she was an active person, but before, when she lived in Phoenix, she knew how to enjoy her own company. She was a reader. Not much of a napper, but she could lose herself in a good book or movie.

"There's a thought."

If she couldn't find a good movie to watch, she could see what there was on Netflix that she could binge watch. Maybe a run first. It was cold out, yes, but that had never stopped her when she was younger. Really what she would like to do was hit the gym and shoot some baskets, but she didn't want to run the risk of running into Dax. Not now. No way she would be able to avoid him forever, but it was too soon.

She slid the pizza into the oven, set the timer, and then wandered to the living room and turned the TV on. Reluctant to commit to TV watching, she perched on the edge of the recliner and aimed the remote at the big screen. Had a flash of Brad doing the same, watching college basketball. NFL Sundays. Catching a baseball game after work. The thought made her sad, and she didn't want to deal with sad. Thankfully, she didn't have to, not the way Leigh did. Karrie settled on a movie station and sat for a moment staring at the TV.

Looked like something from the eighties or nineties. A rom com of course. Just what she didn't want to watch. Still, she didn't have the energy to change the channel, so she flopped back in the chair and watched the guy fight for the girl. When the oven timer went off, he still hadn't won the girl back, though Karrie knew in the end he would. She turned the TV off and went back to the kitchen wishing life was that easy.

She couldn't deal with Dax sharing something she had said to him in confidence. Not just the nature of what she' said to him, but that she'd been completely vulnerable, nude, and in his arms—they'd just made love—when she let the words, the feelings out. He had asked her for her trust, and against her better judgment, she had given it to him. Now her sister and the kids could be hurt—again—and this time it would be her fault.

No telling what else he might have shared. Maybe her ridiculous story about being involved with Dom. Maybe he had talked about the way she reached into his pants and cupped his dick and asked him to fuck her. Maybe he had told someone about how he had her begging him to make her come the first night they were together at his house. Hopefully he hadn't shared that stuff with Jed, but what if Dax and his classmates —Leigh's old classmates—were discussing how loose and easy she was right this very minute? Just something else to embarrass Leigh.

Maybe she shouldn't have come back.

She couldn't change it now, but she gave herself a few moments of regret as she rolled the pizza cutter over the hard, flat tasteless-looking circle. First of all, she had been pretty full of herself thinking she could just come home and make things easier for Leigh. Even if Brad hadn't announced his intention to end their marriage, even if he had lived, and Leigh had been resigned to be his caretaker for the rest of her life, what had Karrie thought she could offer her sister?

She was a nurse, but not a long-term care provider. She sure wouldn't have been able to be a live-in nurse to him. Maybe she could have helped Leigh find someone to do that; maybe she could have helped in the search and the hiring of home care. But their mom could have done that. She supposed she had thought she and Leigh were close like they had been when they were younger, and if nothing else, she could at least be here for moral support.

Instead, Leigh had pushed her away, and Karrie had become someone in the background running the kids around and keeping Leigh's house for her.

She had enjoyed the hell out of Dax Law. She could tell Leigh that and mean every word. Dax had been relentless in bed, selfless in his desire to please her. What woman wouldn't love to be treated as if she were the last woman in the world?

Maybe some women would be okay to carry on with Dax the way things had been going. After all, she *could* do casual sex. She wasn't crazy about it, but she had done it before. The way things ended with Dom had been less than casual sex. If she could forget that Dax had already shared pillow talk, she could go back to his bed and open her legs for him and keep her heart closed.

But she didn't want to.

Half the pizza down, indigestion already raging, she tossed the rest of it and cleaned up the small mess she made. Made her way back to the living room and turned the TV on again, but no more rom-com stuff. She flipped through the channels and settled on a grainy black and white movie that appeared to have just started. She sat until the worst of the indigestion eased, and then restless again, she hurried downstairs and changed clothes from her jeans to running gear.

She glanced at her phone on the nightstand, screen down, and considered picking it up. Dax had called her or texted her at least once if not five times a day since she asked him not to. More than she could say for Dom. But she didn't want to talk to him.

Foolish of her, yes, but she left the room and the house and left the phone behind. Just after seven, it was full dark when she took off at a run. She wondered what he was doing. The season hadn't started yet, not officially, so he wouldn't be at a game. Maybe he already had someone new.

She ran in the direction of the school, though she had no intention of going inside. Even if there were lights on, she wouldn't go inside. But the school was dark; even the gym was dark. The empty parking lot made her sad; the ache inside yawned and stretched bigger as she turned and headed back to Leigh's house.

Thirty-Five

THE INTERVIEW WENT WELL, BUT SHE WOULDN'T DARE to guess how well. She followed it up with two more, though one was in intermediate care and the other at the Colson Physician's Clinic in the obstetrics department. Karrie wouldn't turn down any offer, but she still had her eyes on eventually finding a spot in emergency care.

She spent her afternoons with Hazel and the girls on her basketball team. Though she had come home to coach the girls for their benefit, for Hazel specifically, she found that she loved the time spent in the gym and spent the majority of her days looking forward to that hour and a half every day when she could tune everything out that wasn't basketball or tween girl.

Hazel still cried for her dad, and Karrie figured that might go on for a long time. But Karrie noticed that she seemed relieved to be at the gym, as if Leigh's house right now was so packed with grief, Hazel couldn't breathe there. Maybe the time spent at the gym gave her a way out for just a little while, and it was something she used to share with her dad, so Karrie hoped that Hazel felt free to enjoy herself here and not guilty for feeling anything other than sad now that he was gone.

When the job offer came through—she would be working in intermediate care, fourth floor, Colson Memorial Hospital—she took Leigh and the kids out for pizza. Mom and Bill met them there, and she ended her evening with a phone call later with her dad and his wife. It felt good to curl up in bed that night and not think about Dom and the life she left in Phoenix.

Still, when she finally closed her eyes to relive the best moments of the day—those involved the smiles on Hazel and Gino's faces, and even Leigh's once or twice—she realized she still felt that emptiness inside. She wanted to call Dax and celebrate with him. Didn't matter if he suggested shadow bowling or a beer or if he just climbed into bed with her to hold her, her happy day felt incomplete without him there to share it with her.

She held her breath for what felt like days at a time after she had confronted him about sharing what she said when they were together. Worried that people would talk about Leigh, that they might point fingers at her and the kids, Karrie tried to piece together an apology for her sister. Didn't matter what she came up with, because there was no excuse for what she had done.

She didn't hear anything, though. No one seemed eager to dissect Leigh and Brad's marriage and what state it had been in before his accident. There were no whispers about Brad having an affair or being seen anywhere with anyone besides Leigh. Everywhere she went, someone would ask after Leigh and the kids, but no one seemed to have anything bad to say about Brad.

"You broke up with him, didn't you?"

Karrie ignored Leigh as she set her purse and keys on her kitchen counter—her counter, because yes! She had bought the perfect little house she had loved from the word go—and traipsed through the kitchen. She'd never owned her own place before, and she had never lived alone. Despite how much she missed Dax, she had to admit to being a little bit excited about the new start.

Still, there was room for two in her bed. In the kitchen. The living room. Her life.

She edged past Leigh and stopped to look out the kitchen window. The backyard was small, but she didn't need much. A place big enough for Gino to play, but as long as he was into bug collecting, even he wouldn't need that much space. She had a carport and a paved drive, so one way or another, she could put up a backboard so she and her niece could shoot baskets. Maybe they could even get Leigh to play a game or two of Pig with them.

"Karrie."

"Hmm?"

"What's going on?"

"Hmm?" Karrie glanced at Leigh and then looked back at the window. "I don't like the blinds. I want curtains."

Leigh rolled her eyes, but she stepped up beside her to look out the window. "You need a valance."

Karrie lifted her chin to study the top of the window and then shifted her gaze to see outside again. The nearest house was two yards and an alley away. Probably, she could put a valance here and not worry about anyone seeing inside. Not that it mattered. She wasn't prone to running around nude if she was home alone, and she would most certainly be spending her time here alone.

"You think?"

"Yeah." Leigh nodded eagerly. "Think of the morning sun you're gonna get. It'll be perfect."

Karrie rolled her lips inward and nodded. "Yeah. Maybe. Wanna help me?"

"With the valance?"

"The decorating."

"Yeah," Leigh agreed. "I do."

"Good. I have some stuff still at the apartment. I'll let Sheena know—"

"First I wanna know what's going on."

"New house. New job." Karrie turned sideways and leaned her hip on the counter. Leigh backed up a step and crossed her arms over her chest. "Hey! Did Hazel tell you she hit a three-pointer yesterday?"

"She did," Leigh answered. The smile on her sister's face touched her. It finally felt like she had done something right in coming back and insisting that Hazel play ball. "But I'm talking about you and Dax."

Karrie huffed out a long, frustrated sigh.

"I don't want to talk about me and Dax."

"Why not?"

"Because it's…" Karrie shook her head and shrugged. "It was fun."

"Fun," Leigh repeated.

"Fun," Karrie said again. "Yes. And now, it's done, and I'm going to move on."

"But why?"

"Why what?"

"You're in love with him."

"What?" Karrie felt the blood drain from her face. She stood perfectly still, praying silently that Leigh hadn't said that word.

"What happened?"

"Why are you pushing this?" Her voice a little unsteady, Karrie took another deep breath to calm herself. She turned to press her back to the counter, plopped her hands at her sides, and hoisted herself up to sit.

"Because one of us can be happy," Leigh whispered. "I can't. Brad's gone….Dax is still here—"

"Dax and I had some incredible sex. End of story."

"Is it?" Leigh cocked her head at her. When Karrie nodded, she arched her eyebrows. "He looks like a beat dog now. Like you sucked something out of him —" Leigh shook her head and gave Karrie a stern look before she could make a joke of what she had just said. "Why aren't you with him?"

"I wouldn't think this would matter to you," Karrie said after a moment of silence.

"What does that mean? I can't want you to be happy?"

Karrie sighed. "Of course you can." She dipped her chin to her chest and hoped Leigh couldn't see the heat in her cheeks or the thundering of her heart. Yes, she might be in love with Dax, but she couldn't have him. Not now. Not if she couldn't trust him. "I just thought you might be a little gun shy about love."

"Didn't you tell me sometimes love wins?"

Karrie shrugged and lifted her head to meet Leigh's eyes. "I dunno. Did I?"

"Look. Brad loved me." Leigh's eyes shone with unshed tears. "He loved me right up until he said those words to me—"

"I'm guessing he loved you even then." Karrie's words were small and gruff.

"Maybe we hit a rough spot," Leigh said softly, "but maybe, if he had…I dunno. Maybe we would have worked whatever it was out, and maybe we would have stayed together."

"I believe that," Karrie agreed. "With all my heart, I believe he loved you."

"I talked to Mom." Leigh leaned against the counter. She stood close enough to rest her elbow on Karrie's leg. "About what happened."

"You did?" Karrie couldn't hide her surprise, her relief.

Leigh nodded and leaned over far enough to rest her head on the counter. Karrie reached to stroke her long, loose curls.

"I don't know. Maybe I needed someone who's been there." Leigh's voice was muffled. "Someone who's had that word used against her. Maybe I felt like you were pushing too hard for me to believe in Brad, because of what you did to that other woman."

Karrie flinched. "I'm not proud of that, Leigh."

Leigh's shoulders raised and stretched on a deep breath. She looked up at Karrie and gave her a tiny nod. She had lost control of the tears, and now small black bags circled her eyes.

"I know."

"Do I need to apologize to her?"

"You need to stay the hell away from her and him and their family. She doesn't need a damned thing from you except your absence."

Karrie nodded. "'kay."

Leigh swallowed hard. "I don't mean to judge you. I don't get it, but I don't want to be angry with you, Karrie."

"That would be good, because I'm here now. And I have a lot of time on my hands."

"What happened?" Leigh whispered. "Tell me."

Karrie groaned. She lifted her hands to her face to rub her eyes and then dragged her fingers back through her hair.

"I'm sorry." She smacked her lips together and tried to meet Leigh's eyes. "I'm so sorry."

"For what?"

"The day…" She hesitated, throat too tight to

breathe, much less speak. "Of the funeral. I went to him."

Leigh nodded. "I know."

"After…we…" Karrie licked her lips. "We were talking…and I just…I was upset. Angry at Brad. So worried about you."

"And?"

"I told him. Because he was making Brad out to be a saint. I told him that Brad asked you for a divorce."

Leigh waited silently, eyes wide and innocent, as if Karrie would continue.

"And?" she finally pressed. Karrie looked down when Leigh gave her thigh a gentle squeeze.

"He made a big deal of trust. Before we made love, he said the one thing he wanted from me was my trust. And I guess he had it, because the words were out before I knew I opened my mouth."

"I used to tell Brad everything," Leigh whispered. "What's wrong with that? I wouldn't expect you to keep something like that bottled up. I asked you to keep it to yourself because I didn't want the rest of the town knowing. Not the man you love."

"Yeah, well, Jed Isles asked me about it." Karrie swallowed hard. "Said he was really sorry to hear about it, and that he was thinking of you." She sniffled and swiped at her eyes. "He sounded sincere, but I knew then, the only way he could know about it was if Dax had told him."

Leigh squeezed her eyes closed and shook her head.

"Kare, Mom and Susan Isles are good friends. Brad's mom is close to Susan, too. Mom might have said something. In fact, I'm sure she did. They do coffee together once a week."

Karrie felt her heart sink. A slow, steady slide into her belly. Heavy and aching, it settled like an anchor and pinned her to the counter.

"Great," she whispered. "I accused him of betraying my trust and told him I wouldn't see him again."

"So go talk to him."

"I can't, Leigh," Karrie argued. "He's not going to forget what I said."

"You could try it," Leigh suggested. "Start with *I was wrong. I'm sorry.*"

Karrie felt a surge of hope fill her. It was almost enough to lift her heart, but she remembered the way he looked at her when she had thrown the accusation at him. The way he had taken her in his arms the night of the funeral and asked for her trust.

"It's too late." She shook her head. When Leigh hopped up to sit by her on the counter and slung her arm around her shoulders, her first instinct was to draw away. Instead, she gave in and rested her head on Leigh's shoulder.

"It's never too late," Leigh whispered. She dropped a kiss on the top of Karrie's head. "It's never too late to say you're sorry. And sometimes love wins, remember?"

Thirty-Six

BREAKING IT OFF WITH DOM HAD BEEN DIFFICULT. No one wanted a sticky situation; no one enjoyed the breakup stuff. At least no one Karrie knew enjoyed it. Even the person ready to move on dreaded the conversation. Karrie had wondered a lot about Brad the past few days, after talking with Leigh about Dax and her fear that he had repeated something she said in confidence. Had it bothered Brad to ask Leigh for a divorce? Had he taken a lot of time to build up to it? Or had he just decided one day that he was ready for something different?

Asking forgiveness for misreading a situation, for closing off communication with someone you still wanted to be with was harder. Karrie had wanted to run from the little house she bought and leave Leigh standing alone in the kitchen the same day they talked. Part of her wanted to throw herself at Dax and say she was sorry and ask for a chance to believe in him again.

But she was afraid to crawl back to him. She had been wrong to jump the gun and blame him. She had refused to even listen to him, and she walked out on him as he professed his feelings for her. Didn't get much more hurtful than that.

Still, every day, every night that passed only made it worse. She missed him, and it was dumb to waste time if he might forgive her. The time she spent alone could be time with him, whether they were on the court shooting hoops or painting her kitchen or sharing a cold beer on her cute little patio. The time she was spending alone could be time he was using to replace her, too. The thought pricked her consciousness now and then, and each time it took her breath away.

If he loved her, and he had said he did, he couldn't just move on that quickly, could he?

Could he love her? Was love that simple? Banter and flirting over a few games of one-on-one. A night out for a beer. Hot, dirty sex and quiet words that tumbled out when her guard was down? Was that love? Something like love?

He *might* love her. Might *have loved* her.

Because whatever was inside her right now, making her heart trip in her chest like she had just downed a jug of fire and energy, that might be love. She sure wanted to see him again and find out.

Which only made her heart pound harder and faster. It mattered. Finding Dax—he wasn't at home; she had driven by his house, and he wasn't answering his phone; she'd called twice—and saying she was sorry was the only thing that mattered to her right now.

She drove by Captain's on a whim. She wasn't looking for a drink or a pick-up line, just Dax. She told herself if she didn't see his truck, she would go on home. There was plenty she could do there until she tried again to find him. She had boxes she could unpack. Dishes and other kitchen items that had been boxed up that she could wash and put away.

Most likely, if she didn't find him, she would go back home and not do any of the above. She already passed a few nights curled on her side on the bed she purchased the day before she took possession of the house. It was currently the only piece of furniture there, which was fine because it was the perfect place to lie and wish that he were there with her.

She almost missed it; his truck was parked near the back of the lot. Wondering if that meant he had been here for a long time, what sort of shape she might find him in, she parked at the curb across the street and climbed out of her SUV in slow, herky-jerky movements. Fear made her stiff. But the fear of waiting any longer, the fear of missing out on something with Dax Law, pushed her to swing the door closed and put one foot in front of the other until she was across the street, and she saw her hand reach to pull the glass door open.

The bar crowd was mostly after work folks now, though Karrie doubted this particular bar saw much in the way of hipsters or young drinkers. It was a neighborhood honkytonk, and it was that knowledge that pushed Karrie inside. The door swished closed behind her. She looked around the room, let her eyes scan the bodies at the bar. Only one woman, but none of the guys was hers.

Hers.

Was Dax Law hers?

Hell yes, he was. She just had to show him that was what she wanted.

Nerves jumped in her belly like flame. What if he rejected her? What if he very publicly rejected her and told her to go to hell? He might. He had every right to what he felt, and he could damn sure fire away on her. She smoothed her damp palms over the seat of her jeans and considered grabbing a beer before she looked any further.

But a beer right now would only make her feel worse. Might make her barf. Wouldn't that be pretty?

She turned her head to the pool table at the sound of a break shot. There he was. Not playing, judging from the lack of pool cue in his hand. He stood with his elbow resting on a tall table, fingers wrapped around a longneck bottle, eyes on the table where a woman was taking aim and lining up a shot. Karrie felt a stick in her heart. New interest? Just a friend?

The woman took her shot, and Dax lifted his gaze to a guy at the end of the table. The woman laughed, and Dax said something to the guy, and Karrie hoped like hell the couple shooting was truly a couple, and that Dax was there alone.

Now or never, she told herself. A weird mix of shivers and sweat—it was the fear, rather than the warm bar after the brisk night air—Karrie tucked her hands in her pockets and wound her way through the tables toward the far end of the bar. As if he sensed her coming, Dax suddenly straightened, swung his heated gaze in her direction, and pinned her in place.

He looked angry, though he didn't take his eyes from her as she slowed her steps until she stood before him.

"Hey." She cleared her throat.

He arched an eyebrow in greeting and took a drink of his beer. Karrie waited for him to speak, but he remained stubbornly quiet.

"Do you have a minute?" she finally asked him.

If he would have hit with her sarcasm, she might have walked out. Instead, he leaned in and folded both arms over the table.

"What?" His voice was a low rumble in the loud bar, and Karrie longed to touch him. Unnerved by the intensity in his eyes, she lowered her gaze to his neck. When that proved unsettling—she wanted to kiss him there, to press her lips to that little spot just under his chin—she let her eyes slide down over his chest and rest on his hands. His sleeves were rolled; Karrie studied the sinewy forearms that had held her and made her feel so loved.

Her mouth dry, she tried to swallow. She hadn't thought this through. As often as she sat around mooning over him, and yes, crying, she hadn't practiced this conversation like her friends used to when they were teenagers working up the nerve to ask a guy out. She had always thought it was stupid. Now she wished she would have given it a shot.

"Dax." She rolled her lips inward. A thousand words fought to be spoken, but she didn't know how to do this. Start serious? In a crowded bar? Would he even hear her?

"Heard you bought that house."

She swallowed now, but it hurt, like she had a mouthful of glass. She managed a small nod.

"Congratulations."

She sucked in a deep breath and met his eyes again.

"I'm sorry."

The words were so small, so quiet, they might have fallen before they reached him. But he heard her. She saw the flicker of acknowledgement in his eyes. He huffed out a sigh and took a long pull from his beer. Finally, he looked at her and nodded.

"Okay."

She blinked, waiting for more. What did *okay* mean? *Okay, no hard feelings*? *Okay, let's be friends*? *Okay, don't let the door hit you in the ass on the way out*?

Or…

"I'm really sorry," she said again. "I miss you."

He winced this time. Dragged his eyes away. Spent what felt like an eternity studying the TV over the bar. Finally, he gave her his attention again, his face heavy and unhappy.

"I asked you to trust me. It's all I asked."

"I know." She nodded. "I'm sorry. I just…"

"You didn't," he said simply. "You didn't trust me."

Her throat ached with the emotion she held back.

"Dax—"

"Why would I have told anyone what you shared with me? What would I get out of that?"

Karrie sniffled and shrugged. "I don't know. Some people like the control of information. Makes 'em feel ten feet tall—"

"I don't need that, Karrie Mallory." He shook his head. "You wanna know what made me feel ten feet tall?"

Karrie dropped her hands from the table and stared up at him as he stepped around it to be closer to her.

"What?" Her whisper was thick with dread and hope.

"Making you smile. Hearing you laugh. Making you happy."

She closed her eyes. Warm tears slid over her face.

"Will you forgive me?"

"Brad was a friend, and I wish Leigh only the best," he said quietly. Karrie held her breath when he linked his fingers with hers. "I wouldn't want to hurt her, any more than I would want to hurt you."

She nodded.

"I heard you say you love me." She blinked her eyes open. Dax cupped her chin in his other hand. "Do you?"

"Something like that," he said quietly. "Maybe."

"Dax."

"I sure as hell hate sleeping alone now," he told her. "And I miss your smile."

She lifted her hand to stroke her fingertips over his cheek. "I might…feel something like that, too."

His stingy, reluctant smile tugged at her heart. He moved closer to slide his arms around her waist and haul her up against his chest.

"I've never made up in a bar." She laughed and threw her arms around him.

He pulled back just enough to look her in the eyes. Karrie's heart pounded in her throat now as he dipped his head to kiss her. Lips curved in a smile under hers, she kissed him back.

"There's something I need to ask you," she whispered when he pulled away.

"What?"

"I guess there's a big dance coming up at school." She grinned at him and ducked her head. "I was kind of hoping you would go with me."

Karrie squirmed under his heavy gaze when he remained quiet. He pursed his lips, as if he was mulling it over—the idea of forgiving her or taking her to a dance. She held her breath when he tilted his head to the side and narrowed his eyes at her.

"I think I'd like to dance with you." He nodded. "But it's a Catholic high school dance. So we have to leave room for the Holy Trinity between us. And you'll have to keep your hands off me."

She hooked her fingers around the back of his neck and answered with a slow, pensive nod.

"Maybe after the dance, you could undress me and cop a feel."

"In the locker room?" He wiggled his eyebrows.

She laughed softly. "I was thinking something a little more romantic. Maybe your bedroom."

Dax frowned and lifted a corner of his mouth.

"Okay."

"Just okay?"

"Well." He smoothed his hands down her back to cup her bottom. "God, I love your ass."

Karrie snorted with laughter and rolled her eyes.

"Maybe we should go to your place. Just in case."

"Just in case what?"

"Well. I mean, who knows how long you're gonna live there?"

"I'm not planning on going back to Phoenix, Dax." Her voice was husky with emotion again. "I want to be here. With you."

"I didn't mean anything drastic like changing your zip code, Blondie." He leaned into her and rested his forehead against hers. "But maybe just your street address."

Epilogue

"WHAT'RE—DAX?" KARRIE GLANCED AT HIM AS HE stepped inside and then kicked his foot back to nudge the door closed behind him. "What're you doing?"

Dax all but ignored her as he crossed the living room. His eyes were glued to the big box in his arms, and when he reached the kitchen counter—where Karrie was busy with packaging tape and her own big box—he studied the box with the hint of a smile on his face, rather than look at her.

"I don't know what you're doing, but the object here is to take big boxes like that out of the house and put them in your truck." She slapped one last piece of tape over the box in front of her and set the roll down. A glance at the clock on the wall—never mind the digital clock on her stove and her microwave, she had hung a trendy little wall clock with fancy coffee mugs on the face when she moved in a year ago—goosed her into movement. She had been up for hours and if she didn't get moving now, she would be late.

The girls wouldn't say a word, but Leigh and their mother would surely have some snide comments about Dax distracting her before she could get out of bed this morning. It was one thing for Leigh to tease her like that, but her mother's teasing tended to rattle her. Besides, Dax hadn't even spent the night here last night.

"I gotta go!" She backed away from the counter and looked around for her keys. "The boxes are supposed to go out, Dax. I'm moving out, not in."

"What?" He shot her a quick side-glance, but he was quick to get lost in the box again. "Tie your shoes."

"What?" She frowned. "Have you seen my keys?"

"Why would I know where your keys are?" He shrugged, still distracted.

"Babe." Karrie stepped closer to him and rested her hand on his arm. "Maybe you're working too hard. The boxes leave my house, get loaded in your truck, and then they move into your house."

Dax leaned sideways to drop a quick peck on her lips. "Tie your shoes."

"What?"

"You're gonna step on your shoestrings."

"I'm not five," she reminded him.

"Well, Gino would do better with tying your shoes. I'm gonna put this box in your bedroom for now."

"What?" She shook her head and squatted down to tie her Nikes. "No. The bedroom is cleaned out. The only things left in there are the mattress and box spring. I gotta get going. The girls are gonna be at the gym thinking I'm AWOL or something."

"Karrie?" He finally stepped away from the box as she stood up.

"Hmm?" She dropped her head back to look at him as he slid his arms around her waist.

"You still haven't asked me to go to the dance with you tonight."

She fought the grin, but she lost. Dax arched his eyebrows and lifted one hand to rub his chest.

"I'm crushed. Do you have your eye on someone else?"

"Are you kidding me?" She tipped her head to the side and gave him a long, come-hither look. "After the after party you showed me last year?"

The smile on his face grew into a smug grin.

"It was kind of fun, wasn't it?"

"Dax?" she whispered.

"Hmm?" He smoothed his hand down over her backside to cup her butt in his hand.

"I really need to go. I've got about ten minutes to jump ball."

He groaned and dropped his hands to his sides. "You know how to shut a guy down."

"I love you," she told him as she slipped around him and headed to the door.

"Keys?" he called.

She tapped her hip pockets and sent him a sheepish grin when they heard her keys jingle.

"You comin' to the game?"

"Would I miss Hazel's championship game?" He turned to her and tossed his hands up as if to ask her if she was crazy.

"Then let's go."

"Karrie?"

"And Dax, the box. Not cool. We're never gonna get everything moved. I gotta be out in two days."

"Kare?"

"What?"

"I love you."

She laughed and rolled her eyes. She pulled her phone from her pocket. Ten minutes to jump ball had been an exaggeration, but she was cutting it close on time. The girls were expected to be at the gym for any game —especially the Snowflake championship game—at least thirty minutes early. By those standards, Karrie was officially late.

"'kay. Can we go?"

"Can I tell you what's in the box?"

"Is it a puppy?" she asked hopefully.

Dax frowned and drew back as if she smacked him. "What? No. Do you want a puppy?"

"I wouldn't say no."

"Okay." He blinked, as if he was confused. "C'mere."

She sighed. "Babe, I'm gonna be late—"

"I want you to see this," he said quietly. "And I let Leigh know you would be running a bit late."

Karrie stared at him with wide eyes.

"Come. Here."

She hoped he couldn't see that her legs were a little shaky as she made her way back to the kitchen counter. He held her gaze until she stood beside him and then he reached to pull the flaps of the box open.

"What—?"

Karrie felt her eyes burn when he pulled a trophy from the box. He offered it to her, but she was slow to move.

"You're gonna be late," he whispered as he pushed it at her.

She laughed softly as she took the trophy in her hands. It was surprisingly heavy. She turned it over and examined it. A gold-plated basketball sat on the base.

A sparkly green column and a gold-plated girl posed in a shot topped the ball. Karrie's throat was tight with emotion when she read the plate on the base.

Snowflake Tournament 2017. Championship Game. 7th & 8th Grade Girls.

She lifted only her eyes to look at him, embarrassed at the tears on her face.

"You did this?"

"Your girls have done an incredible job. They fought so damned hard for that third place win last year. And you brought 'em back tougher than nails this year and look at 'em now."

She nodded. She had known that he loved Hazel. But she also knew he had never been a big supporter of girls' sports.

"Thank you," she whispered. "I just wanted to help Leigh." She shrugged. "I wanted to push Hazel." She wiped at her eyes and then laughed softly. "And now I love those girls all so damned much, it hurts."

"If they win," he said quietly, "if they win the game, they'll get blue ribbons. I thought they could hang them on the trophies."

"You're killing me." Her voice came out sideways. She held the trophy in one hand and rubbed her throat with the other.

"There's one for you."

"Dax." She shook her head.

When she didn't move, Dax reached to open the box again. Karrie dabbed at her eyes as he pulled another trophy—exactly the same as the other—from the box. She frowned when she realized there was something on it. Something was looped over the shooter's hands.

Dax took the first trophy from her and put it on the counter. Karrie looked at him uncertainly as he put this one in her hands.

"Marry me, Karrie."

It was a diamond ring. Hanging over the shooter's hands was a silver band with channel diamonds framing a big, round cut diamond.

"Ohmygod."

She watched as he took the ring and set the trophy aside. When he reached for her hand, she snatched it away and rubbed it over her black joggers. Her fingers were cold when she reached for him.

"Dax."

"I wanna spend my life with you, Karrie. I don't wanna miss a minute."

She laughed as tears streaked her face again. He arched his eyebrows expectantly.

"Yes." She nodded. "Yes, Dax, I want to marry you." Her hand shook so badly, Dax had to hold her fingers in his left hand as he slid the ring on her finger.

"Leigh said to tell you she remembers the finer points of the game if you...if we...need to celebrate first."

Karrie made a noise, something between a laugh and a sob. "Leigh knows?"

"Yeah. Had to have some help with this."

She stepped closer to him and slipped her arms around him. "Dax."

"Hmm?" He hugged her. Wrapped his arms around her and pressed her to his chest. Karrie shivered when he kissed her forehead.

"I know this sounds terrible, but can we...celebrate later?"

"We can celebrate us every night forever, Karrie."

She kissed his cheek.

"I wanna share this. With Leigh. With my girls."

"You can show 'em the ring," he agreed. "But you're not sharing me. This body only works for you."

"You get me."

"I do. You gotta see 'em through this game. I know."

She stepped back and eyed the ring for a second.

"You don't like it?"

"It's gorgeous," she answered, a bit breathless. "Just not sure I can get my arms up for a shot, it's so big."

"I'll help," he promised her. "Forever. Always. I'll be there."

"Gonna look pretty funny with you wrapped around my back every time I put up a jump shot."

Dax grinned. "Nah. That's how some guys play defense."

"Your guys," she mumbled with an apologetic shrug. "Not my girls. We don't do lazy defense."

"You're late, Coach," he reminded her.

Hand in hand, they moved toward the door.

"By the way," he said as they stepped outside. Karrie shivered and lifted her gaze to look at the heavy gray sky. Fat, wet snowflakes fell, thick and steady.

"What?" Karrie stepped carefully off the stoop and made her way over the snow-covered driveway to Dax's truck.

"Gino says puppies are overrated."

"What?" She shot him a look and rolled her eyes.

"I told them all I wanted to get you something to make you stay with me forever. Gino said to get you a clown fish."

Karrie yanked the passenger door open and climbed in.

"A clown fish." She nodded and then shook her head. "No."

"Hazel suggested earrings."

"Better," she said quietly.

"Leigh suggested a silver band and a round-cut diamond."

"Damn, Leigh's a smart girl."

"My thoughts exactly."

***

Thank you for reading Something Like Love. If you enjoyed Karrie's story, please consider leaving a review on your favorite bookish site.

TURN THE PAGE TO READ CHAPTER 1 OF JUST LIKE Them.

Just Like Them

THE BLOOD HAD SPLASHED OVER HER ARMS and her shirt and even splattered her face, and she thought of the miscarriage. The second one, the way the blood had soaked through her shorts and then streaked her legs.

The girls didn't even know about the miscarriages, and so she found it funny that she would lie in bed and chase sleep and think about those babies. Keegan was not the middle child, no matter how you looked at it, and so it wasn't about birth order.

There had been three of them, one before Rachel and two between Rachel and Keegan. The first had been hard. So hard to be young...Well, they'd gotten married a little later and gotten pregnant a little later but still...In terms of pregnancies and motherhood, aren't you always young the first time?

She and Bobby had wanted that baby so badly, and she'd ignored her mother's advice and purchased baby clothes and blankets and newborn diapers and then one day, just after the end of the school day, she'd sat at her desk grading English worksheets and felt a twinge in her belly.

The twinge hadn't bothered her. But by the time she left the school to go home to Bobby, she'd been in the grips of full-blown abdominal cramps, and she'd known that baby wasn't meant to be. Her second pregnancy had ended with beautiful Rachel, and she and Bobby had given her the moon anytime she'd reached a fat little hand for something and made a noise that resembled anything like *Daddy* or *Mommy*.

The miscarriage with the blood—the bad one—came when Rachel was just a year old. And though she'd told Bobby it was silly to blame himself, she often wondered if by making love too soon after Rachel and getting pregnant so quickly, if they'd done something to hurt her body or her chances of carrying a baby to term. Intellectually she knew that was ridiculous. Though doctors didn't advocate for women to get pregnant immediately after giving birth, it did happen, and most women and babies were fine.

She'd been further along than the first miscarriage, and she'd suffered through what seemed like hours of labor pain and Bobby had taken her to the hospital. Dr. Cash had said there was nothing he could do. The blood was so sticky and thick, and she remembered how it had seemed unfathomable that this blood had once been part of her baby.

The blood today had been warm like that, and a little sticky, but not thick. If she breathed too deeply, she could still smell the cloying scent, and she gagged, and then Bobby stirred in his sleep. She didn't want to wake Bobby. He had to be on site at six a.m. so he needed his sleep, and besides, what good would it do for Bobby to be awake? He'd held her earlier, until she'd finally drifted off to sleep, but dreams woke her, and she couldn't decide what was worse: the dreams or being awake and feeling the blood splash over her. Funny that she would be thinking of those babies now.

God knows there was so much she should be thinking about. And yet, no amount of thinking was going to change anything. Part of her thought she should get up and figure out how to help Keegan, but then part of her wondered just what the hell could be done to help Keegan. Exhausted, with her body aching from lying awake so long, she rolled to her back and turned her head on her pillow to look at Bobby.

He wore his age so well. Even now, after the blood—there had been buckets—and dealing with Keegan, and the looks her colleagues were sneaking in the hallways, she could look at him and see how attractive he was. She didn't quite feel the stirrings of desire she normally would, but that was okay. Not tonight.

Maybe it was just the blood. The sudden onslaught of warm, sticky blood would disturb anyone, and so maybe it was just the tactile memory of the miscarriage and maybe that's why she couldn't sleep for thinking of her babies.

The second one was a boy. She'd failed to give Bobby a son, though he'd never complained. He loved the girls just as much, if not more than she did. They'd have named him Robert Michael, after Bobby, if she could have carried him to term and given birth.

Maybe it was the pregnancy test stick she'd used just this morning, before the blood.

Maybe it was Keegan. Fear of losing her. Or maybe it was the fear that they already had lost her.

Want to keep reading?

Also by Tracy Broemmer

Women's Fiction Novels:
Luther's Cross 10th Anniversary Edition
Just Like Them
Small Hours
Picket Fences
Two Story Home
Say Everything
Sketching Litchfield Lake
Damsel
The Valentine Suite
Green-Eyed Girl
Ever, Again
Safe as Houses

The Williams Legacy

Women's Fiction Short Stories:
India Falls Read it FREE:

About the Author

Tracy Broemmer is the author of the Williams Legacy series as well as several stand-alone women's fiction titles. She also writes contemporary romance.

Tracy's books have been called gripping, emotional, and timely, and readers describe her characters as real and relatable.

Tracy lives in Midwestern Illinois with her husband of 31 years.

Visit her on the web and sign up for her newsletter at:
www.broemmerbooks.com
or by scanning here: